# THE

# WANING

# CRESCENT

Carrie,
thank you for
supporting my first endeavor
in writing. I hope you enjoy
it and know that like the story, if
God never leaves our sides even
we fail to see him!!

Scripture quotations taken from the Holy
Bible, NIV®, MSG®, KJV®

This novel is a work of fiction. All names,
characters, places, and incidents are either
from the imagination of the author or used
fictitiously. All characters are fictional, and
any similarity to people living or dead is
coincidental.

Published by 3dogsBarking Media LLC

© 2019 by Steven G Bassett
Cover Painting and Design
by Steven G Bassett
Interior Formatting by C.A. Simonson
US COPYRIGHT Registration Number:
Txu 2-138-658
ISBN: 978-0-578-52465-8

# THE
# WANING
# CRESCENT

A NOVEL BY STEVEN G BASSETT

3DOGS.BARKING LLC
stevengbassett.com

# Dedication

If it were not for the grace of my savior Jesus Christ, I would have long ago stayed on paths of poor choices with no desire of a turnaround. I thank Him above all for unconditionally loving me and teaching me how to love and accept others.

I thank my loving wife, Michele, who has stood beside me through not only my many faults but also this process of reading and re-reading, hearing countless ideas bounced around in all hours of the night and day until I'm sure she was near her wit's end.

I thank my son Dylan for his strength in surviving the terrifying experience our family shared that led me to begin this process of writing my first novel. I thank the Lord for sparing him.

Mom, you know how much I love you and credit you for my creative and compassionate side, along with guiding my wandering soul toward the One who gives us life and grace.

This project has been a labor of love and so many of my friends have given me encouragement and wisdom and the willpower to keep on pushing when the outcome seemed never-ending. You know who you are and I am grateful.

Jesus has been there right along-side me in so many ways while working on this story about an ordinary human man man facing life changing challenges we all could or have faced at one time during our journey. He has nudged me here and there and opened doors in my thought process that I was not even aware of in writing this. When dead ends on storyline frustrated me, he would suddenly put a thought in my head that fit perfectly like a single needed puzzle piece.

He led me to my editor whom helped make my story flow so much better with her suggestions and corrections. Thank you very much Nadene Seiters.

---

**I pray whomever reads this will find not only intrigue and entertainment but also valuable lessons of a spiritual nature, such as forgiveness and love for one another and abundant love for our true Master whom longs to reside within us.**

stevengbassett.com

# Table of Contents

# Foreword

I met Steve and his family through church but it wasn't like just "meeting" normal "churchy" people. They were warm, not too aggressive… real. Even more than that- they were deeply caring. Every week, Steve approached me and my young family with a genuine hello followed by a natural conversation. In the years to follow, I watched his love of God unfold into leading our youth group. He was intensely on fire with the love of Christ and it showed the moment you saw him. Even when life happened and his fire grew weary- his faith remained.

Steve and I ended up working together with the youth. He was always open and honest with the teens we encountered. Even the ones that were hard to love- he was able. He shocked me with generosity of his heart. He's the kind of man that's strong enough to wear his heart on his sleeve and I've seen it be an asset to so many others. He's the kind of guy who you can have a beer with, paint with, talk about the problems of the world, or race in separate church vans from a stoplight down the highway. He's the kind of person you want on your team because when you're friends with him, you know that you will have someone in your corner to help make you the best version of yourself.

This book is both heartwarming and heart breaking. It has ups and downs, twists and turns. And yet, although it is fiction it is very much the story of all our lives. Lives that are full of valleys and mountains. Lives that live in the tension of struggle and content. But what my friend Steve has done in this book is he paints a beautiful and realistic picture of God in our corner. A God that's always on your team.

> Colette Patton, Associate Pastor
> Hood United Methodist Church
> Republic, Missouri

# Prologue

## Waning Crescent Moon

I n this phase of the moon, its illumination of light is less than one half and will continue to decrease until the reflected light is completely vanished. This begins the formation of the new moon, which depicts the end of the old cycle and the start of the approaching new.

Spiritually, this represents a time of self-reflection and contemplation. A time to declutter and let go of toxic people, bad habits, or things that interfere with or no longer serve you. A time to detach from the world and seek reconciliation and positive change. As the new moon approaches, so can a new aspect in one's life through growth and acceptance of a new beginning with the understanding and need of letting go from past circumstance and pain. It's a time to turn the page and start fresh on your continuing journey.

# Chapter 1

*Late May 2018*

### Faith Challenged in an Instant

J ason's eyes spoke the panic he was feeling as the current swiftly pulled him away from the reaching arms of his father. The water circled him like the devil pulling its prey through the swirling crevice to its nest. John swam desperately toward Jason, fighting the submerged tangles of the tree limbs and the sucking current that pulled him downward while panicked screams from his wife echoed behind him.

"Jason! Jason! My God John, grab him!"

Jason's last word he called out before submerging for the last time echoed loudly: "*Daddy!*"

John hadn't heard Jason call out 'daddy' in a long time.

His son had turned twelve the fourth of November and like all boys had started to change in the ways he reacted with his parents. It started slowly at first, around the time he turned eleven, but had been amending steadily to less affectionate tones. John had felt hurt, but he knew it was probably normal. The two of them had started to become more adversarial in the past few weeks due to the verbal and visual lack of respect that Jason was showing both his father and mother. It wasn't that he was a bad child; he was entering adolescence and testing his boundaries.

He loved life, his friends, and his church. He recently had to move away from both his friends and his church. Fitting in to a new town and environment with a new school was something he had never had to do, and he struggled with it. Jason was just beginning to find his niche in Ash Grove through his new friends, Sheldon and Cassie, along with a few others. He was excited about the weekend adventure and his chance to have fun again with his parents. He knew deep down that he had not been showing his true feelings to them. He loved them both deeply. He had also begun to wear his famous ear-to-ear smile once again with the announcement of the upcoming camping and float trip. Along with the mischievous wink, of course.

But now, none of that mattered. Jason had been swallowed up by the tumultuous water, and John desperately felt around under the surface with his feet, trying to find a sign of his son's body near the tree-root ball that Jason had reached for in the moment before he had disappeared. The same current that had just swallowed his son was pulling at John's body as he held tight to the roots of the tree and searched, looking downward in trepidation.

He glanced back at his wife, Shelly, just before he decided to try to dive under the rolling surface to find their boy. The current was so swift and unforgiving, for even an instant, and the sound it wailed out seemed to call in a devilish, rumbling taunt for him to engage.

Shelly screamed, "No, John," but her eyes begged for him to do what he must to bring back her baby so she could hold him tight and comfort him.

_____

John grabbed a root as deep under the raging water as he could reach then sucked in a last breath and disappeared into the abyss as his wife frantically shook and screamed motioning to their friends as they paddled closer. They were unaware of what had just happened.

***

John and Shelly were about to celebrate their eighteenth wedding anniversary when close friends from their church had told them about their float trip that they were planning in the southeastern part of their home state of Missouri.

John had struggled lately as his new job placement was consuming large amounts of his time and energy; all the while, his wife's job was doing the same. Shelly also was a big part of their church, volunteering to the point she had little personal or family time. Their new jobs, along with Jason entering the stages of preteen and raging male hormones, had set the stage at home for turmoil between them all. There were bits of hostility in the air almost constantly. John and Shelly had prayed about what to do. They had even sought a counselor, but at this point, the answer seemed to be just out of reach.

The love was eroding all around them, and they saw it but just couldn't find a cure. The counselor that had been recommended had turned out to be such a man-hater that even Shelly was appalled at the way she had talked down to John every time he had attempted to answer her questions.

It seemed to them as if the counselor would bait John every time he would try to answer her questions. She would then interject her own 'personal' feelings of how John was answering her wrong, and that he couldn't possibly think that his answers would be helpful. In her eyes, every maneuver he had made was adding to the family's tension instead of aiding it. John had become confused by the attacks, which he felt were directed personally, yet he quietly continued to participate in hopes his marriage could somehow be improved upon with their communication skills and working together as a team.

Shelly had even started to defend John to the point that Mrs. Gladstone, her name, which seemed totally unfitting, had started criticizing her, and Shelly began to fight back tears. She wanted help, and it seemed to only come in the form of attacking the man she loved. She hadn't heard a single positive statement from Mrs. Gladstone from the moment they had sat down in her office.

The last thing that she had said had crossed the line. She looked directly at Shelly, and with a bit of a sneer, asked a question that felt like a spear shoved deep into her heart.

"Shelly Austin—do you enjoy being told what to do and being controlled by a man who claims to be someone of spiritual beliefs? Because if you do, there is absolutely no help that I can give you."

That was the moment John took Shelly's hand and helped her up off the sofa so they could leave. John saved them both from the terror and mental clutches of this disingenuous "professional." That is how John saw himself, the protector, being able to rescue his family from any situation that might arise. If that was a negative trait, then he would wear it like a badge of honor. They were both too bitter to try another therapist after that. They did, however, get one thing from the session that they both felt was not her intent; they realized their love was still deep enough for each other that they naturally came to the other's defense when attacked. Their love had not perished completely; it seemed to only lack some encouraging nourishment.

***

After talking with each other about their friends' offer to tag along with them on their floating adventure, John and Shelly decided it might be just what they needed as a family. They had exhausted every other avenue. If they could both swing the time away and find someone to watch the family pets, they would take the Pierces up on their offer. John had done plenty of canoeing back in his youth, although he hadn't sat in a canoe since he and Shelly had started dating. Both Shelly and Jason would be newbies, but Bob reassured them that Jack's Fork River was a calm and slow, spring-fed river perfect for first timers and someone who had been out of the sport for a while.

"The rain season has been lackluster, so the water level and current should be slow and sweet," added Bob.

***

17

As John and Shelly packed their little camper and readied for the trip, Jason seemed excited, and some of his familiar traits seemed to take over the less favorable ones of recent. He had really wanted to bring his dogs, but Shelly explained that with three people in their canoe, there would be no room for his rather rowdy boxer and American bully mix, nor would there be anyone to watch them while they were floating for five or six hours. Dozer and Mr. Wiggles would have to stay at home. With a sad and dejected frown, Jason turned to finish packing his backpack. He thought, at least Sheldon and Cassidy would be there!

The Austin family decided, because of work schedules, to meet at the campground roughly three hours away instead of following each other. With plans set, the trip started for John, Shelly, and Jason Austin. The Pierces, Bob, Julie, son Sheldon, thirteen, and daughter Cassidy, twelve arrived at the campground some two hours later and just in time to share dinner. A light rain started to fall as John grilled the burgers.

They talked about what time they needed to meet for tomorrow's float trip, and John asked Bob, "Do you think this rain will amount to anything as far as our float plans?"

Bob smiled a moment and quipped, "Shelly and Julie aren't getting off that easy! So far, plans haven't changed! Rain should be light and end in a couple of hours."

Excitement filled the air for the kids, and even Shelly appeared less nervous than John had anticipated. Shelly loved being around the water but did not relish the idea of being in the water getting her head wet. She wore contacts at times; therefore, being submerged was not her cup of tea. However, she was looking forward to getting some sun.

As the morning sun rose, John and Bob were the first up and making last minute plans across campsites. Both were happy the rain had remained light and was now over. The rest of the families rose and scattered around fixing breakfast while gathering and packing items to take with them.

Their kids had been friends since the Austin's had moved to town three months earlier when John had accepted the pastor position at Deliver United Methodist Church, the only Methodist church in town. It wasn't a large church, but it certainly seemed like a great opportunity for a new pastor's first experience. It was a small town with a close-knit community, and the church had a steady congregation of about thirty to forty-five active members.

While John was no youngster, a man in his early forties, he'd had a life change as he felt God's call while attending their last church's youth mission trip. He had been asked at the last minute to fill in since he had regularly taught junior and senior high Sunday school for several years. When he had returned from that trip to Oklahoma, Shelly hardly recognized him. Although he had been gone for only seven days, he had changed from a quiet and mild husband to one who was so spirit filled that the outpouring of it almost scared her. She didn't understand and thought that maybe she lacked whatever it took to stir this side in him.

What she hadn't realized was until someone experienced God as John had that week, there was no way to explain the feeling adequately enough. It would be easier to explain how air tasted as it filled your lungs. Shelly had lacked nothing in what she had given John because the spiritual inner joy was something only God could pour. The point was, God had filled John up so much that his friends at work, at church, and even his own family could all see his new character as he entered the room. Because none of them had seen this in him before, it baffled them. It was that powerful! His face was brighter and his demeanor more vibrant. No one seemed to understand it, especially John, but nonetheless, he openly showed it.

John almost immediately took on the youth pastor position of their church, and through the grace and guidance of his pastor, he quickly decided to take the steps to become a licensed pastor for the United Methodist conference. They desperately needed leaders that were fired up and willing, because like other denominations, the United Methodist denomination had started a downward trend in membership. John quickly made the commitment and started the training, and two years later, he had been given this church to minister to and lead.

John's mom was elated that his spirit had been so touched and reminded him, "You do realize now that you are working so hard for the Lord, the devil will be working double-time on trying to mess things up in your life!" A notion that had almost made John laugh out loud as he pictured to himself a little red devil with a pitchfork in hand chasing him around, causing him damage and wreaking havoc. A thought that even two years later, still made him smile when he thought of it.

On his first solo appointment from day one, Bob and Julie and their children became close friends. They had shown them the ropes at the church and helped point out the strong supporters and who to turn to when different challenges might come up. Shelly immediately took to Julie as they instantly found similar interests, including music. The first several weeks the transition had gone somewhat seamless. There were however the personal challenges that the family had endured such as leaving their home church, Jason leaving behind friends and school, Shelly's new job as the bank president's administrative assistant, and of course all the transitional challenges that John was making in his career change, such as being someone that people sought out for advice and leadership. The sermon writing obstacles were on their way to becoming a less difficult routine. There was, however, getting familiar with and learning how to balance some of the personalities that were abruptly different than he had dealt with in the past. It was all going well though, truth be told. Even the marital problems and Jason's attitude seemed to be leveling out with the onset of this family adventure.

*** 

The Austin family shared one canoe, Bob and Cassidy sat in one, and Julie and Sheldon in the last. John had thought, since his family had never canoed together, that the Pierces might grow tired of waiting on them. That thought soon vanished as the comedy between Julie and her son quibbling and 360-degree circles began almost immediately. The first several sets of small rapids were traveled backward or sideways, any direction but forward, as Sheldon hollered outrageous commands to his now subordinate mother captaining the front of the canoe.

As the morning progressed, the beauty of the tall bluffs and the magnificence of God's creativity of nature and colors quietly overwhelmed them all. The moments of silence were only broken by the laughter of Sheldon and Julie's antics or Jason pointing out turtles sunning themselves on logs or rocks barely elevated above the slow, moving current of the river. Occasionally, there would be other canoeists that would pass them or that they would pass as they rested on gravel bars and gathered for conversations and laughter. The sky was blue and beautiful, the clouds puffy and white, and a gentle breeze blew and cooled them as the families sliced through water and debated which way to go when the river would split into mild rapids either left or right. They were sometimes a little swifter but never too deep or foreboding, so they all sat comfortably on top of their life preservers to dull the pain of the hard seats. John kicked off his water socks to spread sunscreen. Life was calming and rejuvenating as Jason pointed out large fish swimming below them in the cool and clear water below.

Shelly looked back and smiled a warm, loving smile that John had long missed seeing. It was so bright and turned upward that he knew it was genuine. The sparkle in her blue eyes glistened like the water pellets that would lightly land on her skin as it streamed off the ends of the paddle while John changed from left to right, gently steering the vessel down the lazy stream. Life was grand again!

Two hours later, they stopped at the first take out and decided to eat lunch and discuss whether to take out there or finish the full fifteen miles, which would be another four hours or so. The women pulled out the sandwiches and chips and passed them around while they all laughed at the silliness of Julie and Sheldon's escapades. Julie had stated that she was absolutely done and finished just twenty minutes into the float, but an hour and forty-five minutes later, she and Sheldon had worked their system out, and she was feeling more tolerable and considering continuing the last half. The kids talked about all the turtles they'd seen and skipped rocks across the river. Shelly looked relaxed and settled and was enjoying the scenery of the beautiful outdoors and the sounds of the water. She so loved the sound of ocean waves, but the light sounds of the water rippling through the rocks in the rapids had been a close resemblance and brought tranquility to her usually busy thought process of everything and everyone she always had counting on her.

The decision seemed unanimous, onward we go on one term, according to Bob. "Slow down! Floating is for relaxing, not working out at the gym on the rowing machine! Cassidy and I have fought to keep up with you guys! Enjoy! Relax!" And with that, they ate, emptied the water from their canoes, packed up, and shoved off for the last half of their adventure.

Forty minutes had passed since lunch, and they had run into new groups that were slowing up and crowding the entrances before the rapids. The river had become a bit faster it felt, and a couple of times, as they entered their chosen path through the obstacles in the rapids, other canoes had charged in and bumped them and redirected their path into stumps and barely submerged rocks. By the third set, John asked Shelly if she was ready to power paddle and lose the large group of unruly and likely intoxicated canoeists that were playing dangerously in the entrances of the narrow, rapid-moving turns.

As the Austin family powered through with deeper and more directed strokes, they started seeing more barn debris and corrugated metal sheets twisted in the tree limbs, some as high as thirty feet overhead. Larger trees overturned with huge root balls were appearing more frequently and closer together in piles at the entrance to the rapids.

"There must have been some serious flooding not too long ago." Shelly turned back and continued, "I think I remember hearing about the bad flooding out this way last year; it looks like this must have been the area affected. How amazing that it was bad enough to put debris up into the trees that high!"

A soft rumble emanated from ahead, and it looked like another choice would need to be made as they drew closer to another split in the stream. John looked back, and there were no signs of the Pierces behind them; in fact, the river looked empty. They must have really powered ahead. "Oh well, I guess they will catch up with us at the take out. I think we are surely only an hour or so away; let's take the right side, the left looks too shallow." Jason turned and nodded in agreement.

Had John known ahead of time just how swift and deep the river would turn just around the blind corner and just how big the overturned tree was that blocked a good portion of the entrance of the more raging turbulence—he would have pulled over onto the gravel bar to the left and had his family put life preservers on or even waited for the others to catch up. But John didn't realize until it was too late. Their canoe headed into the turn, and the current quickly sucked them toward the bank and a log that was jutting out toward them, drawing them into a wedge. Like a boat pulling quickly into a dock slip, they slammed hard to an immediate jolting stop. The boat quickly leaned right as the water rushed over the edge of the canoe, filling it almost immediately and dumping all three into the devil's mouth. *In an instant, they all disappeared under the surface.*

John was the first to shoot his head out of the water, and he quickly looked all around scanning for his wife and son's heads. Shelly then popped up beside him, and he yelled *"Where's Jason?* Did you see where he went?"

Shelly *choked* from the water, and the pull of the current kept yanking her down and toward the large tree root ball in the middle of the twisting, swirling river. *Suddenly*, Jason's head appeared from the churning water, and Shelly grabbed onto him and screamed, "He's here!"

John swam over and, scanning the area, determined that he could shove them toward the gravel bar about fifteen feet away to the left and worked at getting them to where he believed they were safe. He aimed them where they were in the clear and then turned his attention back to the wedged and submerged upside-down canoe. John glimpsed back at Shelly and Jason who were almost to the gravel bar in what looked like knee-deep water. John quickly worked his way through the limbs back toward the canoe, believing his family was safe, then concentrated on the ensnared canoe. He pushed on it and pulled to no avail. He grew tired, and his muscles began to cramp. His legs and bare feet wildly banged against limbs and rocks under the surface of the water as he felt his skin being torn and cut. His breaths became more strained as he fought the pull of the current when he again heard Shelly's blood-curdling scream, *"My God, John, Jason is gone again!"*

John quickly pushed off and swam back toward his son's bobbing head just five or six feet in front of the tree root ball. The water moved Jason's body in a full circle, and for an instant, he was facing his dad and frantically splashing and reaching for him. John swam faster than it seemed physically possible as he heard his boy yell, *"Daddy!"* His fingers barely catching a piece of Jason's shirt as the current pulled and stretched until the sleeve tore away. His son disappeared into the root ball and then under.

# Chapter 2

*7:38 p.m. Day of the Float Trip*
**The Reckoning**

J ohn sat at one end of the gravel bar, Shelly about twenty feet on the other end, her face buried, sobbing into Julie's shoulder. Bob tried to console John, but there was nothing that could be said to soothe the emptiness.

John couldn't cry, he couldn't speak, nor could he get up off the gravel near the river's edge. Complete exhaustion and more than that . . . total and irreversible devastation. He had failed. John had always come through in the end when defending and providing for his family; yet this time, he was ineffective in his attempt to deliver the one thing his wife had so desperately pleaded for.

He was fruitless in his attempt to save their son. His spent muscles and short breath could not sustain him long enough under the turbulent surface of water to locate his son. The son that, just a week earlier, had sat next to him during the service in the front row pew at their church listening to their previous pastor and mentor, Jim Whitley, guest minister. The son that, even at twelve, sat nestled into his left shoulder and pulled his dad's arm tightly around his neck to feel secure in his loving arms. Jason was the son that never held grudges. If he was angry before bed over something his parents had said to him or had punished him for, it was always forgotten by morning, as if nothing had happened. *Always.* He woke with a smile every morning.

One of John's congregation members had come up to him after that service and commented how she had witnessed the way Jason looked at him while snuggled in and that he was so lucky to have a son at that age who still showed this kind of true and pure love for his father.

"It doesn't happen often, John! Enjoy and treasure it. That boy of yours loves and admires you so much. You can't fake what I saw." Her eyes watered slightly with emotion as she had reached to pat his shoulder. "You and Shelly are so fortunate to have had him delivered into your family; even true blood rarely delivers that kind of admiration." Yes, John quickly reflected, that was the son he had just failed *miserably and irrevocably.*

John now sat a broken man beside the river that had swallowed them up in the blink of an eye. His son was missing now because he couldn't perform his fatherly duty of protecting him. *Irreversible devastation.*

How could he face his wife, his friends and family, his congregation, or even the mirror ever again? Then it hit him like a solid punch to his gut—how could he face his Savior?

\*\*\*

*"Come," he said.*

*Then Peter got down out of the boat, walked on water, and came toward Jesus. But when he saw the wind, he was afraid and beginning to sink, and cried out, "Lord, save me!"*

*Matthew 14:29-31*

***

At 7:38 p.m. on May 25, 2018, their son Jason Allen Austin was officially declared deceased when another canoeist found his battered body some quarter of a mile downstream.

There was no comforting John and Shelly. There were also very few words between them as they rode off in separate cars after the helicopter had landed them in Mountain View, Missouri. Their precious boy's lifeless body had been taken to the Mercy St. Francis Hospital.

Darkness fell quickly upon the Austins and so intensely there seemed no way for them to come together and love each other like they had before. The day that had begun as grand had now ended in complete desolation.

John knew deep down that Shelly held him responsible for their loss. He knew that she counted on *him* to keep them safe and protect them. He also knew that he had never imagined the little red devil with the pitchfork running around causing havoc, as his mother had cautioned him about, would have come in the form of a swift and ruthless river, born from the calm, spring-fed estuary they had entered earlier that morning. He also knew that ultimately, he would need to come to terms with his horrible loss and face his heart-vanquished wife, his congregation, and the new best friend who had *needled* him into going with them.

***

Defense and division forming in John's mind had already begun to play cruel games and turn him on those closest to him. He knew, somehow, under the layers of self-guilt that Bob had not pushed him into this trip. He knew even in his muddled mind that surely Shelly didn't blame him, that there had been no way he could have known the river would change so quickly.

He did, however, remind himself, as he reflected the events, he shouldn't have brought that one beer with him in the cooler, and he shouldn't have enjoyed consuming it in the heat of the day as they lazily drifted down the then quiet river. He discerned that one beer had not slowed his mental capacity to govern their vessel, especially as it had been over an hour before the incident he had savored it. Yet, his guilt was chastening him early on, and his internal defenses were manipulating his exhausted mind as the events seemed to be looped in his brain, over and over, relentlessly playing every time his eyelids would attempt to close. When they would slightly close from exhaustion, he pictured his son's fear emanating from his terror-stricken eyes, and that last word would echo again thunderously in his head.

"*Daddy!*" Jason's final plea for his father to save him.

How could he live with that in his head? How could God have forsaken him after calling him to his service? How could He have taken his only son from him? For a millisecond, he thought of the irony of that question and then to the memory that God had NOT taken Abraham's son, Isaac, in the end. His angel had spoken just before Abraham had brought the knife to his son's heart in sacrifice. *'Do not lay your hand on the boy or do anything to him, for now I know that you fear God, seeing you have not withheld your son, your only son, from me.'*

Then his mind moved on to the next internal question. Did I not *fear* you enough God? And where, he thought, was the strength that **He** gives us in our time of desperation and need? The lesson that he had taught in Sunday school and preached about? He wanted answers. But most of all, what he wanted—no, what he needed— *fiercely*, was his son, Jason, nestled tightly under his shoulder with his arm pulled tightly and protectively around him so no harm could come. He also needed the closeness of Shelly and the words of comfort that only she could deliver as she lightly touched his neck.

He looked across the stark hospital waiting room at her and briefly watched as she battled her own war with what reality had so coldly dropped in their laps. The tears rolled from her eyes as she sat trembling under a hospital blanket. John then quickly realized that none of that was going to happen, not ever again. He started to stand up to walk over to her, but then she looked up at him emptily then back down toward the floor, nestling tighter into her blanket. He discerned his legs would not let him stand up and make the journey over to her. His head dropped back down, and he too stared again at the cold and stained floor. A teardrop fought its way out and slowly slid down his cheek until it rested in his mustache. The bitter taste of saltiness entered his mouth.

\*\*\*

The rest of that fateful weekend was lost in a whirlwind of darkness and confusion. Honestly, John didn't even remember how he had ended up in the little, cramped, furnished cabin behind the church that was behind the community garden behind the tool shed that sat on the edge of a small line of trees blocking the sight of the tiny stream running quietly about forty feet from his corrugated, metal-covered back porch.

Shelly was in no better shape as she lay curled up in a ball on the couch in the hotel room her parents were staying in. Each time her mother would reach over to comfort her, the tears would flood even more. She was inconsolable. Her father paced the floor not knowing how to comfort his little wildflower, a nickname he had given to her as a small child, and he certainly was unable to change the outcome of the tragedy she was now living.

The funeral was arranged by Jason's grandparents on both sides because Shelly and John were not communicating with each other and were too mentally overwhelmed to be cognizant of arrangements that would be fitting for their son. It was a wonder that they were even able to attend. Shelly was moving back home with her parents after the funeral because she was not able to cope with being in their once-happy home. It contained too many memories she was not willing to confront yet. She was instead staying with them in the motel while they were in town. John had not even been through the front door of their home since they had packed for the camping trip. He had let his folks gather his personal items he would need and drop them in his new place of refuge.

The funeral was the first time since they'd lost Jason that John and Shelly had seen each other. Confusing how a week and a half could seem like years, but that was how it felt to John. He wondered if Shelly was feeling the same way about how time had lagged. That was how long it had taken for the arrangements of Jason's body to be prepared. Time had stood completely still in John's mind—nothing to do each day but question why he was unable to save his son or find a way to console Shelly.

They sat quietly side by side, both sobbing and speechless. Jason's body had been cremated because neither could conceive having others parade by his tattered and torn body caused by the river's rage. They both wished they had not seen him looking that way, so the meek wooden urn with the cross rising up from the lid sat on a small table in the middle, surrounded by flowers and a family picture of them all together. The last picture of Jason that had been taken at the picnic held at the church after Pastor Jim had delivered the message just a week before their world shattered. John quietly looked up at the enlarged photo of the then happy family and sighed slightly before glancing back to the urn, tearing again as the realization hit him. His son's remains were encased inside.

Somehow, they pressed through the day and listened to the sea of well-meaning words of encouragement from family, friends, congregational family, and others who had heard the tragic news in the community. John seldom communicated to God recently and felt out of his skin sitting in the church. He imagined everyone had been watching closely and murmuring amongst themselves about what a tragedy for such a sweet family to suffer and how horrible it must be for the pastor who was unable to save his own son, let alone now his marriage. He felt sickened by the thoughts that were running amuck in his head.

The day finally settled to a close, and he found himself alone, sitting on his tiny back porch being taunted by the trickle of the stream just past the trees. He barely heard the knock on his front door. It was the first of many knocks ignored. The knocks of concerned friends wanting to offer what they could were unanswered by the broken shell of a man that used to lead and inspire them to look past their temporary circumstances on the journey through life and reach toward the saving arms of Christ. He would always tell them it was tough lessons from the loving Master—not punishment at the end of an unloving master's whip. If only he would listen and hear his own Master calling, reaching out. His pain was becoming resentment that was residing deeper and deeper in his darkening and sorrow-filled soul.

# Chapter 3

*Early July before the Town's Summer Festival*
**Spreading the Venom**

Beverly Snodgrass had begun getting busy with her usual dose of gossip and spreading venom throughout the body— the body of what she considered her church. After all, she had been the longest standing member, having been born and raised in the small, quaint town of Ash Grove. She had been christened at birth there, along with her parents and their families, whom had attended all the way back to the cornerstone being set.

But with this new pastor and his family, it was quickly becoming an abomination of what her church was becoming. More so recently since their ornery little boy had drowned. She would indeed be the one to 'deliver' Deliver UMC from the slow death that she insisted John was bringing it to. She wasn't sure just how, but it *would* be done at her hand.

"John," she coldly spoke, not even able to bring herself to call him Pastor John, "has stayed tucked away in the little church rental house except for Sundays. Why he doesn't even do much congregational care anymore." She chatted to one of the town's ladies that didn't even attend DUMC (Deliver United Methodist Church).

"Did you know that little boy wasn't even any blood of theirs? *Adopted I hear*, I can't see why he is still so torn up about it; it's been over a month already. And then walking out on that poor wife and mother. Shame, shame—that's all I got to say." It, of course, was not all she had to say.

Beverly spit poison out to whoever would swallow it. She would get so fired up that tiny pellets of saliva would fly out of her bright ruby-red decorated lips, causing instant infection to those that were unfortunate enough to be on the receiving end. It never mattered to her that most of what she passed along was unverified drivel. Whatever way she could twist things into to benefit her point was just fine.

"Why his sermons were elementary to begin with, but now that he's been a recluse in that squalor of a shack, they are becoming even worse! Cursing God at the top of his lungs all hours of the night from that crusty old porch. It's an abomination, I declare!"

"Morning Mrs. Snodgrass," interrupted Henry Tanner as he strolled by the two ladies on his morning walk. "Surely is a beautiful day on the Lord's earth isn't it?" he stated as he marched on by sporting a gentlemanly smile but then followed by an eye roll when his face was out of sight. He often pictured Beverly's husband, Billy, tied up in their basement just begging her to apply the noose around his neck and knock the blocks out from under the chair he was surely hogtied to. A dangling end would be so much quicker than to perish slowly, dose by dose, in constant agony, from her poison.

"Well, thank the Lord for things other than this beautiful day on the Lord's earth, Mary," Beverly sneered. "At least Henry didn't stop to spread *his* version of the Word today!"

Mary rarely enjoyed her conversations with Beverly. She found them a challenge to bear, but so few visitors come to see her at her home, and she was unable to force herself to go to theirs. Mary disliked the fact she struggled leaving the confinements of her comfort zone, but travel away from her home was difficult for her to endure. The town gossip was that she suffered from agoraphobia. She could make it down to the end of the street to Pennington's Market for short amounts of time, but that was her limit. It hadn't always been that way, but a few years ago, after her brother had passed, she began her spiral downward into the inability of leaving the comfort of her close surroundings. Now, after hearing this talk about the preacher, she started fearing that maybe he too was caving to the clutches of 'fear leaving' as she called it.

"Pitiful, just pitiful, the whole situation," was all she could say as the voice in her head started whispering it was time to start heading back to the front porch. She glanced nervously toward home and then began walking back while telling Beverly, "Thank you, Mrs. Beverly, for dropping by. I'll be praying for you and the families at the church! Give the preacher my prayers, and tell him I wish I could come hear him give his message."

Beverly's mouth turned upward in a bitter, forced smile, making her bright-red painted lips appear more clown like and said quietly to herself out loud, "Yeah, honey—like hell I'll give him THAT message." And with that she turned and marched off to find her next victim with an ear for wickedness and verbal venom.

# Chapter 4

*Late Afternoon on the Way to the Pastor's House*
## Henry Comes a Calling

H enry was known around town as the 'walking reverend,' even though he had no official credentials of spiritual education. He was a towering man in the dawn of his sixties but still in above-average health because of all the walking he did daily. He had started this daily ritual about the time his wife had started to lose her ability to get around easily. She was now in one of those motorized chairs, and because of her diabetes and lack of exercise, she had become rather large and cumbersome. Molly was, however, a sweet flower of a woman with the most loving heart a person could possibly have and, of course, the apple of Henry's eye.

She had taken her fall to poor health in good stride, but her husband, Henry, had struggled in denial of it for years and started walking so he wouldn't be faced with watching her struggle throughout the long days now that they were both retired. He quietly questioned why God would let her be stricken with this burden so early in life. They were, after all, both very devoted children of God. Henry kept those thoughts to himself because he imagined surely they were temptations from the devil. Nonetheless, he knew he needed to talk to Pastor John about his thoughts because they were becoming more of a temptation that drew him into darker thoughts.

He turned the corner as he headed toward the pastor's new place

***

John practically lived on his back covered porch now that overlooked the line of ash trees, which partially obscured the sight of the creek. He had almost become entranced by the subtle sound of the water trickling over the rocks because it gave him a small dose of peace and, oddly, a source of comfort. He would try to scan his bible and come up with sermon ideas while he sat swaying in the porch swing.

He was coming to terms that he had lacked substance in his messages since he had lost Jason and Shelly. He had no desire to go out and face the town's people unless one had been admitted in the hospital or called his cellphone in desperation. John knew he was just pressing through each day and was most likely losing some support of his church, but still, he settled into the habit of sitting and swinging while listening to his new muse.

He had a phone app that allowed him to pick any type of music that fit his mood without going out and purchasing it. The music he enjoyed lately was acoustic guitar on the folksy side. It was calming and went well with the breeze blowing through the trees and mixed with the reticent sound of the stream. The concoction seemed to orchestrate contemplative thoughts of what life used to be like.

But like clockwork, the rage in his soul would start
to bubble up and then begin battling with the faith that
had been so deeply rooted within his soul. The loud
screams of anger he would yell toward the creek were
directed at *God* himself, but those who didn't
understand his torment would hear him as they
knocked on his door and turn back not knowing how
to support a pastor acting out so wildly. Most were at
such a loss at what to do they would turn to Chief Bob
and beg him to reason with Pastor John. They knew it
was still very soon after the accident, but they feared
they were losing him to his battles of guilt and hostility
toward God, fearful he had been instrumental in taking
his family. But even Bob was unable to break the walls
down long enough to crawl in and reason with him.
People were listening more and more to the poison that
Beverly was spreading, and the town talk was that the
pastor parish committee should call the district
superintendent. The serpent in the grass seemed to
know when and where to strike to cause the most
damage.

Bob had tried to call John's former pastor and
friend, Jim Whitley, to have him come meet with John,
but he had recently left the country on a mission trip
with the Clean Well Water Initiative for three months
in Botswana, South Africa. The receptionist reiterated
to him that Pastor Whitley was totally incommunicado.
Bob was worried because if the district superintendent
came and witnessed one of John's episodes, he knew
John's chances of retaining his charge were slim, and he
might possibly lose his license. Bob felt in his heart that
John could be saved from this horrible chasm he had

fallen into. It wasn't pity he felt; it was an honest, deep friendship that they had shared, and what man wouldn't have some hard falls before he could climb back up after the horrific tragedy he had just suffered? The things he had given to serve God and then by such an abhorrent chance accident have everything dear to him ripped away like a painful scab that is unexpectedly pulled from a fresh deep wound. Who wouldn't need time to recover?

The truth was Bob did feel some sense of responsibility. After all, he had wanted his friends to come with them floating. Maybe he hadn't researched the river enough. Certainly he hadn't kept up and been there soon enough to try to help rescue Jason. He held himself accountable to a point because he was the town police chief, and he questioned every action from every angle like he had been trained to do his entire career. And now, a true friend seemed to be drowning, and he couldn't get through to help save him. The irony of his predicament seemed coldly cruel and perplexing, along with painful.

\*\*\*

Henry knocked on the door and waited. No answer. He knocked again even *harder* and pressed his ear to the door trying to listen for movement. He could hear the faint strum of guitars and someone singing. It sounded soft and distant, so he reached for the doorknob and turned it. The door squeaked as it slowly swung open, and Henry could see past the living room and through the kitchen. The back door was wide open, which seemed to be the source of the music.

Henry looked around the room as he quietly made his way toward the kitchen, the old rough-sawn floorboards *creaking* with every step that Henry's large frame took. He had never been in the old shack and noticed not only how humble it was but just how clean it was. It looked as if no one lived in it. The kitchen was spotless! *No dishes left out or discarded boxes of food lying around the table.* He was curious because most bachelors' homes he had been to all looked the same: clothes strewn across the couch and soiled dishes piled on the table and sink countertops. As he reached for the screen door handle, a face peered from around the corner of the porch outside, nearly giving Henry a heart attack as he jumped backward and grunted.

After he regained his composure, he quietly spoke, "Pastor John, I'm sorry to intrude, but I felt the Lord nudging me to come see you." Henry paused to get a response from the pastor.

John pushed through the door and reached for Henry's hand, taking it into his and lightly squeezing. "Henry, it's good to see you! I'm sorry for the mess, but I wasn't expecting company."

"Pastor, I'm going to skip all the pleasantries and get right to the point. I'm scared. I'm getting bad thoughts again, only more frequent. I know you have so much more on your plate than I, but I'm scared— I'm really scared and Molly . . ."

"Molly is, *okay*, isn't she? "John pressed. "She isn't in pain or—*anything* is she?" John questioned thoughtfully and gingerly.

"No, no Pastor, I haven't done anything, and she is fine, except I'm afraid . . ." Henry began trembling as his emotions overtook his ability to speak. He had held his dark thoughts about as long as he could since John had gotten back from Mountain View those several weeks back. Knowing that these were temptations from the devil, he had the wherewithal to repress and fight them, but his control was about to collapse. "I—I think Molly can read my mind lately, I—I think, I think she knows I have these hateful and dark thoughts in my head, and she has—star—started to question me when I—I leave for my walks," he stuttered as he explained. Henry did not *normally* stutter. This seemed rather abrupt to John.

Before John's family had suffered their loss, Henry had been walking over regularly to their house, and the two of them would take evening walks together as Henry confided in him. He had started suffering doubts about God because of his wife's physical circumstances and about his very own value to the world now that he no longer worked at the hardware store. And of course, one of his main ongoing sources of frustration for years was a certain person in the church that tested his very self-control to not take physical action to snuff her verbal, venomous lies and gossip, a shared concern of more than just Henry in the town of Ash Grove. As Henry had gotten more comfortable sharing his deepest conflicts, John had begun to worry that maybe Henry was slipping into early onset Alzheimer's. Inevitably on their next walk, Henry would start again as if he'd never shared the exact conversations with John before. He was very likely suffering from depression too, he thought to himself, because of his concerns about self-worth, which surely was a red flag. Of course, John wasn't trained in any psychological field, but he had been witnessing some rather recent abrupt character changes in Henry before his absence from the walks.

But now for John to suddenly, as a first inclination, think that Henry might be capable of hurting his wife, a woman he loved and cared for so dearly, well, it brought reality back in a flash to John. He couldn't let Henry hurt anyone. But who would he share this concern with? Who would listen to a pastor who had just had his own world turned upside down and could very well be spiraling into a nosedive to earth himself? John scratched his head, stroked his beard, thought deeply, then spoke plainly and slowly.

"Henry, I want you to know that I love you as a brother, and I am praying that you will find an answer. We can search together for answers because, as you know, I'm in a similar boat, so to speak. We can ride this river together Henry, you and me, just don't do anything rash to anyone—yourself included. Stay focused, and let's start back again with those walks together. Lord knows I need someone to talk to also."

And with that the world shifted noticeably for the two of them. It was like as a child when you first got off the merry-go-round and your step felt off-kilter at first, but as you regained your balance and your head stopped spinning, you felt normal again. *Normal again*, it was a nice feeling for the thirty seconds John absorbed it and began to revel in it, then he realized the analogy he had just used, riding the boat together down the river.

John, in that somewhat glimmer of a hopeful moment, had no idea of where the ride in that metaphorical boat with Henry was going to take them. Was his faith moving forward with hope and trust? Or was he subconsciously using it to drive himself deeper into his battle within while drawing a helpless and tormented passenger to take the trip alongside him?

His head dropped down in shame as he turned to head back to his refuge of the back porch he now knew so well.

As Henry walked out the front door and down the small walkway around the tool shed, through the garden and toward the church parking lot, John had felt as if maybe—just maybe—he should and could work his way back into some sort of normality. It was time to stop hiding in his little shack of self-pity and venture back into the world. After all, it was a small world in Ash Grove, Missouri. What is the worse that could happen, he thought to himself. He had nothing more to lose; he also felt that he had nothing more to gain. There lay the dilemma. The void in his heart from the loss of Jason could never be filled again he feared.

Unfortunately, he was oblivious to all the possibilities, and the sadness and grief settled back in as quickly as that moment of hope had come. He sat back down on the porch swing and doubtfully picked up his worn bible and started reading.

*In your struggle against sin, you have not yet resisted to the point of shedding your blood. And have you completely forgotten*

*this word of encouragement that addresses you as a father*
*addresses his son? It says,*

*"My son, do not make light of the Lord's discipline, and do*
*not lose heart when he rebukes you, because the Lord disciplines*
*the one he loves, and he chastens everyone he accepts as his son."*

*Hebrews 14:4-6*

John then thumbed backward toward the front of
his bible and stopped abruptly in Proverbs. His finger
traced across the page and stopped at Proverbs 3:11
almost as the Ouija board planchette had been
magically directed to the letters that spelled out an
answer he had silently asked with his teenage friends
when they brought the board out one night long ago.

*"My son, do not despise the Lord's discipline, and do not*
*resent his rebuke . . ."*

John pondered the scripture for a moment,
slammed the cover closed over the passage, tossed the
book to the side of the bench in the corner, let his head
fall back against the backrest of the gently swaying
swing, and let his eyes slowly roll closed. He listened
for the crackling water and almost instantly fell into a
deep sleep. It was the first truly boundless sleep he had
experienced since—His heart had *died*.

# Chapter 5

*Sound Asleep for around 48 Hours Late June*
## John's Body Goes into Hibernation

T he beautiful woman with the golden blonde hair slid quietly and seductively under his sheets. He tried to see her face but was never able to focus in and visualize more than an outline in shadow. Every time he thought he was about to catch a glimpse, she would turn away at the last moment or the light of the moon would backlight her silhouette brightly, and she would remain a darkened blur.

It had been so long since he had felt so aroused and virile that the urge to pull her into his arms and ravage her right then had to be carefully and willfully wrangled. He was so afraid that a rushed movement might chase her away, and he longed to hold her in his arms and look into her eyes and be loved again. The old, familiar feelings had been lost in the whirlwind of recent pain mixed with years of intimacy taken for granted and left to wither.

He knew who he wanted her to be. Who he longed for her to be. If he could just see her face and be certain.

John's body tossed back and forth on the swing, and his head would lift momentarily before turning one way then the other only to return resting back down on the backrest of the wooden porch swing. For someone watching, he would have looked like a puppet being whimsically controlled by strings leading upward to a puppeteer's hands. With each movement of his head and body, the swing would gain momentum gently at times then more swiftly at others, rock back and forth, and move in circles.

The moon shone brightly through the tiny holes in the rusty, corrugated metal roof, highlighting little moonbeams down on John's face as they danced a peculiar dance across his forehead and cheeks. John's head moved back and forth with the motion of the swing, enabling the flashes of light to perform across his face like a scene from a ballet. Every now and then, a smile would begin to appear in the corners of his mouth, but his brows would quickly furrow, and the smile would transform back to a straight line. Sounds of deep, inhaled breaths and occasional sighs mixed with the breeze blowing through the trees. The trickle of the stream and the wind whistling through the same holes in the roof that the moonbeams shown through seemed to mesmerize his body further and deeper into his resting slumber.

Lightning bugs quickly blinked on and off in the distance but would disappear when they landed up in the high tree limbs. It was mating time for them, and they flashed their beacons of yellow codes hoping to find the right mate for the night, and as they did, they would land and copulate in the cover of the leaves. All the while, John seemed adamant in his sleep-induced movements to search and find the face of the woman who was playfully sending him ciphers of what her body also seemed to ache for.

***

The night before their float was the last time that John had felt the effects of raging adrenaline and carnal arousal. He had teased Shelly with his wandering fingers as they lay in their bed with only the sheet covering them. The thin, hollow panel doors separating them from Jason's room some twenty feet across the echoey camper floor to a thin fabric folding door was all that gave them and their son subtle privacy.

Shelly kept saying *no* to John's advances quietly because Jason may be awake, or he may wake up with the noise it would make. "Besides," she whispered, "the camper rocks when you merely walk across it. Do you really want to be the one to shock your son John Allen Austin? You're his father! It could ruin him for life seeing his dad doing that!" She smiled wickedly with the same desires awakened but playfully pushed him away as she rolled over to her sleeping side, a position in their bed at home that had become such a familiar habit.

***

John's heartbeat slowed down as the faceless, naked body slowly turned and began to slip from the cover of his sheets and fade into the darkness of the surrounding space that he was lying in. He tossed around as he tried to calculate in his slumbering mind what he had done to cause her to vanish before they had shared their moment connected to each other in a passionate and lustrous entanglement.

50

The rhythm of his heartbeat began to fluctuate in tempo while his eyes moved wildly back and forth under the flesh. The orchestration caused tiny wrinkles to shimmer quickly on the eyelids that kept the light of the full moon from waking him. Every other muscle lay motionless as he seemed to transport to another place of his past.

\*\*\*

John's body hovered above a little, dilapidated house with rows of cracked and sometimes missing wooden shingles. The wood siding was in shambles and most of the white paint had long since peeled and fallen into piles around the cinderblock foundation. The windows were thick with dust from the dirt road that led through the long field to its front, and there were piles of discarded junk scattered everywhere in the yard. A broken refrigerator laid on its side, and long-dead auto parts and skeleton vehicles were scattered throughout the yard up to the front porch that held many boxes and sacks of refuse filled to the top, spilling out. He could almost smell the rancid scent from the bags that lay below the buzzing flies circling in and out, from bag to box.

But around back, on a cracked concrete patio, gathered a small group of three boys playing a game around a circular table made from a large wire spool with an odd board covered in large gothic letters that lined up across it in alphabetical order. In the middle of the board was a small arrow-shaped object with a tiny, clear window in the center of it. The three boys had their resting fingertips on the outside edge of the arrow while it slowly waltzed around the board, stopping on certain letters, causing the boys to laugh and giggle.

As if John were a ghost, he was able to hover just above the scene of the three boys. As he awkwardly maneuvered in closer, he recognized the place as the home of his childhood best friend.

None of the boys seemed to stir as he clumsily flew close above them, almost banging into the sides of the structure or the trees that circled the outer boundary of the patio where they were tightly gathered.

As John dared to move closer so he could see what the boys were doing, he suddenly felt queasy in the pit of his stomach. A knot tightly formed in his lower intestine as he instinctively understood exactly what they were in the middle of. He silently hovered in closer and saw himself with the two neighborhood friends of his youth. He at once recollected without hesitation what question he had asked the Ouija board that night after being relentlessly prodded to take his turn. What nauseated him so overwhelmingly was that now, by recalling the question, he also recollected the answer that was spelled out that night by the game's pointer.

As his friends had each one placed their fingers on the planchette, it had slowly guided the tiny clear window on the arrow-shaped tool to slide over specific letters, hesitating on certain ones before moving to the next. The boys would speak the letter aloud before it would glide on to the next. One letter after the other, it finally came to a stop on the last one, which was N, and the word it had spelled out was 'DROWN.' The boys all lifted their heads up in unison and scanned each of the other's shocked eyes. They then both looked inquisitively at John before breaking into a nervous laugh again. Quickly, they moved on to a different game of hide-and-seek in the shadowy field of a full-moon evening, swiftly forgetting about the silly board game of Ouija that his best friend had gotten for his birthday.

John remembered that before the game had begun, his friends had read the directions and warnings of things you should not ask because the 'spirits could deliver *disastrous* consequences if you do!' His best friend read the last line in the book of rules in a deep, haunting voice. "*Under NO circumstances should you ask the spirits how you will die!*" Then of course, they all burst into giggles before starting the game.

John's heart pounded painfully against his chest, and his stomach twisted into knots exponentially as he stated the question aloud again for the first time since he had spoken it silently to himself all those many years back as he had sat around that small round table surrounded by his neighborhood cohorts. "*How will my best friend Jason die?*" He then glanced and smiled at him and winked—the game had started—too late to ask a different question even though he now remembered wanting to.

*** 

Back in John's childhood, he had two best friends that he had considered close enough to be brothers. In fact, they had performed the ritual that close friends often did in that day. Each one had cut his palm then passed the blade to the next until all had completed the task, and then they had pressed their bleeding palms together, saying a silly chant he could no longer recall, making them official blood brothers who would then promise to stand by and protect each other until the bitter end. He remembered that evening precisely as he now pictured his very best friend's face vividly. He had bright-red hair and freckles that bled together covering his mischievous face in a patchwork of white and light tan. His bright-green eyes almost pierced through you when he stared at you, and he had a thin, chiseled body even at thirteen.

After all the years that had passed, and though they hadn't spoken since they'd each grown up and moved away to distant places, to this day, John had considered him a brother and close enough in his memories to name his own son after him. His friend's name was Jason Tyler Dean. His father was a mean, scary man who would only come around when he was drunk and out of money. John befriended Jason out of pity at first, but they quickly grew to be like brothers. Jason's dad would sometimes beat Jason. His mother and Jason quickly learned how to fight back and cause his father to retreat. Something neither of them should have had to learn.

Then John's memory quickly flashed and re-focused as if someone clicked the switch, and his thoughts moved to the outcome of his and Jason's history that night so long ago in their childhood.

*My God!* He thought. What mistake had he made all those years ago? Had he angered his Creator so badly when he played a foolish board game with his friends that God had allowed the spirits to mix up the two Jasons and take his son instead of his best friend? Or was God's intention always to punish him for his childish and unwitting sin against him? Would God really be so jealous and vengeful as to set up the conditions for Shelly and him to a chance meeting that led to them to adopting their son, only to take him from them years later? His thoughts began arcing off each question like sparks flying from crossed electric lines. Had his Master sat back and allowed them to love and teach him for twelve years while they worshiped *His* son Jesus, only to steal him away in such a horrific accident? And why would Shelly be so harshly chastened for the sins of the father?

John cursed aloud as fiercely and defiant as he could, "Damn you for taking my son! I gave up everything to serve *You*! I put *You* above my family! I sacrificed the needs of Shelly to spread *Your* Word and bring in more sheep to *Your* flock!"

John at once felt more like the wolf than the humble shepherd he'd been, and he wanted to exact his wrath against the one who had robbed him of his world.

Then he thought to himself, was he somehow the evil person himself for placing his best friend in danger by breaking the game's rules so blatantly? Maybe he truly deserved to lose everything for carelessly risking his friend in that wicked game. The thoughts were so numbing that their sheer existence left him to melt into a pool of emptiness.

\*\*\*

Now John found himself standing at his pulpit giving the message to what was left of the congregation. He gazed out at them, scanning their faces one by one as his hands gripped the edges of the lectern tightly. He conscientiously hesitated over each face mentally marking them as either a good sheep or wounded and mentally unstable one. He didn't care if they could comprehend what he was doing. It was his dream or nightmare after all. If he wanted to pull the small handgun from under the shelf just under his bible and take out the spiritually challenged ones, one after the other, he could. If instead he chose to give them grace, he was perfectly content with that. It was only a dream, and he was only marking them by how he had seen them interact with one another anyway.

He abruptly stopped his thought process for a moment. The eyes out in the pews showed no fear or knowledge of what he was thinking. He let his eyes close momentarily as he strained to filter through his anguished mind. John suddenly scanned the room one more time and pulled out the already charged pistol and raised it to his chin. He *HAD* caused his own ruin. He *HAD* let down his loving and faithful wife, and he *HAD* failed to save his son by trading him years earlier in his adolescence when he foolishly gambled his life for his best friend Jason's life. It was supposed to be a prank that he would divulge afterward but when the answer had revealed itself, he felt like Judas betraying his master Jesus with the kiss.

The faces never changed, not so much as an eye blinking. They continued to focus on him expressionless, as if they were waiting for an answer that only he could deliver.

John lowered the gun from his chin, never removing his sight from the congregation as he slid the executioner's tool back onto the shelf under his bible, and covered it with a cloth after wiping his brow with it.

He had just experienced an epiphany in the nick of time. He had to search out Jason, Jason Tyler Dean, his boyhood companion, no matter where he may be. He had to seek forgiveness to appease his angered demons he had tempted so many years earlier.

Again, darkness fell upon him as he was pulled up and above the sanctuary and disappeared into the hollow darkness of the tall, wooden, shiplap covered ceiling.

***

John's body still lay on the porch swing as the sun had set and risen and was setting again for a second time, meaning he had slept without waking for his first full day. His clothes were wrinkled and moist with sweat, and his forehead would have been hot to the touch if someone had been there to check it. He had lost considerable weight throughout his whole ordeal as he barely had eaten for weeks. Most of his clothes were fitting much looser than they had. If truth be told, John looked more like he was a homeless man passed out on a park bench than the town's pastor and community spiritual caregiver.

\*\*\*

Beverly Snodgrass was hoping John's demise was close. Either he would buckle from his mental state, or she would succeed in getting him removed by the committee . . . or there could always be other options. She had thought about standing up during a service and berating him openly with *dirt* . . . if she could only find something. *Anything.*

Deliver United Methodist Church's existence was counting on her, and she wasn't about to let this go on much longer. If only others would be as brave as she had been and stand up, she thought to herself. In truth, she had never once talked to Pastor John about her feelings toward him. Every venomous bite she had delivered had been behind his back. He was the victim of the serpent but had not once been injected by it personally. Her victims had just been innocent bystanders that found John and his family very pleasant and giving until she would cautiously slither up and deliver little nibbles of poison to them like a coral snake, without them realizing they had been contaminated by her venom until the ill feelings had hit them in their guts. Most of the members would resist the toxin, still hoping he would recover and that possibly Shelly would move back after the pain healed in her heart. After all, no one had heard anything from her since she had left and the word divorce had not popped up at all in the local chatter.

\*\*\*

As John lay lifeless on his swing, the motion as dead quiet as he was—the pastor had no idea he was about to enter the final chapter of his dark journey before waking some twelve hours later. As he slept, he would go unaware through the gentle night that would soon evolve into a rain-filled day full of thunder and lightning. There was a storm that was on the distant horizon, and it was about to consume him and the town of Ash Grove in a way they could never have predicted.

The end of this unfolding story that would take place in these final hours would decide what fate lay ahead for John as a plan of action would be laid in his mind to follow without variance and with no turning back. There was only one entity that could intervene. *Would that happen?*

\*\*\*

John's body stirred on the swing again as he found himself back at the pulpit with words coming out of his mouth that he seemed to have no control over.

He looked out over his congregation, and they listened intently. John moved his body and hands around, both from the swing, which mimicked his movements in his parallel dream-world, and from behind the lectern as he delivered God's word to them saying, *"One day angels came to present themselves before the Lord, and Satan also came with them. The Lord said to Satan, 'Where have you come from?'"* John paused scanning his crowd and memory to determine what verse he was speaking before he continued, *"Satan answered the Lord, 'From roaming throughout the earth, going back and forth on it.' And then the Lord said to Satan, 'Have you considered my servant Job? There is no one on earth like him; he is blameless and upright, a man who fears God and shuns evil.'"*

John now recognized that it was from the book of Job. A man so blameless and yet was punished so unjustly when God had let Satan have control over him. With what the book contained, John started to shake his head as if he could personally relate with Job and his troubles. John then stood up a little straighter and broadened his shoulders wider as he continued to deliver the message that he did not recollect putting together himself. *"Does Job fear God for nothing?' Satan replied. 'Have you not put a hedge around him and his household and everything he has? You have blessed the work of his hands so that his flocks and herds are spread throughout the land. But now stretch out your hand and strike everything he has, and he will surely curse you to your face.'"*

There was a bright stream of light that suddenly lit the back of the church up as the door opened wide with a loud *creak,* showing two backlit silhouettes starting to enter through the arched doorway. Every eye turned back to look as Pastor John also strained to make the faces out against the brightness that illuminated them from behind.

A loud gathering of gasps arose from the pews simultaneously before the hushes started to come from here and there in the room as to try to quell a spectacle. Their faces were all white and frozen with looks of surprise.

As the two walked in slowly, moving down toward the front pew hand in hand, a trickle of tears followed one by one down John's face until they came so quickly it formed rivers streaming down his face, and his shocked and overwhelmed smile gleamed boldly when the two quietly sat down in their usual spots. Front and right as they looked up at John, husband and father to them, standing at the pulpit to their left. His family hath been returned to him with nary a scar nor saddened demeanor. John's hands warmed as he clutched the wooden edges of his pulpit and smiled at his family.

He shakily continued to speak with much difficulty: *"The Lord said to Satan, 'Very well, then, everything he has is in YOUR power, but the man himself, do not lay a finger.'"* John fought back the flood of tears and yet managed to continue: *"Then Satan went out from the presence of the Lord."*

At the very moment the word 'Lord' fell from the tip of his tongue—John noticed the water starting to trickle down the isles from all sides of the church, flowing toward the spot his wife and son sat motionlessly watching. Slowly at first but rising steadily, the sound of rushing water grew louder, and the sound became stronger echoing off the wood-clad ceiling and walls as the rising rivers became deeper and swifter, encircling his family in front of him.

John remained perfectly dry, he tried to move forward toward them, but each of his feet felt as if they were encased in a thousand pounds of concrete, and as he pulled and tugged at the pulpit to no avail, the water kept coming. The last thing he saw before he was whisked up to the wooden ceiling above, was the two loves of his life plunging up and then under and again up out of the water and back under like fishing bobbers as they stiffly flowed back through the front door and out of his reach and sight. Not a word was heard from anyone in the sanctuary as they watched their pastor disappear into the seams of the shiplap boards that covered the ceiling of Deliver United Methodist Church. And then a single loud gunshot rang out. *BANG!* It echoed from the distance followed by a strangely dead quiet within the sanctuary. His congregation sat calmly and stared at the empty pulpit as if the sermon was continuing.

\*\*\*

As quickly as the dream ended, the rainwater dripping through the holes in the corrugated tin roof began landing on John's forehead waking him from his deep sleep. All the while, the thunder in the distance barked out its anger, and bright flashes of lightning backlit the row of trees that concealed the now-rising stream. John felt like he had just experienced a revelation. He had deciphered the answer he had suspected from the beginning. He got up and headed into the living room, a room he hardly recognized, but the couch was dry, and he felt sheltered from the storm.

He fell back asleep quickly with a new calmness. It was as if his resolve had tucked him in neatly like a mother comforting her child at bedtime, tucking the sheets snuggly around them for warmth and protection before dousing the light for the night.

# Chapter 6

*The Day of the Ash Grove Festival July Sixth, Friday*
**Shelly is Back in Town?**

Boone Days! The summer festival was about to start! There was a buzz in the air, and the week of scattered thunderstorms had ended just in time for the town to dry out. The vendors were arriving early and setting up their wares, while the few shops that existed were lining the sidewalks with summer bargain items. The town had a sparkle on this morning.

The Pastor was out and about and being more visible today; he looked very good for a change. Thin and paler but very good.

Henry was glad to see Pastor John walking around in public, and they would surely have to walk the streets together today! But of course, this would be just a happy stroll with no talk of darkness on such a, "Fine gift of a day from the Maker above!" Henry spoke aloud as he passed by a group of people he didn't recognize. He fanned an exaggerated wave as he quickly headed for the pastor to shake his hand.

"Pastor John! Am I glad to see you! I was beginning to believe you were going to hibernate the entire summer!" Henry felt as if maybe he knew the pastor more than anyone else in town. He realized that Chief Pierce was a close friend, but after the river trip he had taken John on, Henry suddenly felt he had moved up the chain of confidant to number one. A position he felt very comfortable in

***

Shelly had always loved small town festivals. Since her earliest recollection as a little girl, she always looked forward to them or any carnival that might pass through town. The excitement that they brought, the crowds, and all the lights at night. Oh, the lights at night and the way they blended with the stars in the distance! Festivals also brought new visitors and new friends! Shelly had always been the girl that could converse with any new stranger, no matter what age or sex. Her daddy had always told her that out of a field of roses, she would be the wildflower that would draw all the attention, especially since she refused to bend to the conformity of the rest. He also whispered to her that she was a keeper, and that her qualities made her extraordinary. Shelly loved her daddy greatly and admired what she would hear him say. He was the sun and moon to her.

And now his wildflower's heart had been broken irreparably. Her beautiful pedals seemed to be drying up one by one and falling away. There she sat 869 miles from her husband and unable to shed the misery of losing her baby boy or figure out where her marriage with John now stood.

They had been through a lot of shifts in their journey together but never questioning the partnership they shared. Obstacles had always drawn them closer until . . .

65

***

She suddenly looked back up at the road. The loud *growl* of the rumble strip scared her when she veered over it unintentionally. Shelly snapped back to the present and straightened her car back to the center of the lane. The beginnings of a tear poked its salty edge out of the duct then pushed down her cheek, resting on her chin before spilling over the edge and onto her hand that gripped the steering wheel tightly. She had fought internally with herself about making the trip, and of course her parents had mixed emotions as they had watched her suffer alone and without the comfort or even phone call from John. They knew he had to be suffering also, but the pain of watching their Shelly hurt and the cries they heard regularly from the closed door of her childhood room had turned them more and more bitter about their feelings of John. Her daddy had resorted to cursing him more frequently to her mother but never in front of Shelly.

He had tried to reason her away from going back to Ash Grove and meeting with him but to no avail in the end.

"Daddy, I *have* to do this, I can't take the never-ending days and nights without at least asking him why he stopped loving me. I'll be okay. Remember, I'm your wildflower that doesn't bend. I'm strong! And the drive will be mind-cleansing, I promise to call you when I stop for the night and then again when I get there."

And with that, she had loaded her bags, gave some loving to Mr. Wiggles and Dozer, hugs and kisses to her parents, then waved out of the window of her SUV as she pulled onto the dusty road that led away from the home she'd grown up in on the outskirts of Tularosa, New Mexico.

She had spent countless recent nights and days holed up in her bedroom. Every thought she had led back to the fact she had lost not only her precious son but also the man of her dreams and her best friend. That day at the river would play over and over no matter how hard she would try to move forward. The tears would flow, her stomach would twist, the nausea would set in, and then the images of that day would replay. Shelly's hands would shake so violently that she couldn't even write in her journal that she had kept for so many years.

The hard part was looking back through the journal reliving the moments with either one or the other that she had scribbled onto the pages. She had put them there for memory's sake, not ever imagining that the memories would hurt so deeply in her future.

Occasionally, she would glance up and catch her reflection in the mirror that hung on her bedroom wall. She would try to picture herself as a teen, dancing to music, pretending she was talking to the boy of her dreams, while checking herself out, looking at her responses and smiles. Trying to hide her current circumstances by imagining her youthful ones. It would work sometimes, for a few moments, then she would get up and look closer at herself in the reflection, seeing the dark circles under her tear-filled eyes along with the newly forming wrinkles from age and surely the stress of late. Who could be excited about seeing you, she thought to herself. Sure, you used to be pretty and vibrant, even exciting . . . but now, now, you are just a broken shell of the previous version. Her head would dip back down, looking at the pages sitting in her lap, pen lonely in its place beside her on the bed.

She briefly thought for just a moment as she fell back into the pile of pillows on her bed—how was John handling all of this? Surely he was having some rough days and nights also, not that she would wish these hard times on anyone.

\*\*\*

Shelly pulled off the road for the night in Texola, Oklahoma after a day of driving on her two-day trip. Her eyes were getting heavy, as she had mulled through her thoughts for hours to the point she felt nauseated and knew she would surely throw up the minute she could exit her vehicle. Four-hundred-and-forty-two miles she had made it without stopping once on the side of the road because of the many tears that had caused her vision to blur. Tears had started rolling out of her eyes steadily since she had turned onto I-40 East. But now she was pulling into Texola, which sat quietly perched on old nostalgic Route 66, a road that originally led directly to the outside of Ash Grove through Halltown, Missouri which appeared to be close to the half-way point of her journey. She had never had to watch for directions or pay attention to her surroundings while traveling in the past because that had been John and Jason's job. But now, she was the one searching for a place to spend the night and rest her worn and red eyes and hopefully unwind and ease her queasy stomach.

The town was very small, and as she passed a little restaurant called the Tumbleweed Grill, she decided to turn back around for some hotel advice along with a moment of friendly conversation as the silence had been more maddening than she had planned. Shelly had seen some small towns in her days, but she thought to herself, this town had not likely seen the sites or heard the exciting sounds of a festival even once in its days. Nonetheless, she pulled in and stretched her tired legs and started for the door.

"Why honey, we got no hotel in this dust squabble of a town! You'd have to go up the road about twenty miles to Erick, but don't be expecting anything fancy! Sure, they have about ton more dust than we do—and yes, they do have a hotel or two, but nothin' else is more special there than whatcha see here, especially the food they got." The waitress smiled a friendly smile then winked back toward the kitchen to the cook. Shelly smiled back as she tried to ignore the empty spaces between the teeth that remained in the big grin she wore. Her name was Lila. Shelly had politely asked.

And when the conversation slowed, Shelly said, "Thanks, and you have a wonderful evening," as she headed out the door and on toward Erick.

When Shelly pulled into the West Winds Motel that was nestled barely off highway Route 66, she said out loud, "Oh my Lord help me," as she now wished she had taken her daddy's advice of bringing Dozer, her son's American bully mix with her. She could only imagine what the innkeeper was going to look like and what shape the rooms would be in that were lined up side-by-side down the dirt parking lot running parallel to the highway.

Upon closing the door tightly and propping the chair back up under the doorknob of room number five, a trick John had taught her on an adventure trip to a bed and breakfast on Bourbon Street in New Orleans, she dialed up Daddy to let him know she was safe and tucked in for the night. After cleaning up and eating the sandwich she had purchased from Lila back in Texola, she turned the nightlight out and lay quietly rummaging through her thoughts again.

"Hmmmm," she said out loud, thinking about NOT being superstitious when she had glanced at the clock hanging on the wall, but there she lay in room five on the fifth at just past 5 p.m. "Oh, the coincidences of life; at least it's not the sixth, room six, at 6 p.m." And with that, she fell asleep.

\*\*\*

Shelly looked out the rearview mirror of her vehicle as she pulled onto the old Highway 66 headed back to the interstate and noticed the salty, old gentleman waving at her as if he were flagging an incoming airplane onto a landing strip. Her mental alarm clock had gone off early after her reasonably restful night. She smiled to herself when she realized she had survived the night in the scary rundown, fleabag 555 hotel room and that her fears of some monster serial killer innkeeper had turned out to be the sweet old man waving her goodbye with a smile as wide as the distance between here and Ash Grove.

70

Giggling to herself as she relished her silent folksy analogy and accent, thinking she was actually pretty good at it and could possibly fit right in if a necessity arose. She took the entrance ramp back onto I-40 and smiled yet another time as she passed the Motel 6 AND the Days Inn she would have seen last night had she'd not taken the old Route 66 exit to Texola but instead stayed on the interstate to begin with.

"Oh well, it was just a part of the adventure!" she spoke aloud as she fumbled in the console to find a CD for the rest of her trip. She searched around not finding any in her console or glove compartment, so she ran her hand under the front of her seat, and after startling herself again with the rumble strip as she crossed to the right, she pulled out a CD case while lining back up on the road correctly.

"Gary Jules. Trading Snakeoil for Wolftickets?" As she read the cover aloud to herself, it was the star which was tattooed on the gentleman's fist in the photo that caught her eye for a second. "I don't remember ever seeing this," she said out loud, but then decided to poke the disc into the slot on the stereo.

She thought again about the star on the guy's finger, so she lifted the case up and held it resting on the steering wheel, he looked a little like John in his younger years she noticed, but the face was so blurred it was impossible to get a clear visual; she glanced back at the star noticing it was on his ring finger but opposite hand of where a wedding band would sit. Odd, she thought for a moment and then the music started coming from the speakers, and it was frolicsome and acoustical. Good traveling music, she thought as she tossed the case down on the passenger seat beside her and returned her focus to the empty highway ahead.

About six or so hours of driving she thought would put her in Ash Grove around noon. There would be time to wander the downtown in the middle of the festival. Boone Days as it was called. The town where Daniel Boone's son had settled. They had merged it together to the weekend after the Fourth of July, making it a combined celebration this year, so it should be very full and fun with visitors from all over. There would surely be live music and fireworks galore in the park to enjoy also.

She tried to think happy thoughts, but they were mixed with the anticipation of how John would react to seeing her after all this time. She had lost several pounds, not with intention—but *dang* I look good, she thought to herself. Would he notice? Would he even talk to her since he had no idea she was coming? She hoped he hadn't moved on. And could she make herself walk into the house she'd left? The questions she was asking kept planting seeds of doubt, but she kept counterpunching back with thoughts of how he couldn't do better than the wildflower among the roses he had picked.

As the CD continued to spit out mellow song after song, the singer's voice seemed to somehow make her feel closer to John. She couldn't put a finger on it or make any connection or sense of it, but her heart seemed to warm and feel a refreshed connection with his as the songs melted into her ears. While her thoughts continued to dash back and forth between warm fuzzies and streaks of nervous fear, the miles rolled on that drew her nearer to her goal. The goal that had not come from a plan but a desire to test the waters again with the man she had fallen for that crazy day they met. So many memories rushing back like waves rolling up on the beach after forming in the never-ending horizon of the ocean. Swish,swish—she smiled with a small tear in each eye's duct gently pushing their way out to meet the light of day.

*** 

The lyrics of the song that was playing to the haunting melody suddenly caught hold of her, and she backed the song up again to listen closer to what it said. Its music was mysterious, and the lyrics made her feel sad yet closer to John, maybe closer than if she was sitting with him right now at this moment. She hit replay a third time as she looked for a spot to pull her car off the road.

She listened again intently after finally simply pulling as far off the edge of the highway that she could. She reached over and looked at the song list on the CD that had laid in the seat next to her. After scanning down the list, her finger stopped on "Mad World." Yes, that was it, she hit replay again and turned the volume way up, laid her head on the backrest, and listened with her eyes closed.

Shelly must have replayed that haunting song at least ten times before she gathered up her now willowy senses, turned the stereo off, moved the shift lever into drive, and silently pulled back on to I-40, steering her down the highway toward Ash Grove to her chance rendezvous with her estranged husband, following the shared anguish over the death of their most prized gift in the world, exactly forty-three days past from today.

The last thought she could recall as she drove the final miles of her journey was the single word "Macabre." She spoke it out loud as she hit the gas and pushed her way forward without a single car in sight, only the disappearing center lane dashes as they quickly raced under her tires, swiftly disappearing into a solid line of where she had come from.

\*\*\*

Ash Grove's Boone Days was in full swing. People were on every corner of downtown, and there was a constant line down Parkway Street to the city park where live music was being performed and visitors milled through the food and craft tents that scattered across the open field.

\*\*\*

Mary James' home backed up to the park where she lived on Wells Street. It sat halfway to the city park from her back porch and halfway to Pennington's Market from the front porch, where she was able to venture to for limited amounts of time to gather her daily needs and hopefully some quick conversations.

She had a humble home, but it served her, and later her brother, well. Mary had never felt like she needed possessions other than the basic needs: the clothes on her back and place to rest her head in the evenings. Her brother had moved in with her after he returned from serving in the Army over in Iraq. If you were to go inside, the furnishings were sparse, but she did have the walls filled with pictures of desert scenes from all over the Middle East. They were encased in olive-wood frames and were photos taken by her brother Jake from his overseas travel. Mary enjoyed looking at them frequently since the accident.

Shelly had grown up in New Mexico, desert country; it was one thing they had in common to talk about when Shelly visited. She would answer Mary's questions such as what the hot dry climate was like or how was the temperature when the sun went down? Since Mary had never experienced it firsthand, she would hang on every word Shelly spoke. After each visit, she would study the pictures on the wall and in Jake's scrapbook trying to imagine how he felt and what he had seen *minus* the war parts. Mary disliked thinking about the evil that war creates.

But Shelly was gone now also, and Mary looked out across the field full of people and breathed deep the smell of fresh popcorn mixed with deep-fried pork rinds, and she felt the charge of electricity surging from the music being emitted by the band performing on the high-rise stage that towered over the crowd. *Exceptional!* she thought to herself as she prepared mentally to walk through her garden gate and into the mass of movement. It would be quite an undertaking, but this year, she knew she could do it. There were people to talk to, and she so longed for people to converse with and share thoughts and smiles. The thought brought her true joy that soon sliced a path cleanly through the anxiety that had made her hesitate.

\*\*\*

Mary's background story; she had just turned thirty-two when her brother had suffered the boating accident. He had been out fishing with their dad, while on their way back to the dock, they were speeding across the lake and his tackle box had bounced onto the floor from the seat. Jake let go of the steering wheel to reach over for the box, and the boat suddenly made a sharp turn and threw them both out. Jake's father had a life preserver on while her brother did not.

Jake, out of instinct, swam for his boat as it made large circles surrounding them in rough waves churned by the motor. His immediate thought was to swim toward the moving boat so he could climb in and kill the motor. He quickly dove underwater the first time he saw the boat heading at him and it passed over him, dodging the spinning prop by inches. Jake could feel the thunder of power that had raced over him as he re-emerged from the surface.

Jimmy, their father, was hollering, "No, Jake! Let it go and swim for shore!"

When the boat circled over Jake a second time, he was too exhausted to go under and avoid the spinning prop again. Jake suffered horrible slices across his back and legs and sank below the surface before Jimmy could swim to his son to help him. Another thing that she and Shelly now had in common, in a way, but thought to herself they would never share those stories together.

Now at thirty-five, Mary had transformed from a young, carefree, runabout-town single woman into a trapped, vibrant, and beautiful soul encased by a tight boundary of something indescribable even to herself. An internment much like the one her father was held in the day he was surrounded by the circle of churning water that was guarded by the unmanned boat that had taken her brother. Mary was destined to live alone without ever experiencing the gifts of a soulmate—not that she really thought she needed it to complete her story.

*** 

The crowds instantly became apparent as Shelly crossed the railroad tracks at the entrance to Ash Grove from the south side, coming up the highway toward the first of only two four-way stops in town. Looking over to the right coming out of the 'Man Cave' was the first friend to spot her and wave in a loving and welcoming way. Wayne Renfroe owned the local lumberyard and hardware store. The hardware store that had employed Henry Tanner since he had moved to town forty-some years ago and up until his retirement.

She slowed and rolled her passenger-side window down and greeted him with a, "Gee, Wayne you're looking younger every day! I hardly recognized you! But really, trim that beard down if you want the lady's attentions!"

Wayne passed through the crowd quickly and leaned in the window of her vehicle. He gleamed as if he'd seen a friend from his distant past. In many ways, it did seem distant. The gleam dissipated quickly as the reality set in of the last time he'd seen her—Jason's funeral.

"How are you doing Shelly, are you holding up okay?" He suddenly had no idea of what to say or how to react.

"Hanging in there, Wayne, day by day—day by day." She pushed a smile across her lips to give Wayne comfort and help set him at ease. "It's okay good friend," she continued. "Let's let the awkwardness fall to the ditch and come over here and give me one of those big bear-hugs you used to dole out so sparingly! I'll pull in your drive, and you can deliver it properly!" She turned in toward the open gate as the crowd slowly parted. Wayne trailed behind her, and the crowd quickly closed the gap again.

Wayne scanned the mass of moving visitors funneling into town; he thought to himself—the money would be flowing into Ash Grove this weekend, and he then reminded himself that it had desperately needed it. Answers to prayers he had sent. He then looked back toward Shelly and looked quickly upward toward the clouds with a smile and said under his breath quietly, "You're one outa two so far God. Let's shut the opposing team down today."

# Chapter 7

*Early Evening while the Festival Rolls On*

## Miscreants Bask in the Shadows of Night

hen the time of day starts to slip into the *antecedents of evening, a loving parent whose home lies anywhere on the outskirts of town near woods or fields will warn their children before play that this is the time snakes crawl through the grass searching for their evening prey. Be mindful of your surroundings!*

"Whilst creatures that slither and clamber in the dark steadily comport more treachery than those espied in the lightness of day, their sting produces naught greater toxin, hitherto the sum of thine fear of things which lurk in the shadows, therefore, doth add exponentially to the feelings of uneasiness."

~ Unknown

*So, things are scarier in the dark. Everyone knows this and most everyone feels this. Ever try tucking your hand down deep between the cushions on your couch while watching a scary movie in the dark? Or at night start to slide your arm under the pillow that holds your resting head and then suddenly feel the urge to jerk it away for fear of what spider could be resting there?*

Beverly thoroughly loved the anonymity that the cover of darkness afforded her. It gave her greater opportunity to slither closer and eavesdrop undetected on conversations of unsuspecting prey. She could then collect tidbits of dirt, like a rodent collecting nibbles of cheese, and scurry back to her den to lay it out and play with it and mold it to fit her strategy. A plan that would consist of when and whom to dole out the little smidgens of excrement to, her targets, as to manipulate them for her advantage. Make no doubt, Beverly Estes-Snodgrass was a predator. She had been trained and polished, honed if you will, to evil perfection in her ways. She had always been tactical from her earliest childhood up to and including today's sun which rose this morning. It was a family heritage of sorts that had been passed from mother to daughter through the generations. She had an agenda to work on, the Estes's, her maiden name, always did—a plan that may at first seem devious to others but would eventually be justified through the means to an end. And by virtue of its warranted outcome, she knew she would be admonished and revered.

Deliver United Methodist Church was *NOT* going to collapse under her watch. And it mattered not that her pathetic example of a male husband would not collaborate. Beverly knew deep within that she would be adulated in the end after John had been decamped.

But now was the busy eve of Boone Days, and under that cover with the bonus of darkness, she walked out of her front door and toward the horde of faces she would so coyly blend in with. Her blood-red lipstick stretched ear to ear, fitting well with her smug and devilish smile.

It hadn't taken very long before she spied her first possible victim. She had to do a double take as she almost swallowed her own tongue with the mere sight! Had she really stepped out of her door and in a hundred or so steps spied the crème de le crème?

There standing on the steps of her beloved DUMC was Wayne Renfroe. Standing tall and proud with his coal-black hair stood a nibble of dirt that she'd so hoped for. The thrill of the pre-kill sent shivers of anticipation from her cold and ruthless heart up to the roots of her hair planted in her scalp.

Beverly wouldn't have taken any notice of Wayne had he been alone. She was no fan of his, but he was no threatening foe either. But standing next to him, and rather closely, she surmised—*stood wantonly*—in his clutches, she would later add from her own accord to the dirt morsel of a story she was already concocting, was no one other than the bride of her arch nemesis.

"Shelly Rose Austin, you poor, tortured infecund tart," she said quietly to herself but suddenly covered her mouth with her hand as if the words were an accidental belch from deep within her diaphragm.

If she could only get a compromising angle and snap a picture for proof. She laughed out loud but muffled the snort that quickly followed by her hand that was still parked by her painted lips.

"Pictures?" she questioned quietly. "In this scandalous town and with my wit . . ." She wouldn't need any pictures she quickly calculated. *When John gets wind of the way I will paint this, in his mental state, like pushing a baby cart into busy traffic. No matter where in the road the cart enters—someone's baby is getting run over.* And with that thought, she turned to begin her assaults with nary a secondary thought.

As Henry walked by Beverly on the opposite side of the street toward the park, he swore he witnessed her perform a shuck and jive step and squeak out a 'Can I get an amen?' He paused a second, shook his head, and put the silly thought out of his mind.

Behind him, Molly was headed his way in her 'HOVEROUND' motorized wheelchair at top speed screaming, "Henry! Stop!" at the top of her lungs. Pedestrians were scampering off the street to either side to keep from being run over by the rather large woman swaying back and forth down the middle of Park Street, whom upon closer examination seemed to be wielding a small handgun in one hand. "Clear the way people!" Molly hollered. "Out of my way—stop Henry!"

Beverly looked across as the pandemonium moved down the street like the surge of a tidal wave moving ever-closer toward her. As her eye focused on Molly leading the crest of the wave toward the park, her red-painted lips moved from a circle shape of shock to the more familiar shape of a monstrous smile.

"Molly ole gal—shoot that crazy old curmudgeon!" She cackled to herself.

***

"Chief, what we have is total chaos and a freaking quagmire on Park Street. You gotta get here quick before someone gets shot or run over!" Mayor Thomas snapped his flip phone closed and rushed back out to his porch to witness the turmoil.

# Chapter 8

*9:15 p.m. July Sixth on East Park Street*
**Chaos Equals Quagmire**

T he night's festivities had been relatively calm and without need for law enforcement stepping in with any reinforcement. But Chief Pierce and his officers were counting their chickens before they had hatched, and now, incubation was over, and they were about to be up to their ears in baby chicks!

After the chief received the mayor's call, he and all three officers on duty ran out to their squad cars and would have quickly converged onto the scene had it not been for all the people and mayhem. The station was merely five blocks, but with all the visitors walking to and from the park and Main Street, they ditched the idea of their squad cars and advanced to the scene on foot.

The scene they found after pushing through the crowd involved Molly confronting her husband Henry. She was yelling at him full volume with hands flailing toward him as she circled around him. In her hand was a small handgun just as the mayor had reported. Poor Henry was standing there receiving his wife's rants in horrified awe.

All he could muster from his mouth was, "Oh sweetie, baby—I just got it for protection for us.

Please put it down, please." He spoke the same words repeatedly as Molly seemed to be stone-deaf to any communication spilling from his mouth. She just continued screaming and waving the gun in her hand uncontrollably as she continued to drive around him in circles.

Chief Pierce quickly pushed his way through to the scene with his officers splitting from each other and taking control of the audience, maneuvering them back and clearing the area.

Chief Pierce looked at Molly directly in the eye and gently spoke, "Molly—it's okay now. No harm done by anyone, and we surely don't want anyone to be hurt by accident, so can you look at me and follow my directions?" The chief had such a calming and tranquil voice in situations that called for it. His training always kicked in, and he was always able to take control and bring things like this to a positive close.

Molly looked at him face to face as she brought her chair to a halt, and tears started pooling up as she talked directly at the chief. "I'm sorry Chief Bob," her hands shaking, "I found this gun in Henry's sock drawer, and with his crazy talk lately—I just don't want him to do anything foolish." She sobbed as she slowly lowered her hand holding the weapon to Bob's hand and pushed it into his palm. She then dropped her head down into submission.

Chief Pierce turned to the hushed crowd and disbursed them saying, "Show's over, folks; please move on toward the park or Main street and vacate this general area. The festivities will continue until midnight as scheduled. Fireworks should be happening anytime soon." And on that note, there was a loud *boom* that lit up in the sky, signaling the beginning of the show with a thundering report.

He then turned to Molly and Henry and noted, "I'll return this after we talk next week." Looking at the handgun and then back to them. "I don't think we need any charges brought up tonight; this feels like a big public misunderstanding and no one was hurt—but we *WILL* all three get together and talk about this after the weekend, okay?"

Henry turned to Molly as she rotated her electric scooter a hundred and eighty degrees, pointing it back toward their home. Henry reached and shook Bob's hand then turned and followed Molly home, dejected and humiliated.

After the crowd moved on, he gathered back up with his officers; they walked back toward the station, each headed around different parts of town hoping there would be no more action needed tonight but aware that chaos can break out in a New-York minute, even here in Ash Grove, Missouri.

*** 

Beverly was so glad that the chief hadn't shut the evening down. She had watched carefully from cover as the scene had played out. She knew that by coupling what had *unfolded* with the Tanners along with the juice she had concocted between Shelly and Wayne, it would surely help seal the authenticity of the web she was weaving!

Yum, yum, she thought to herself as she slithered off to spread the news. "What more flavorful contagions could I stumble onto tonight?" she said aloud to herself as her first step attempted a small skip, almost causing her to tumble to the ground.

Beverly had a busy evening spreading her stories and adding more juicy details to the Wayne and Shelly saga to anyone that would show the least bit of interest and a few that had shown no care at all. She did her best to spread it like butter on hot toast so the talk of the town in the morning would take hold of the community and cause as deep a pain for John as she could. She never once hesitated, thinking of what it would do to Shelly or Wayne. It didn't matter if it expedited John away as quickly and as far away from Ash Grove and Deliver UMC as possible. After a full evening of prowling, she snuggled into her nest with her unsuspecting mate and fell asleep with an evil smile brightly glimmering from the evening's moon that shone in on her just outside her bedroom window.

\*\*\*

Wayne was home at the Man Cave finishing off a cool, frosty beer thinking that maybe, just maybe, his friend who was also his pastor and Shelly would soon be a couple again and a normal life could get back to Deliver United Methodist Church.

\*\*\*

Shelly settled into bed feeling awkward that she had not seen John yet and wondered how he would react to her being back in town. The truth was Shelly really didn't sleep a wink even though the bed in Jake's old room was soft and comfortable, as were Mary's words just before she tucked her in. She always felt strangely warm when talking to Mary. She had sown a deep friendship with Mary that had grown more with each visit as they would spend time together sharing stories about Jake and looking through his desert pictures. Photo memories of a period past for sweet, sweet Mary.

As the first night of the weekend festival came to a sleepy goodnight, the visitors and partygoers dispersed. Chief Pierce turned out the light at the station, radioed the third shift officer that he was the man in charge, and then headed home to snuggle in next to his wife, Julie. He was to get some much-needed shuteye; he had to be ready to face day number two of Boone Days in the tight-knit community of Ash Grove, Missouri. USA.

## Chapter 9

*The Town's Immunity Systems is Tested, July Seventh*
**Fever Sets in For the Austin Family**

J ohn woke up for the first time in quite a while from his bed instead of the porch swing. He had enjoyed walking around amongst the crowd yesterday, feeling a connection to the world that he had disconnected from after the death of his son and the following immediate estrangement of his wife. He had also tired himself by noon from the crowd and headed back to the sanctity of his little shack to reflect. He smiled to himself, feeling refreshed, but then in subtle fashion, the guilt edged its way back in on the fringes of his thoughts. His dreams had still planted doubts in the ways he had failed protecting his family, and with that pain, he again was reminded of the suggested cure that had metamorphosed from his sleep-induced overview of his recent life.

He fought the negative persuasions off enough to drink a cup of coffee then shower and head to Main Street for some breakfast. He thought to himself as he headed out the door and down the path, passed the tool shed, then through the community garden into the churchyard—that maybe from now on, he would be dealt winning hands in his poker game of life. And with that final thought, he put a new foot forward with a jolly little step.

As the door swung open to the Copper Grill, John grabbed the edge and held it wide open while saying, "Good morning, ladies, how are we today?" He thought he felt a hint of uneasiness between them as they seemed to look him over on their way out without so much as a word.

"Good morning, Pastor J!" said the smiling waitress that had just started attending Deliver UMC. "It's good to see you out with a smile! Pay no attention to the snobby hens that just waggled through the roost's gate!" she said with a snicker. "You know hens—they get mean if they don't get any rooster time! Sometimes, it's just the egg that gets laid!"

John cracked a smile and said, "I believe that comment just made my morning! Enough so to enjoy a couple of hen's eggs whipped into an omelet and a side of bacon."

"You got it, Pastor J," Becky answered quickly. "I'll have 'em out to ya before you can get to the opening prayer!"

Yes indeed, John thought quietly, today is a new hand, and so far, the flop has dealt three hearts to the one I'm holding!

***

Shelly, whom never actually got past a wink of rest the night before, was jittery and bouncy as she readied herself to search out her distant husband, John. Wayne had told her last night where John was staying since he too had not been able to live in the parsonage after losing Jason. When Wayne had said Jason's name the night before, it had felt like the sting when you touched your finger to the stove but deep within her heart. It was painful, but then again, it was also a comfort because it kept him close to her thoughts. It was her new existence, and she was still trying to make it fit like a glove that so far was still too small to pull over her palm.

Her thoughts returned to her immediate dilemma. How would she greet her husband? As a long, lost friend? Maybe an old adversary willing to put down the sword and console each other in a truce? The internal stage in her brain played over and over with different outcomes each act could bring. It was causing her nerves to unsettle along with the nausea in her stomach.

"Oh, please, tummy, not now," she said aloud as she climbed out of the shower. "I need to focus, focus, focus! I don't have the time or room in my brain for this queasiness now." Her words didn't seem to matter though as she rushed to lean over the toilet just in time.

***

Mary had breakfast ready in the kitchen when Shelly entered the room looking frazzled. "Oh, girl come over here and let me hug some comfort into your sweet little body. It's going to work out Shelly—I feel it. In God's time, you're going to heal and find happiness again." At that, she pulled Shelly in tight and gave her the longest, most comforting and caring hug she thought she'd ever received. *Warm and bone deep.*

After breakfast, Mary said she'd be praying and to hang in there. And with that, Shelly was out the door. She thought about driving but then realized it wasn't far, and she could use the air and exercise. Besides, the beauty of a small town like Ash Grove was that you really didn't need a car to get around!

***

As John was finishing breakfast, the next batch of ladies was seated to his back. He was sipping his coffee when he started to hear the local gossip. It didn't take long to hear the story of Henry and Molly's escapade last night, and it brought concern to him, but it was the second story that landed harder on him and sucked the air from his lungs as he sat motionless, unknowingly spilling hot coffee onto his crotch from the tipped cup. He sat so stunned and numb that he couldn't feel the scald on his legs over the scalding his heart was experiencing.

Not Wayne, he thought to himself. He wouldn't do that to him. Between the searing in his heart and the rage of possible betrayal from a friend and his wife—he reached in his wallet, pulled out a twenty, and threw it onto the table as he arose and exited past the women without a word spoken either to or from anyone. Becky glanced over just in time to see John's back as the door closed, then she glanced over to see his plate almost untouched.

***

As John felt each heavy-laden leg force its way in front of the other toward his fortress of solitude, he thought again to himself and spoke out loud, "Shelly is in town? Wayne and Shelly? My God! How can you lay another burden on my shoulders?" He asked God as he rounded the corner, realizing just then that the four hearts he was holding in his Texas-hold 'em game of life—had just received the flop in the game play of 'life poker' and the last card dealt was a two of spades, the cheating pair he'd just discovered. Seems the river had dumped him once again, robbing him of his wife and a two-timing friend this time. His dreams had been correct all along. *Instructions of what should follow!*

\*\*\*

John's head hung low, and he was moving swiftly as he rounded the corner. He hadn't looked up to notice who was moving toward him from the other side. It was of course Shelly. She hadn't been privy yet of the talk around town and had no clue why John would say what he was about to say to her when their eyes would meet for the first time since laying Jason's body to rest in the small, wooden urn.

Shelly had a beautiful but cautious smile as their eyes scanned each other from bottom to top. Then the world's rotation seemed to slide to jarring halt as they slowed to a dead stop, face-to-face, arms-length apart from one another. The silence felt like it lasted a lifetime while each searched for words to speak from the thoughts that were churning deep inside each of their brains.

Shelly made a garbled noise as the first word got hung up in translation, getting caught up by her twisted tongue. It was at that moment John's vocal rendering broke through the sound barrier like a missile from an anti-aircraft gun.

"I hope you burn in hell, Shelly Rose; I know I will. Maybe I'll bump into you there, and you can stab me in the back yet again while we share a burning flame together in Satan's ole hot tub, wouldn't *THAT* be fun?" It had been delivered, and with the visual he saw in her face, it had hit its target hard and with devastating accuracy. He had delivered a smart bomb that cut through the intended victim's barrier and exploded at her core. *BOOM!*

John didn't stay long to ponder the carnage he had just delivered. He quickly moved each heavy-laden leg again, one after the other, as he forged his way back to his porch swing so he could lick his wounds and continue the docket toward his final curtain call.

\*\*\*

Shelly stood melting in the apocalypse that John had just delivered and quickly vacated. She couldn't catch her breath no matter how hard she gasped and sucked deep for the life-giving substance. Her head felt light as her vision dimmed just before she lost consciousness, falling backward, hitting her head hard on the pavement as her body tumbled to the ground. Clutching the side of the building had done nothing to slow the speed of impact.

It seemed that, indeed, Beverly had orchestrated, strategized, and by third party delivered the ultimate plan of perfect destruction. In one evening, she had been able to collect the enemy's secrets then artistically modify them into a quick-spreading contagion that took not only the weak, embattled pastor out of her way but would be sending his only reason for living to crawl back to Tularosa, New Mexico in a wounded state of ruin. Make no mistake, when the chatter would get back around to her later that day, there would be one heck of a party in the Snodgrass den. *All associate snakes invited!* It would, however, be a party for only one.

***

The ambulance showed up fifteen minutes after it had been called and dispatched. The trouble was, at this point, no one could calculate just how long Shelly had laid unconscious on the edge of the sidewalk that morning or what could have been the cause. She was being taken to Springfield because that was the closest hospital, and at seventy miles an hour, it didn't take long to arrive there. It beat the town gossip wagon by mere seconds.

# Chapter 10

*Saturday Early Afternoon at Mercy Hospital*

## It'll Take More Than Stitches to Heal That Wound

**M**ary was the first to arrive along with Chief Pierce. They had almost caught the ambulance even though they'd had a fifteen-minute lag from starting. Bob's squad car had been flying. Bob, knowing that Mary was a close friend of Shelly's, had quickly picked her up after hearing the call go over his radio. It was a whirlwind stop on his way into Springfield with Mary frantically climbing into his patrol car without time for worry about her 'special' problem of 'fear leaving.'

The doctor came out, and Mary quickly rushed up and asked about her condition. He turned in close to Mary and with a concerned look told her she was lucky that the head wound was a concussion and that the swelling had been outward and not inward. It could have been much worse, but she had required five staples that would need to be removed in four or five days.

"I'm going to send her home in a day after overnight observation as long as she has someone to stay with her for twenty-four hours. And of course, she'll need bed rest for at least forty-eight hours after she leaves the care of the hospital. She'll need to try to lay flat on her back, only sitting up to eat and help getting to the restroom."

Mary said that Shelly would be going with her and staying in her home where she had been visiting before the accident. The doctor leaned in and talked to Mary in a hushed tone, directing Mary closer. Bob felt awkward and started following the nurse to Shelly's room as the doctor and Mary continued their conversation. Bob looked back, and he couldn't help but notice that Mary was responding in an acknowledging fashion with some looks of seriousness.

Bob knocked on the door and peeked in slowly at Shelly. After focusing a minute, she looked Bob square in the eye from a procumbent position as he sauntered slowly in with his hat in hand. She simply stated, "Bob Pierce, I detest you as sure as I'm lying here. My husband hates me now, and I hold you personally responsible. You took us to that river knowing we had no experience. I lost my only baby boy, and now I've lost John. You helped destroy my family, and I hope to God you feel the pain you've brought on me."

It cut deep. It cut directly to the bone, and it didn't seem like anything from left field. It sounded like she had rationalized it out to be direct and concise.

Bob leaned over and quietly said, "Shelly, this too shall pass. It will take some time, but you will heal. I know John, and believe me—I know it seems dark and distant—this world you two are sharing. Don't give up, the relationship can heal as surely as that nasty bump on your head will. You and John and this whole situation has been—and will continue to be—at the foremost of mine and Julie's prayers as it has been since that horrible day." And with that, he turned and exited the room, walked over to Mary, and told her he would send another squad car when she needed to be picked up. He had something come up and couldn't stay.

As Bob walked out to his car, his head was mulling over the possibilities of just what might have happened that would have changed Shelly's attitude yesterday into what he just witnessed. Mary had said she had been in a great mood with only anxiety about seeing John and how he would react to her. It had been a horrible and quite frankly odd situation from the point they had found Jason's body until now. Yes, relationships frequently split from tragedies like the loss of a child, but not usually so instantaneous, especially from a couple so close to God.

Chief Pierce was a logical man who found answers that weren't always normal, but they were predictable many times if you thought them through thoroughly. This one, though, had baffled him from the start. It was almost like Satan himself had chosen to rattle the very foundation of their beliefs. He wasn't sure that the doctor's sutures in Shelly's head were going to heal the much deeper problem, and that perplexed him. But more than that, it made a tough guy sad. Officers of the law cannot show emotion. One of the top ten rules. He was having a hard time following that rule today.

In the thirty-five minutes it took to drive back to town, Bob tried to forget the look Shelly had in her eyes as she had fired those direct hits aimed squarely at his chest for maximum damage. As he pulled up to the police station, it dawned on him when he reached over to the lockbox in his squad car that contained Molly's handgun that he needed to meet with Henry and Molly soon—*very soon*.

One more night of this danged festival, Bob thought to himself as he closed the door to his office and locked the handgun in his safe. "Lord, let us make it through the last night eventless and I promise I'll be at Deliver with Julie and the kids tomorrow," he said quietly while marking his calendar for Monday in big letters. TANNER'S ONE P.M.

# Chapter 11

*Sunday Morning Service at Deliver UMC*
### A Time for Reflection of Our Sins

T he morning came early for John. He had spent the remaining hours of the last day of the festival reflecting on what had happened between Shelly and him. He had suspected her disdain for him because of his failed attempt at saving Jason, but he never would have expected her to move on so quickly through the pain and seek out intimate pleasures. All he could picture was her drowning her pain in a pool of lust with his friend who was also part of the congregation that he was responsible for spiritually feeding.

John used his guilt and hurt to form a scalding message to his flock that he would deliver this Sunday morning. Stabbing or subtle was the question. He supposed that would depend on who showed up and who would cower from him.

He tapped his personal bible a couple of times with his pointing and middle finger in a drumming fashion before sliding it under pulpit on the shelf.

\*\*\*

John busied himself setting the scene for the service, arranging candles and the giant bible that sat

99

open on the altar. He tried to calm himself with self-assurance that there had been a mistake of some kind. A misunderstanding or the gossip was just that—gossip. Untruths.

It seemed as it came closer to service time his anger began backsliding. This was his new normal, the war within himself between evil and good. John's anger would fill his inner being when circumstances would develop and then start to subside as he would pick apart the possibilities that things were not as they seemed. He had begun to realize that his love for Shelly was not dead as he had previously presumed. It was good that he had been researching answers for adultery and forgiveness in God's word. John still hadn't given up to the point he wouldn't seek answers by seeking God's wisdom. Answers were usually attainable if he only picked up the book and searched for them.

\*\*\*

John looked out over the crowd as they entered the arched doorway; he noticed several new people walking in. Visitors from the festival, he imagined as he greeted them with smiles and nods.

Internally, he knew he didn't want to deliver a message like a radical evangelical would. He really didn't go for the hell-fire-and-brimstone approach, although the scripture he chose was condemning. It hadn't been in his upbringing, and his mother would certainly have feelings of disappointment in him if he used fear to scare people into their faith or punish them from the pulpit for personal reasons. With that thought, he realized he was unprepared for the message today. John instantly acknowledged his conscience still existed. He glanced up toward the ceiling at the shiplap boards and then over to the stained-glass window portraying Jesus looking upward to his father in prayer. John bowed his head and began praying that he would receive the Lord's help in putting the right words in his mouth today. John knew the congregation had probably heard the gossip and would be listening even more intently to his words, and he fervently prayed for guidance. He asked that he not use God's pulpit to dole out personal retribution to those that may have hurt him. It was the first true sincere prayer that he had communicated which hadn't been based on his own needs but rather focused on what God wanted from him.

After he said Amen to himself, he looked over to his organist and nodded to begin the service. The door opened and closed several more times, lighting the room with the sun's brightness and then dimming as the door would close. The organ played softly "How Great Thou Art."

John had expected a smaller than normal crowd because of the festival and people sleeping in, but as he went through the opening traditions before his message, he was astounded that the sanctuary was almost filled to its capacity. There must have been at least ninety people seated. This fact would put the pressure on him since this would be the largest congregation he will have preached to. After the receiving of joys and concerns and then the passing of the peace, the liturgist began reading from Jeremiah 5 verses 7-13.

*"How can I pardon you? Your children have forsaken me and have sworn by those who are no gods.*

*When I fed them to the full,*

*they committed adultery and trooped to the houses of whores.*

*They were well-fed, lusty stallions, each neighing for his neighbor's wife.*

*Shall I not punish them for these things?' Declares the Lord; and shall I not avenge myself on a nation such as this?"'*

*"'Go up through her vine rows and destroy, but make not a full end;*

*Strip away her branches, for they are not the Lord's.*

*For the house of Israel and the house of Judah have been utterly treacherous to me, declares the Lord.*

*They have spoken falsely of the Lord and have said, 'He will do nothing; no disaster will come upon us, nor shall we see sword or famine.*

*The prophets will become wind; the word is not in them.*

*Thus, shall it be done to them!'"*

Pastor John stood silently for an uncomfortable moment. It could be felt by all seated in the church, and then he walked up to the pulpit. He took in a deep breath and looked across the entire room scanning each face that was in the crowd from left to right and then back.

"That is some intense and foreboding scripture don't you think?" He paused again to notice the nods in the room as he quietly tapped his fingers on the pulpit sides. "The Lord had seen what the people of Israel had become. There were no true followers of his word. They had taken up other gods and ignored the true God's warnings of punishment. Life doesn't seem so much different today than it did as far as how we push God away and pretend that he has no punishment for us, for our sins, until some later date if at all. The harm was only dealt out in the early days, right?" John shifted his weight back from one leg to the other, a nervous habit he had when he was uncomfortable in speaking. "We do tend to expect a blanket of forgiveness when we mess up, and we don't even think of a punishment that might be bestowed on us, no famine, no death by sword." John looked out among the crowd and then back down for a moment in contemplation. He started to speak but choked a bit and cleared his throat.

Pastor John smiled before continuing, "We expect instant forgiveness for our sins and transgressions against our Father with no real repercussion even though it is written that he can be a vengeful God. But a quick 'I'm sorry, please forgive and forget—' and it is all supposed to be forgotten as we move on toward the next slip up. But if we are wronged, do we give quick and simple forgiveness?" John's eyes began to water as he reached up to brush it clear with his left hand. "Are we emulating the same treatment that we expect our Lord to give us? Or do we extract a self-determined amount of revenge called justice and punishment before we decide it may be time to forgive? Let the offender dangle a little while longer from our nooses before we consider forgiving them and cutting them loose. I know I have!" John nodded in conjunction with others in the congregation, acknowledging the guilt they have suffered together.

The pastor stepped away from the pulpit and walked to the middle of the altar between the pulpit and lectern. "You surely don't think I'm any different just because I'm a preacher, do you? I wasn't always you know. I am reasonably new at it. I'm just like you, I'm human! I'm a sinner, but like you—I am also one of God's children, whom he loves with such vigor." John put his right hand over his heart and pounded his left hand down on the top of the piano top, startling some who were about to doze.

"Yes, I sin. I did before, and I sometimes sin the same sin over and over! Don't be shocked! I too expect to have that instant forgiveness with absolutely no punishment from the Lord. When I ask for it, I expect quick forgiveness. When I declare that I am truly sorry and repentant, I don't even consider that he would punish me!

"He didn't punish me for something I did by taking my son away or causing marital problems for my wife and me! He *forgives*! He paid the price of my sin and your sin already long ago with his *life*! His Father offered him up to be falsely accused—tortured and beaten—nailed to the cross for all to see. He was taunted and spit upon for no other reason than one, *so we can be forgiven daily*! For the sins we commit and for the ones we haven't even dreamed up yet!" John walked back over to the pulpit and reached under, pulling his personal bible out and holding it up high in his right hand.

"Can I give that kind forgiveness to those that have hurt me? I'm supposed to. Every person who claims to follow Jesus is supposed to. But it's difficult if not impossible when we are sinned against personally. We see holding grudges as the easy way; I'm telling you right now that that kind of thinking is dead wrong!" John slapped his bible down on the pulpit, causing another loud *bang*!

John scoured each of the faces sitting in the pews before continuing, speaking in a hushed tone, "The truth is I'm having trouble right now. It's painful! It doesn't seem like the offending person deserves my forgiveness! It doesn't seem like I deserve the Lord's forgiveness. Some of those that don't seem like they deserve grace are those that don't even believe in grace the way you and I do!" He raised his voice a little louder as he continued, "Why, oh why, would we waste our time forgiving people who might even get personal enjoyment from hurting us? Or stealing from us—or coveting what is ours?"

John persisted, "Why they even seem to target us believers sometimes, like they're testing us! Toying with us. Testing our faith and if we truly live the way we claim to. Laughing and pointing at us in ridicule when they see us fail at what we so easily profess to do as believers but often blunder in practice."

John looked down toward his feet for a moment in self-reflection and then looked up to the ceiling at the seams of the shiplap boards. He almost expected to be pulled up like gravity had ceased existence in the room as in his dreams. But that did not happen. The room was quiet, and as he glanced around, he saw that no one was snoozing, not even the regular sleepers!

He then smiled to himself briefly as he noticed Beverly Snodgrass roll her eyes when they met momentarily. He looked over at Molly and Henry, who were starting to well up in tears. He glanced over to where the Pierce's were seated, and Bob winked at him. John then glanced at Becky, his waitress friend who was smiling even though tears were streaming down her face and gave him a quick thumbs-up gesture.

John returned back again to the pulpit while continuing, "If I have to forgive this person without punishing them—how will they ever understand how badly they have hurt me and what in the world would ever keep them from doing it all over again? Can I get an Amen?" Several people across the congregation responded back in like. "How many times do I have to forgive? Seven? Seventy? Peter thought he was clever asking that question. And Jesus answered back, 'Seven times seventy Peter,' or in other words—boundless times."

Then John spoke with a clear smile on his face, "Well, you know what folks? Those questions are really above our pay grade. It's not yours or mine to even contemplate if we will be sinned against again from the offender, or if he gets punished or not. It's not our worry. We need to learn our place and our rank in God's world. You and I are his subordinates, God's followers." Pastor John winked at the congregation as if he was letting them in on a little secret.

"You see, forgiveness doesn't mean that you are forced to reconcile, folks. That's right, forgiveness and reconciliation are two totally different animals. Forgiveness is what the one who was hurt or offended or wronged is supposed to seek out from God to help themselves let go of the pain and animosity that was caused by the other. Let me say that again so you hear this plain and simple. When you are hurt—you seek God so He can forgive *YOU*, and *He* heals you from that pain because Jesus knows the sin festering in your heart from being sinned against will continue to grow without *HIS* forgiveness." John's hands were clasped together tightly as he began to speak again.

"Forgiveness isn't necessarily something you seek out to give the one that hurt you so they can be let off the hook. Forgiveness is a healing of one's self that you seek so you can continue in God's plan that *He* has set for you. *He* wants you free from that burden and pain. *He* wants you set free from that pain and imprisonment that comes from not asking for His forgiveness when we are sinned against by another."

John took a deep breath and then continued, "You see, by failing to ask God for forgiveness, it lays that heavy burden upon our shoulders and we continue our journey bogged down, and then we begin to veer off onto paths of revenge and punishment of those that offended or attacked us. Those are *His* worries of how to punish. Those are *His* battles—not ours. If you go chasing those battles, your path will never lead to the *CROSS* my friends. That path will twist back and forth, leading you wrong directions and taking so much longer to get where you want to end up."

John looked back over from the pulpit as he scanned God's followers, and then he looked over again to the stained-glass window depicting Jesus looking skyward. God had answered his prayer once again. He scanned the room once more, and it seemed the words God had given him instead of what he'd written had hit home with several people seated in the pews. John began to pray aloud as he nodded for the organist to start the closing music.

"Brothers and sisters in Christ, there are some people out there in such denial of our Lord that all they feel they have to live for is to make you and I and everyone they come in to contact with miserable and filled with pain. We are going to be hurt, each one of us here today. Time after time for most of us. The difference between the offenders and you and I as the recipients—is that you and I know and love the Lord." John walked out from behind the pulpit and down the stairs into the congregation, walking amongst them and touching shoulders as he wound around the sanctuary.

"We know that *He* wants us set free from the pain and anguish and that through coming humbly and graciously to *Him* to work out forgiveness doesn't mean that we leave our hearts open for repeated offenses. God will take control of that burden the minute we give it up to Him, and then we receive *His* Grace." Pastor John walked past Billy, Beverly's husband, and touched his shoulder.

"To hurt someone is a sin! We all know that, or we wouldn't be sitting here today. But we also need to remember that to deny forgiveness to an offender—to NOT go to God for help in rendering that forgiveness is also a sin. It's a sin against the offender and a sin against God himself." John started to wind back around toward the altar and back up to the pulpit.

"We are to love others as we love ourselves. Not just a select lovable group chosen by us—but all, even our enemies. A very hard lesson to practice but nonetheless a very important commandment to follow.

"As we go through this week, I want you to try to remind yourself to have those conversations with God and get that burden that is on your shoulders off and hand it over. It's so much easier to walk with our heads held up and smiling if we lighten that unnecessary load. Smiling is a way of proclaiming our faith to others. You can't smile without asking for and giving out forgiveness. It won't happen. Trust me! I'm living proof of that. Are you? Now let's sing the last song "Amazing Grace" together as we close the service and head back out to the battlefield. Amen?"

Most of the crowd responded back with an amen. The real question that was left on several of the people's minds, those who were members and knew the community's circumstances, could Pastor John practice what he just preached, after the wrong he had just recently received?

Bob looked over at Julie, and she whispered to him, "I pray that John has crossed back to the land of the living. I also hope that when he finds out that Shelly was here and is now in the hospital in Springfield that they can work things out."

Bob nodded back and merely responded with, "Pray for it to be because I so miss that girl and her smile and John's smile too."

# Chapter 12

*July Eighth Monday Morning, Festival Over*
## Not Your Typical Monday Morning in the Grove

B ob rolled over in bed and looked at Julie who was still soundly sleeping as the alarm on her side of the bed repeatedly buzzed the most awful sound that ever existed. How could she continue to sleep through that racket? As Bob sat up and leaned over her to reach the off button, their noses almost touching. Julie's eyes opened *abruptly*, and she leaned up to peck her husband on the lips.

"You were fake-sleeping again weren't you? Dang it Julie, all you need to do is ask for a kiss—you don't have to snipe one; you know I hate your alarm, and I am going to take it outside and shoot it one of these mornings!" Bob's eyes rolled and then zeroed in, meeting Julie's square on. He tried to keep the stern look on his face but failed as his expression became overtaken with humor.

"Yeah, but stealing one is more fun—forgive me? After all, you are required to or you're sinning against me, and I know you don't wanna do that!" She smiled at Bob and then said, "Too soon?" She changed subjects abruptly and stated, "I'm going into Mercy to see Shelly today. Hopefully, she can remember how she ended up on the sidewalk. I can't believe in this little bitty town she hasn't at the very least bumped into

John! I do however wonder how that will go? I assume she came here with a plan?" She continued to ramble, but Bob had other things on his mind for the day. He had become accustomed to doing some fine-tuning and filtering the rapid-fire thoughts and questions off to the back corner of his brain without letting Julie perceiving what he was doing.

He had failed to mention Shelly's statement to him before he had left the hospital. He wasn't sure now how to break it to Julie, so he led off with a different question. "Julie, I forgot to tell you who rode with me to the hospital. You will never in a million years guess ..."

Julie peeked around at him with a toothbrush in her mouth and mumbled that she had no idea, and somehow, Bob could tell what she had spoken and said, "Here goes—Mary James! I don't know how, but she never glanced back at her house nor mentioned needing to get back while I was there. She told the nurse that she would be keeping Shelly at her house and watching over her while she recovered!"

"But she has that phobia thingy ... Julie replied as she spit out the toothpaste and rinsed. "Have you noticed this town is more and more on edge? I mean, not just at church, but the whole town—for that matter the whole area, it must be all this political stuff is finally getting to people."

Bob looked up from tying his shoe with the most shocked, dumbfounded expression and said, "Really? You are just now noticing that? What's it like living in your world? Because me living in my world trying to figure out how you live in yours—is maddening!" And with that, he slapped a big juicy kiss on Julie's neck, which she hated wet kisses on her neck, and Bob headed down toward the kitchen.

Bob had been surprised that there hadn't been more altercations over the political turmoil that was ever-present every single day. Ash Grove was becoming divided just like the rest of the country, and tensions were mounting. Already, lifetime friends at church had started changing sides of the sanctuary to sit in. "Totally crazy," Bob said aloud as he grabbed his coffee and headed for the door.

The minute Bob opened the door at the station Wilma Rae started filling him in on the latest town gossip. Normally, he didn't pay attention, but when she said that, "Shelly and Wayne had been seen holding each other at the door of the church," his ears perked up, and he paid closer attention to his secretary. After listening to all Wilma Rae had to offer up, Bob surmised that something just didn't sound right.

"I'm going over to the church rental and see if John has heard any of these crazy rumors. I know Wayne and I know Shelly, and those puzzle pieces don't fit. I'll be back by 1 p.m. to talk to Henry and Molly. Would you please call and remind them of our meeting, Wilma Rae?" He had leaned in closer to her and nodded his seriousness about his need to talk to Molly and Henry.

\*\*\*

Bob knocked on the door several times then banged harder than he felt appropriate doing, but he was getting frustrated as he walked around toward the back porch where John spent a good deal of his time. *Empty*. Door closed tight. He peeked in a window and could pretty much see through the whole small house from the vantage point of the backdoor window. He walked over to the garage and peeked in through the door. The old Ford F250 was gone. John had obviously left on errands. He pulled out his cell phone and found John's number and hit dial, *right to voicemail*.

"Uh, yeah, John—I'm trying to get in touch with you buddy, got some info I need to talk to you about. Could you give me a call back when you get this? Thanks—It's Bob."

***

John pulled in to Bass Pro Sporting Goods store in Springfield and parked in the back lot. He hadn't been there since the camping trip with the Pierces. He really wasn't a hunter or a fisherman, so he rarely had reason to visit.

He reminisced about the times Jason would hammer on him until he would cave and go looking at all the firearms and bows. Jason, like most pre-teen boys, loved guns and bows and outdoor things. He had always promised him that one day he would buy a handgun of some sort when Jason got old enough to be responsible, and that they would take up target practicing together as he and his dad had done. He held it over his head as a tool of discipline on many occasions. Shelly had never been too gung-ho about the idea herself. With that, a rush of guilt flushed across his face. He was again reminded that Jason was never going to get to target practice with him. He fought back the urge to tear up and then faked a smile to the gentleman at the door greeting customers as he walked in.

John tried to think of why he had come and turned his attention to that. He was going to be making a road trip to Wichita, Kansas where yesterday he'd traced Jason Dean, his childhood best friend's, last known address. He told himself that he needed protection because of today's crime and road rage, but he also was telling himself a slew of other reasons why he should purchase one.

He now just wanted to hold one and see how it felt again after all these years. He wasn't sure why he was feeling guilty for thinking about purchasing a firearm, *but he did*. He was in his forties, he was knowledgeable of handling firearms, and he was a preacher for God's sake! And one that had never been in any serious trouble! No police record! Yet, he felt like everyone was staring at him like he was a criminal as he asked to see the first revolver that caught his eye.

The salesperson, whom was surely no older than twenty-one, was telling him he had made a good choice. It was a Smith-Wesson Body Guard .38 caliber revolver. Lightweight and very easily concealable. It also had a built-in crimson trace laser to help acquire your target easier and faster—especially in the dark.

It felt comfortable to John in his hand. Thirty minutes after filling out the paperwork, John was headed out to his truck with his new purchase along with a single box of ammo. He thought to himself how crazy it was that buying a gun was so quick and easy. No wonder there were so many protests lately with all the recent school shootings, he thought. How would anyone really be able to know what a person's plans for a weapon were? He had been conflicted about how he felt on gun rights lately. He climbed in his truck and locked the box that held his new revolver in the console that sat between the front seats.

"Well, that's done." He contemplated his actions for a moment, then started the truck and turned in the direction of I-44 West that headed to Oklahoma and toward Kansas.

John was anxious about finding his childhood best friend. He wondered how Jason's life had turned out. He'd had such a rough start compared to his own. He still remembered the day that the police came and picked up Jason's dad and locked him up for beating his mom and him. He had hurt them both seriously the last time he'd come home drunk. John remembered Jason's blackened eyes and bruised arms and stomach and his dejected, lost look. He also remembered after they sent his dad to prison that it was the next day when Jason came to school for the last time. He'd pulled John aside and told him he and his momma were moving back to his grandparent's house in Kansas. It never seemed fair. John couldn't tell if it was something that Jason wanted to do or if he was being forced. They never really had a chance for any deep conversation before he left.

It was the end of the blood-brother club. John felt like he was losing a sibling. He had taken him under his wing and had been his only true confidant. John had always hoped and prayed that Jason would move back, but he never did. They did share letters back and forth for several months and then came the day when the mailbox never held another letter for him from Haysville, Kansas. But that was then, and this was now.

John was rolling west down the highway on a journey of reconciliation. John needed forgiveness. Not just the forgiveness that God gave us when we humbly knelt with our folded hands together in prayer but the kind that John felt he should seek out as the unknown offender who had possibly changed the life path of a good friend through an unwitting childhood mistake. He knew it sounded crazy, but life had dealt him some bizarre realities recently, so this didn't seem that far off base.

John's mind drifted from thought to thought before landing back on Shelly. He felt guilty for the words that had quickly shot from his mouth, launching the pre-emptive strike. The fact that he hadn't even given her a chance to respond or retaliate his attack was now laying heavy on him. His stomach rolled as he tried not to think of her and Wayne together as the town hens had cackled about. Was life with Shelly irreconcilably over—forever? He wondered if she'd sought forgiveness. Maybe she was going to ask him for it before he drew his verbal sword?

He asked himself out loud, "Did I purchase this gun to solve that problem?" Hearing it aloud made him sick. He knew he could never take someone else's life. No, especially not people he cared about or had ever cared for. He had never caused harm to anyone in all his days. Sure, he'd been self-destructive as a youth, experimenting with drugs during his latter teen years and college. But, no he could never cause physical harm to even the darkest of foes—with only one exception.

Possibly himself if things got too bad. But that couldn't happen. He could never let his mom down in that way. He couldn't let his creator down either, he told himself. Yet, he knew the thought still lay dormant in a back corner of his mind, occasionally poking its head out like a badger, but he had learned to chase the thought back in deep from sight. He did wonder from time to time how much longer he could weigh the disappointment of family and friends. How would death compare as opposed to the relief of inner torment and question of his failures that he perceived himself guilty of?

Driving down the highway, John continued questioning the inner demons he knew he had and the dark challenges that had been laid at his table ever since the beginning. It seemed to begin with accepting God's call and answering it with total faith and commitment. Was there really an evil force that had fallen over him to conquer him from his closeness and dedication with Jesus?

John was physically strong with the stamina to get through any physical challenge, but his mental strength was being impugned as close to its boundaries as it had ever been. He wanted to stand firm and confront these obstacles. Surely, he thought to himself that this is a good sign. He hadn't given up yet, even though he'd suffered major loss and immense mental anguish. His faith was being calculated and shaken to its core, but the foundation had not yet crumbled. Finding Jason Dean and getting his forgiveness would surely be adding a block to his cornerstone where it was foundering in disrepair. The word 'conflicted' came to his mind. He had certainly been entertaining the reality of that word lately. Life had been a teeter-totter, with an emphasis on confliction.

John looked over at his cellphone that he had tossed over onto the passenger seat as he pulled away from the parking lot earlier. He noticed the flashing blue light that was informing him he had at least one missed call. He turned his sight back toward the path ahead. His brain was too scrambled to add on to the pile of mental debris from something like a cell call.

It would have to wait until later. He was already busy unpacking deep thoughts as he reached for a CD to pop in the player.

\*\*\*

"Henry, do you really need a handgun?" Bob asked. "This is a pretty quiet town, and I can't think of one incident where you would need this. I can, however, imagine someone hurt seriously the way all of this has played out!" Bob tried to look serious, but not too harshly.

"Chief, I want to be able to protect my wife. She wasn't supposed to find it. I can't apologize enough I know—for the trouble and public embarrassment." Henry lowered his head in shame.

"You two are very fortunate that no one was accidentally shot. I really don't have a good legal reason to keep this firearm from you without charges, which I truly do not want to bring up, but I need reassurances that it will be kept safely locked away at home and not ever brought out in any similar fashion again. *Ever*! I just want you to think this through and maybe reconsider your needs. Are we square?"

"I just don't know why Henry bought it or even when." Molly looked over at Henry. "It scares me, Henry! I don't believe you're thinking straight these days. *Please* get rid of it!"

"Darling, I just can't imagine how horrible I would feel if someone broke in and tried to hurt you, and I couldn't stop it, that's all. I'll keep it locked up in a lockbox. I promise that is where it will stay unless I need to protect you; I have to be able to do that. I have failed you in so many ways. I can't let myself fail at that."

"Oh Henry, you've never failed anything for me. You're my rock. You're the love of my life! If being able to protect me means having that thing in a lockbox, then so be it." Molly looked over at Bob. "I am so sorry for my actions Chief Pierce. I'm embarrassed. It just scared me when I found it. I had no idea that Henry was that worried about me. I can make you a peach pie if that will help make amends." Molly continued to look sheepishly at the chief, waiting for his nod of affirmation.

At that, Henry and Molly were dismissed to head home with an unloaded .9 mm handgun in a brown cardboard box marked 'EVIDENCE' and containing the 'Ash Grove Police' stamped in red ink across the top of it. Chief Pierce had one of his men package the firearm this way, hoping it would make a point that would sink into Henry and Molly Tanner.

***

Beverly Snodgrass paced her living room back and forth. She had gotten almost no sleep Sunday evening after scoffing to herself about how the Sunday service had gone awry. It had been *too* good, message and delivery! She had sold the skin before she had killed the bear. Sure, she had clearly wounded the bear, but she hadn't seen to it to put it out of its misery. When it got right down to it she had just plain been outwitted. How could she have failed to see the cleverness that John might be capable of?

"The man should be writhing in pain and agony still wasting away on that dang porch swing cursing at his maker!" she said coldly but softly to herself as the anger began to boil over.

Even the pestilent 'walking reverend' and sympathy seeking Molly had somehow escaped any harm from the evening. She had so thought that they would be collateral damage of the noxious poison she had spread that evening. She wanted to see an end of Henry's preach walking, almost as much as John's bush league ramblings!

Beverly had heard through the grapevine that Shelly had been hospitalized and was quite confident that her plan had come to fruition at last. "I rue the day that man came to Ash Grove . . ." she said as she began trying to calculate another scheme.

Beverly's enfeebled husband called out from the other room, "Bev, what in the world are you fussing around this house about?"

"Nothing for you to worry about, just go back to your golf game or whatever is on the television; you can't help with what I need done," Beverly chided back and then quietly berated him to herself as she headed out the front door.

She seemed to quickly retract into her own skin as the bright beams from the sun hit her, much like a vampire would as it came out of the darkness into the brightness of day, *flesh searing*! Repelled by the lack of dark obscurity in broad daylight. One could have more than likely heard a loud hiss had they been standing near as she stepped onto her porch before dropping her sunshades down, applying a thick coat of red lipstick to her lips and heading down the sidewalk.

\*\*\*

The main phone at the police station rang, and Wilma Rae answered in her monotone voice, "Ash Grove Police, Wilma Rae speaking, how may I help you?" It was Mary James on the other end, and she asked if she could speak with Bob. Wilma Rae patched her through to the chief's phone. "It's Mary James, Bob."

"Hello, Mary—have you got Shelly back home with you yet?"

"Well, no not yet. I was hoping maybe you could send one of your officers here to pick us up. I wasn't really thinking yesterday of my return trip when I jumped in the car with you to race here. And now, I'm in a bit of a quandry. I—uh—well, I am feeling very uncomfortable and out of sorts about being away from my home, and they will release Shelly to leave shortly. We have no way back, which is the point I'm trying to get to, and I'm feeling very uneasy." In the rush to make sure that Shelly had a friend at the hospital with her, Mary had somehow forgotten her 'fear leaving' and was now suffering from the effects of being away from her boundaries.

"You know Mary, I'd love to come there myself, but you are probably aware of the way Shelly feels about me presently, aren't you? Anyway, I can call around and get someone to pick you two up. Let me do some checking, and I'll call you back. This a good number to do that?" After a brief second, the chief realized Julie was headed that way now. "I just now remember Julie is headed your way at some point this morning. I'll give her a call and send her there shortly." Bob gave his wife a call, and she told him she was pulling into the hospital parking lot as they spoke.

Life in a small town had its benefits in the fact that everybody knew almost everybody, and it had its disadvantages, such as everybody knew almost everybody. Soon, another page in Ash Grove's history book would turn as the day settled into another evening, bringing another tomorrow and another new chapter with its own little stories and chatter. Life was usually a bit different in the first couple of days after the festival ended and everything was packed back up. Then things would slowly begin to settle back to the mundane rituals of everyday, small-town existence.

Tomorrow would bring a new question to the town gossip, though, as to where in the world Pastor John disappeared to?

# Chapter 13

*July Tenth, Tuesday in Wichita, Kansas*
**John's Discovery in his Search for Jason Dean**

J ohn had pulled into Wichita around six in the evening on Monday. He had taken his time driving there while he cleared his head and began preparing for what he had hoped would be a good reception from his childhood blood brother. It had taken some mental searching, but he had finally recalled Jason's mother's name. Carissa. He could picture her clear as day, but he really had to dig deep to come up with her name. He remembered that from his mom's strong insistence to social manners that he had always called her Miss Carissa whenever he spoke to her. John finally fell asleep after hours of replaying the possibilities of how meeting Jason again may go. When he did finally drift off, John slept deep and awoke mentally and physically rested.

Today was hopefully the day he would get his chance at an apology and then reminisce the old days and share what life had dealt each of them. John was excited, yet also very apprehensive, of the unknown. He had prayed to God that Jason would give him the reconciliation he so needed. Would they recognize each other? Would Jason's eyes be as piercing green as he had remembered them in youth?

He looked at his phone's Google map again. 136 Estelle Street. He would head there right after some breakfast. It felt like it had been forever since he had been out and away from his little shack in Ash Grove. It felt good. It felt new, and it felt as if it could be a new beginning. John felt he was re-emerging into the world of commonplace that had dissipated from his existence since he had lost his family. He relished in the moment as he loaded his plate of the complimentary breakfast foods provided by the hotel he was staying at.

***

Bob was getting worried that John had not returned his phone call when he awoke and again as he drove by the church looking back at John's house and garage. It appeared no one was home, so he decided to try calling him again.

As John looked back to his phone, he quickly swallowed his food that was in his mouth and answered it since he had forgotten to call Bob back. "Hello there, Chief—what's up?"

Bob quickly responded, "Oh, I see how it is; now I'm downgraded to Chief instead of Bob, huh?" Bob chuckled a little but was mildly annoyed if truth be told.

"I'm sorry Bob, just being polite and professional, since I have been neither lately! What can I do for you?"

"Well, John, I was hoping to track you down and chat with you in person today. I have some information that I need to talk to you about. I really don't want to talk over the phone though. It's on the personal side.

Any chance of meeting you today somewhere, maybe coffee?"

"That could be difficult today Bob; I'm about four or five hours out of town on a little quest! Trying to touch base with an old friend from my past. I'm hoping to meet up with him right after this delicious little breakfast I'm staring at! Can it wait a day or two? I'll definitely be back by Thursday or Friday. I have to get prepared for Sunday service!"

"It's good to hear you're out and about John. I got to tell you, friend, you have had me concerned the way you've been staying hidden in that little shack these days. Your message Sunday gave me hope for you and all of us in our little community. Why, even Julie was talking forgiveness with me just this morning!" Bob smiled to himself as he quickly pictured Julie's expression while asking for forgiveness. "I suppose it could wait, but I'd like to see you first thing when you get back. You know how gossip is in this little town, and I'd like to touch base with you before any tales get told! All is good, but I'd like first dibs with chatting— sound good?"

"Well now, Bob, this is beginning to sound a little like a professional call and not a personal one! Should I be worried or call an attorney?" John snickered a little, but he started to feel a little apprehensive.

"No, no, John, nothing like that. I just don't want you to take any steps backward when you seem to be moving forward. Nothing to worry about; in fact, I wish I hadn't said anything now."

"Bob—I'm curious now, does this have anything to do with Shelly being in town during the festival? We bumped into each other, and I was totally taken by surprise. I have to say, I wasn't very pleasant and was most assuredly not speaking in a Christian fashion. In fact, I'm ashamed of the way I acted. I should probably be seeking out forgiveness from her since I was preaching about it last Sunday!" John stammered a little in his speech and felt the embarrassment of being caught acting hypocritical. "I assure you, though, I have followed my own advice and sought it from my maker!"

Bob interrupted, "John, this is exactly what I was wanting to talk to you about. I would feel so much better if we were sitting across from one another instead of having this conversation over a phone. Did your being upset have anything to do with any gossip you might have overheard?"

"Bob—let's talk about this when I get back. I need to be in a good frame of mind when I see my old childhood friend, and I have a feeling this may change that. I promise I will call you just before I hit home. I want to get all this stuff behind me. I just can't do it right now because I'm working on clearing some past forgiveness issues out now. I appreciate you, Bob, and I want to talk to you—as a friend too. I'll call you buddy. I promise."

"Sounds great, John, and actually, you sound great. Your message was spot on Sunday, and you sound like the old John everyone loves and misses. You be careful out there, by the way, where are you if you don't mind?"

"Wichita, Kansas. Cowboy town! I've haven't been here for twenty-some years, but it still seems like a nice place. Thanks for reaching out Bob, and I'll be talking to you."

Bob felt like progress might have been made. He sure didn't want to destroy any with what they were going to talk about. Their conversation did raise some questions to him though. He now wondered where John and Shelly's chance meeting was and just what happened between the two. He surely hoped it had nothing to do with Shelly being found on the sidewalk with a head injury.

"No—no way could John have anything to do with that." Bob wanted to talk to Shelly also; in fact, he knew he needed to. He thought he would first hear what John had to say when he got back. Shelly would still be recovering at Mary's at least until the weekend, he imagined

*** 

As John pulled up to the front of 136 Estelle Street, his shoulders slumped, and he slapped the steering wheel of his truck. There was yellow tape surrounding the yard, and the duplex looked as if it had been under construction. No one appeared to be living in it.

John parked his truck and got out to walk around. He could see there was a note up on the front door just up a few stairs to the porch. He glanced around and noticed a balcony that was almost covered from sight from pine trees growing up against the structure. The brick on the place had been recently painted, and there was lumber stacked on the porch.

John crossed under the tape and walked over to some windows and peeked in. It was empty. He walked to the right and up the couple of steps to the front porch where two doors with glass panes were. The building appeared to be a duplex with a residence upstairs and the other on the first floor. He read the note while glancing through the glass. It seemed to be a work stoppage order from the city for permit violations. He looked around searching for maybe a neighbor sitting on a porch or walking down the sidewalk. He spied an older gentleman across the street and a couple of houses down.

John mumbled to himself, "What the heck, I have nothing to lose . . ." as he turned to head over and chat with the man.

"Good morning, sir," John spoke to the man that sat on a chair and appeared to be in his mid-seventies. "I was wondering if you could tell me anything about that duplex across the street from you? My name is John, by the way."

"Whatchoo wanna know 'bout it?" he answered back.

John glanced around the neighborhood quickly and then turned back to the elderly black gentleman sitting and responded, "Well, I'm looking for an old friend from my childhood that I haven't seen for many years. I tracked him down to this address across the street as his last known residence. I've come all the way over from the Springfield, Missouri area in hopes of finding him and reconnecting with him. His name is Jason Dean. Did you know him?"

"Oh yes, sir, yes sir indeed, I knew that troubled soul. The Po-Po used to be there on a regular basis. Yellin' and screamin' going on all the time. Some say he was beatin' his momma over there every time he got drunk. You see that balcony over there up in the trees?"

John nodded, "Yes."

"Well, that boy got so drunk one night he done fell over the railing and broke his neck. I heard it took him over a month in the hospital to let go and die. Sad, sad state of affairs. I can't say I miss him though. Can't say that at all, but his poor momma—she was a sweet lady, she was indeed."

"How long ago did this take place?" asked John.

"It was beginning of winter last year. One of the coldest nights there was. I always wondered what he be doing out there on the balcony that late at night. Too drunk to feel the cold chill, I imagine."

"You don't know what happened to his momma by chance, do you?"

"Ms. Carissa? Why what a sweet woman she was . . . always wondered how such a sweet lady could give birth to such a devil of a boy. She done moved out after he passed . . . I reckon she wanted to run from bad memories. She gave my wife her number though. I reckon I can go inside and see if she still has it. Lord, I haven't talked to Ms. Carissa in a minute or two, yep, it's been awhile fo' sure." With that, he shook his head and chuckled as he struggled off the chair and headed in through the door. He turned and said, "My name is Jordy— Jordy Wells. You might as well come on in. It's gonna take a bit to hunt that number up for ya son.

130

Momma! We got us some comp'ny—make sure you decent now!"

John smiled and followed Mr. Wells into the front room and glanced around at all the knick-knacks that were scattered about. It almost looked like a museum to him, and then it quickly hit him that his friend Jason was gone. He had lost his chance at the forgiveness he so desperately sought and the ability to ever reconnect with a friend. He had put so much stock on this trip and talking to Jason. John's head dropped downward as he fought to keep his demeanor pleasant for Jordy and his wife. They had been kind enough to invite him in and try to help . . . He fought his inner demon that poked at his will to break right then and there.

As Jordy rounded the corner into the back of the house out of sight, John quickly closed his eyes and turned to the Lord for strength. He prayed to himself internally. *Dear gracious Father, please take some of this burden from me. You say that you won't let one's burden become more than they can bear. I'm not as strong as the credit you are giving me. I know that you know me, even better than I know myself, but I'm crumbling here at this very moment. Please give me strength to overcome these circumstances. Please give me the power to pull myself away and closer to you who is my strength. Please take my hand like you did Peter's outstretched hand when he lost his faith and doubted before beginning to sink . . .*

With that last word, John fell to the floor in tears that would not cease. As soon as he had spoken the phrase of taking Peter's outstretched hand, he suddenly thought about his son Jason's hand reaching out to him and pleading, '*Daddy!*' The look in Jason's eyes that screamed of his desperation for his father's help—his father's help to save him from the struggle he couldn't overcome himself. The help he was unable to give, no matter how hard he'd fought to be there for him, no matter how swiftly he had forged through the turbulent water to reach him. It was too late. Was this plea to his Creator and Father also too late? Maybe he did deserve each burden that was being stacked on top of the other, neatly piled on his shoulders like boulders. Maybe he was meant to *sink* to the bottom of the abyss.

# Chapter 14

*John Slips into Unconsciousness in the Good Samaritan's Home*

**Angels Dispatched to Watch Over You My Son**

J ohn slowly opened his eyes, not knowing or
recognizing where he was or how he had
gotten there. As he glanced around the dimly
lit room, he saw the shadowy figure of an
elderly black woman sitting in a rocking
chair. She was reading a book or something and a small
creaking sound would squeak out with each slow rock
forward she made. It must have been the sound that
had awoken him because his body felt heavy, like
cement formed to the contours of the bed in which he
was laying. His limbs felt numb as if he'd been there
for days, and if it were not for the repetitive rocking
chair noise, the silence and dimness of the room would
have felt almost heavenly. He felt oddly comfortable
even though he had no idea where he was. He felt
nothing but calm and kindness and warmth in the
room. He didn't want the woman to notice he was
awake because he didn't want the feeling of calm to
leave, so he lay there motionless and quiet, trying to
soak in his surroundings. Moving only his eyes to catch
the shadows painted on the walls and ceiling.

He almost felt as if he had passed and now lie
waiting to be judged before knowing if he would be
moving forward or not. He had no fear though, no

feelings of presage. In the distance he could almost make out voices that seemed to come from another room close by. They were muffled and mixed together, sounding like a rhythmic conversation. John imagined for a moment that it was Saint Peter from the gates of heaven—possibly trying to advocate for him and his actions so he could pass through to the safety from Hades. All John knew at this moment was he felt a calmness surround him as if he were protected by angels sent from above, and he didn't want the tranquility to vanish. John thought he would close his eyes for only a second or two, but in a short moment, he was asleep again.

\*\*\*

Jordy sat on his chair in the front room, sorting papers in a box that sat on his lap. The preacher on the television was loudly evangelizing. Jordy would look over occasionally and nod in agreement then concentrate on the paper he'd just picked up. He'd study it from top to bottom and then methodically set it on the stack that he had previously viewed. Jordy wasn't sure where in the world he or Mariah had put Ms. Carissa's phone number, but he knew it must be very important to the gentleman resting in the spare bedroom.

He had never had a person pass out in his home before, especially a young white man. It had shocked him when he had come back in and found him unconscious with his face soaked in sweat. He yelled for Mariah, and when she came in, she'd yelled, "Oh

Lordy, he done died. There's a dead white man in our living room, Jordy!"

But as they looked closer, they had realized that he had fainted, and they helped him into the spare room onto the day bed. It had been quite a task for them to manage. He was semi-conscious but faded back out quickly after getting him settled in. Mariah had checked his forehead, but he didn't feel hot. She ran and got a cool, damp washcloth anyway and put it to his head. She stayed in the room from that point on, keeping watch over him.

Jordy went over their conversation with Mariah almost word for word looking for any clue about why he was there. They thought about going through his wallet but decided to wait and see how he was before being that invasive. "Now Jordy, if he don't wake up in a bit or so—we gonna investigate his wallet and call somebody!"

"Mariah, it's gonna be okay. I have a good feelin' 'bout this boy. I think he just collapsed 'cause I told him 'bout his friend dying from falling off that balcony when he was drunk. I just gotta find Ms. Carissa's telephone number for him, that's all. It's gonna be okay. You just watch over him and check on him while I do some lookin'."

*** 

*Jeremiah 29:11*

*For I know the plans I have for you, declares the Lord, plans*

*for welfare and not for evil, to give you a future and a hope.*

135

\*\*\*

When John awoke for the second time, he knew as he glanced around the room and saw the woman in the rocking chair still there that it was time to let her know he was awake.

When Mariah saw John stir, she got up from her chair and walked over to him, comforting him with, "Lordy, you are awake! How we doing here? It's okay; you gonna be fine now. Take your time and git your bearings child." And then she hollered out to Jordy, "You come on in here; he's awake!"

Jordy came in holding a small piece of paper with Ms. Carissa's name and number scribed on it. "I found it, John! I got Miss Carissa's number for you. I knew we had it. You be feeling better there now?"

It was all taking a minute for John to comprehend, and the feelings of warmth and comfort that had felt so surreal were now slowly morphing into feelings of confusion. Reality was settling back in as he re-acclimated himself to his surroundings. He almost felt like he did when he'd experienced a couple of nights of restless dream sleep. *Out of body.*

John quietly asked about the number. "So you found Miss Carissa's number?"

Jordy responded, "Yes I did! I knew it was here somewhere!"

At least he would hopefully connect with her and close as much of his past confliction as possible.

"Now that you're awake, you hungry? You been asleep for several hours," Mariah asked.

John took the Wells' up on their dinner offer, and he decided to share some recent history with the couple so they could understand better why he was there and why it was so important to find Miss Carissa, now that he had learned about Jason's passing. He opened himself up more than he had to anyone since the accident, and they listened intently. Tears were fought back by all three of them as they sat sharing dinner and conversation at the table. John had found new friendship in Jordy and Mariah of Wichita, Kansas. He told them he felt like they were angels of God in the flesh when he needed them the most. Jordy asked John if he minded that they pray together before he left to continue his journey.

As they bowed their heads holding hands together, Jordy spoke, "Dear Father in heaven watchin' over us here today, thank you for your boundless blessings that you bestow on us daily. Thank you for bringing this young pastor here into our lives and enabling us to help him with his continuing personal journey. Please continue to have your watchful angels look after him and guide him and keep him safe in his travels. Please Father God, help him find the answers he is in search of and to be able to close his past up and allow him to move to the future in continuing your teachings and showing others the love that we are supposed to have between all us brothers and sisters. In your ever-present and loving grace, Amen." They each squeezed each other's hands tightly at the closing of Jordy's prayer and smiled to one another.

John hugged both Jordy and Mariah and told them they were welcome to come visit Ash Grove, Missouri and him any time they wanted. Jordy stated to come back and visit them soon, and with that, John thanked them again for being there when he was in need. As John drove past them standing on their porch waving, he gave his truck horn a double tap and headed off toward downtown Wichita via Douglas Ave.

It was about 6:45 in the evening as John pulled into the parking lot of the Exploration Place, just slightly northwest of the downtown Wichita area. He pulled into a parking spot, killed the ignition, and reached into his pocket to pull the piece of paper out that contained the number of Miss Carissa Dean—the mother of his childhood best friend who had recently passed away and apparently had become somewhat of an incarnate of his father in disturbing ways.

He looked down at the paper silently questioning what good would really come from calling the number. What would it do to Miss Carissa, besides open old wounds? Was he doing this with no concern for her and only himself? Was this just a selfish act to try to clear his guilt from his childhood past? Or was it truly to make amends for a wrong that possibly changed the direction of a best friend's life? It was now too late to make a difference for Jason Dean. His life had gone awry and ended tragically. Could his plea for forgiveness help Miss Carissa in her feelings of the loss she had already endured? Her son had been gone already for months. Could his own shoulders hold yet another stone of burden? He already felt like Sisyphus, from Greek mythology, a king who was condemned to roll a huge boulder up a steep hill only to have it roll back down and then begin over and over in an endless endeavor to try to complete his task.

John so wanted at this very moment for God to speak out or give an obvious spiritual sign to him so he would know what choice to make. He just wanted to be normal again—like he was before he'd gone on that damned float trip. Back before his entire world collapsed around him. It hadn't been perfect between him and his family, but at least they were a family. John longed for the time before when his faith in God was solid as granite and he felt like he was changing the world for the better, steering people toward Christ and showing how the bible was still relevant in their lives today.

Why was everything and every day bringing a different and more difficult burden? He shook his head in question as he looked out the front windshield and upward. His attention was drawn to a large, tall metal statue of an Indian Chief looking up with open hands held upward as if he were asking God for the same thing that he was. Amazingly, he hadn't even noticed the tall slim object as he'd pulled in. It was just beyond what appeared to be a pedestrian suspension bridge.

It intrigued him. He had a sudden urge to go see it. To walk around it and experience it up close. To take in the air and possibly clear his head. He felt a connection with the Indian as if they were both begging for something from the heavens. He instantly related to it and felt compelled to explore.

John glanced over at his console lockbox. He looked back over at the bridge toward the statue. He decided to open the box and remove his recent purchase. He held it below the level of his truck window so no one could see it if they were looking. He opened a lone box of ammo and then rolled open the cylinder of the gun and loaded each of the five chambers with a bullet and then snapped the cylinder into place. He studied it a minute and then slipped the snub-nosed revolver into his right-hand suit jacket pocket and exited his truck as he scanned the parking lot and surrounding area. It seemed relatively quiet. There were very few people in the lot or walking around. It seemed safe.

John started walking toward the modern suspension bridge that crossed the muddy Arkansas River toward the statue. The sun was slowly beginning its descent in the humid summer evening. The only thing that made it tolerable was the breeze that was blowing across the bridge as he made his way closer to the rusty iron sculpture. The quietness and solitude began comforting John as he let his thoughts wander around the outer fringes of their boundaries, like the fringes hanging from the clothing on the statue. If they hadn't been formed from metal, John imagined them flowing freely in the breeze that became stronger and more consistent.

Birds flew overhead in scattered patterns through the crosswinds and gusts, circling back as if they were searching for acquaintances. Groups of them were scattered in small social passels perched high on the power lines, overlooking the river and 'the Keeper of the Plains' as if they were living gargoyles watching over the chief with vigilance as he prayed. Like the disciples of sorts on the night before Christ's crucifixion.

John had pulled his phone out while crossing the footbridge and Googled the statue, finding out that it was created by a Kiowa-Comanche artist named Blackbear Bosin. It was erected where the Arkansas and Little Arkansas rivers converged. The statue itself was forty-four feet tall and sat high above the ground on a thirty-foot mountain of rock to elevate its stature even more. It was surrounded by rock formations at the bottom, and some of those formations contained fire pits known as the 'Rings of Fire' and were lit at night to illuminate the statue.

John felt at ease walking around and observing the reverence that the statue seemed to exude toward the heavens above. He realized at that moment he had not really ventured out much in his own life, instead choosing to stay close to his roots in Missouri. Sure, he'd moved away a couple of times and as a child had been fortunate enough to have a loving family that vacationed every summer, seeing new places when they could afford it. But generally, he had not ventured out or explored the world much.

John started feeling emotions of regret as he looked out over the river while the lights from the city in the background began to slowly twinkle out from the approaching darkness. The sun began dropping even lower in the sky. He felt regret that he had not shown their son more of the world outside their own box. Jason would have loved this western Cowboy-and-Indian-based city. Jason, like every young boy, had an interest in new places and sights, his eyes lighting up at even the suggestion of going into Springfield, the neighboring 'big city' to Ash Grove. This spot would have been a playground to dream about for him.

John again started feeling fault in the way he had controlled his family's lives, it was from the fear of what could happen if he let the reins too loose. We somehow had let the world become something to fear instead of embrace. Shootings, abductions, gangs—even drivers on cellphones oblivious to everything around them. It was nothing like when he was a child. He'd had no video games to play, no five hundred channels of trite television garbage to entice him in from the neighborhood friends playing outdoors. He was thankful that stuff didn't exist as he now pictured how different his son's childhood should have been. John was able to grow, experience, and enjoy the unknown world around him without his parents having fears that he may not come home for suppertime because of some evil devil lurking around the corner. John steered his thoughts back to happier ones as he made his way on the path toward the base of the effigy and river's edge.

He began to imagine Shelly and him, standing together holding hands and watching Jason run about on the trails or trying to climb the huge rock mountain as many boys have surely done.

John sat down on a rock ledge at the base of the statue that was close to the water's edge. The river moved so quietly it was almost as if it were pavement. The sky had slowly become like a painter's palette of oranges and pinks mixed with brilliant shades of blues and an ominous black-filled mass surrounding the meld of color. Smaller grey clouds looked like tiny islands surrounded by the brushstrokes of color.

"My God, you are a master of beauty; how could anyone doubt your existence?" he spoke aloud.

The Ring of Fire pits lit one by one and brightened the area around him while creating flickering shadows against the rock base that held the chief high above him. He looked over at the bridge arches that held the suspension cables from high up, stretched downward connecting to the bridge. They glowed in the light, creating complimentary shapes that appeared like spearheads pointed into the brilliance of the brightly painted yet darkening sky.

John sat there, longing to hear the laughter of his son. Desperate to feel the thunder in his heart that happened when Shelly would snuggle close into his arms.

He imagined her long blonde hair blowing in the breeze with strands trying to hide the beauty of her bright blue eyes and Jason hollering, "Hey Dad, come here—I want you to see this . . . " just as Shelly was about to give him a kiss, her lips so close to his he could feel the heated breath.

Those blue eyes looking up to him in awe and filled with unquestioning love but then playfully turning away and glancing at their son as he vied for their attention. It felt so real in this moment, in this place. John didn't want this moment to end; he couldn't let go and come back to the reality where it was all gone. As he stood up, his head spun, while joyful memories swirled, quickly mixing with the grief of the present.

The dark unknown of the future quickly became an incomprehensible blur in his brain.

Emotions came fast, as tears once again streamed down his face. He loved his family. He longed for their return and struggled with the reasons that had brought him to this place in this very emotional snapshot in time.

"Please, God, I'm sinking—I'm begging, take my hands and pull me from this," he cried with his arms stretched up to the heavens.

His tear-filled pupils made the dimming colors of the sky and city lights blur into a salty mixture that stung as he tried to focus upward past the shadowy figure of the Keeper of the Plains that towered above him. It seemed to mimic his appeals with his outreached hands cupped, shadowing his, ready to catch those pleas if granted as they fell from the heavens.

But John's hope seemed to instantly lose its patience, and his hands dropped down beside him as he fell back into his seated position on the rock ledge. He realized these dreams would never become real again. He only felt the pain of betrayal. It seemed endless and unbearable to bear any longer.

John's right hand reached into his right-hand suit coat pocket. He glanced skyward again as his fingers instinctively scouted the metal tool in his pocket, searching for the proper way to grip it.

John immediately realized that he was somehow brought here tonight to this specific spot to face his internal demons, much like a suspect would be led to the interrogation room to be questioned for crimes he was suspected of. He looked around again at the flames in the Ring of Fire, expecting to see black, shadowy apparitions darting in and out of the flames, hissing in laughter and taunting him in to dare join them. He then turned all the way around in a complete circle, looking for any sign of other people that might be walking by. Someone who would reach out to him and convince him life would get better. He noticed there was nary a soul. He peered upward one last time toward the sky, scanning the darkened infinity that twinkled from the thousands of stars and planets that had come to watch him fall from grace. He questioned again why God hadn't given him an answer or sign of hope as he believed he had been promised , with the silence closing in and surrounding him,  the burden had finally become too cumbersome to carry, and it overtook his will to survive. His load of stones seemed to fall, crushing him under their weight as his shoulders slumped in surrender.

John began the sequence of muscle and nerve movements that were to lead to the finality of his existence as he pulled the revolver from its hiding place. He calmly pushed the muzzle into the pit of his chin, pointing it upward so it would target the projectile into his calm but dejected and numb brain. Neurons and synapses fired back and forth as the electrochemical signaling took control, and he relinquished all hope and will to move forward in faith. He was resigned to the fact that his life would end tonight. It really had ended on May twenty-fifth at 7:38 p.m. this year anyway. The time granted after that day had just been borrowed and a tormented existence at best he surmised.

"It's time to pay my debt—for failing you Jesus. Please forgive me," he spoke quietly but aloud as his brain sent its last command to move John's finger to the trigger and begin the mechanical movement of his final curtain call that would end with the small lever being pulled.

No stay of execution or sign from God....

# Chapter 15

*At the Base of the Keeper of the Plains Under the Stars*
**Not Our Will be Done, But Thine**

J ust as John's finger muscles retracted back and began squeezing the trigger that would end his journey, there was an immediate burst of sound that echoed loudly from the opposite pocket that had contained his revolver. The sound startled John from his concentrated effort, and his muscles quickly released the tension on his finger that had tugged against the trigger. He instinctively looked up toward the heavens then to the slim waning crescent moon that had been high overhead watching the entire scenario unfold.

Just as his eyes became focused through the stream of tears—he witnessed two separate falling stars as they tumbled simultaneously downward, just off the tip of the lower crescent. They rolled and spiraled gracefully, twinkling and sparkling in a multitude of glimmering colors. It seemed to last forever and yet only milliseconds, all at the same time. It was a sight in which he had never seen in his forty-four years of existence. Their brilliant, blinding descent quickly faded into the blend of darkness and the shimmer of stars that remained behind. It was over in a nanosecond.

The phone continued ringing as he lowered the revolver down to his side, nestling it back into his right-hand pocket, then he reached into the opposite pocket to retrieve it. The screen displayed 'Unknown Caller.' John hit answer out of curiosity and drew the phone to his ear to hear a distant haunting voice calling out, "*Johnny?* Hello—is this you, *Johnny?*"

Her voice quickly sucked him back to his youthful days and times of trouble-free summer nights. John struggled for his answer to exit his mouth as if the words were caught in disconnect between his brain and tongue and lay tumbling in circles. Moments later, he managed to force them into the microphone of his phone. "*Miss Carissa?*"

"Johnny, it's so nice to hear your voice again—all these many years and a little lower pitched, but you sound just like the Johnny I remember coming over to see my Jason."

"How in the world did you get my number, Miss Carissa? I mean, I'm so glad to hear from you, and I was actually thinking of calling you but—I'm speechless."

"Well Johnny—let's just say that the hand of God reached out to you through me tonight, and we can talk all about it when I see you. That sound okay?"

John drew from his memory a picture of her face so clearly as he listened to her talk and tried to decipher what she was saying. He suddenly felt very warm under his skin, and yet, he was shivering as if he were frozen to the bone.

"I don't understand, you—um, you caught me at a very—um, time—I, uh, well, of course I'd love to see you. You—you just tell me where and when. I will be there Miss Carissa."

"Oh Johnny, stop with the formalities already; you're not the young boy you were the last time we saw each other—you're all grown up, please just call me Carissa. We can surely be on equal levels now after all these years!"

"Of course, Miss—I mean, Carissa. And, actually, I—um, I just go by John these days, but you can call me Johnny if you like; it makes no difference to me. It's just such a surprise, and of course, a joy to hear from you tonight. You have no idea. No idea at all what this moment means to me."

The night sky seemed to open wide with a plethora of twinkling stars as John sat on the rock ledge near the river with the chief towering over him, either catching God's blessings in his cupped hands for John or possibly offering thanks up to the heavens in appreciation for what God had given him. It didn't matter which one it was. It had been his saving sign— his miracle. John realized it almost instantly. The Keeper of the Plains stood staunch and silent above him as if he were now his personal advocate to the Lord.

The conversation between John and Carissa went on for hours as they reminisced and shared stories from the past together. Occasionally, the quiet evening air would be broken when John would laugh out loud. Yes, John laughed out loud. Many times. There was an instant transformation in his perspective of life. It was the miracle that he had asked for, and though it had not come in his time—the Master had offered his hand in the exact moment that was most auspicious for John. God's grace and the power it holds, saves.

***

Darkness can fall on us so quickly when we let the poison enter our bodies and our minds. John had fallen very fast from the moment he'd found out his son was gone forever. The demons inside that he never knew existed quickly began adjusting the flow of toxin into his thoughts at their opportune moments. The evil one is wise and crafty, and like the shark gliding close to the ocean floor, always looking upward, searching and smelling for its prey in distress. And when it senses that desperation, it will launch its attack from underneath while its target is unsuspecting. Once he smells the blood in the water, the feeding frenzy is next to impossible to escape without outside help.

John had fallen quickly. He had come from a happy-go-lucky, newly appointed pastor and loving family man down to the darkest, dampest pit of self-deprivation a person could ever conceive. It happened within a matter of two months. He was stuck in distress. He was easy prey now. Satan had found delight and began to quench his thirst from John's misery and suffering. The devil had become more and more ravenous through the work of others to bring John down into his darkness where light does not exist, yet Christ always keeps, at the very least, a small glowing ember of hope in a twinkling glow. You only need to reach out and touch it in order to receive it.

John had consciously fought those demons back without asking help from God, but even more so, demanding answers *from* him. He had failed to keep his conversations with his Creator regular as he had before the circumstances brought tragedy. He overlooked the hand reaching into the water to help pull him out. John had begun to arrogantly believe he had to fight these battles on his own. His inner demons took advantage and filled his thoughts with guilt that was not his to own. The darkness creeping in like the black-wall cloud surrounding him before the storm, quickly swallowing the entirety of light from above, yet that light was always there if he only had looked and accepted God's help.

John had only talked to his Savior when he made demands and questioned him for what he assumed *He'd* taken from him. He forgot to look back and see the single set of footprints in the sand for the times when God had carried him. Such a long and black-filled journey he had been on. One that had come so close to ending tonight as he sat alone feeling all hope was out of reach and yet still ignoring Christ's light until his divine intervention.

John tested his Creator all the way to a point of certitude because his faith had been shelved and replaced with doubt and anger. He had heard boundless words of encouragement on the many walks he'd shared with Henry, but they seemed to drift into obscurity after they would part.

John remembered Henry telling him, 'This too will pass, John,' but those words seemed only like syllables from the mouth of a friend that quickly dribbled down to the floor and evaporated as soon as he'd leave. It was of course not the fault of his friend but the emptiness that John had allowed in to swallow his hope. Without hope, the will to live dissipates quickly.

***

But now, the silhouette of John sitting on the rocks by the edge of the river, backlit from the light of the flames in the Rings of Fire, was different. He now appeared as a new treasure that could only be created by one. The *One* that can take a spec of dirt and breathe life back into it or paint a sky so vibrant as the one he'd admired in awe earlier. Christ, Creator, and Master of all seen and unseen. John felt healed at once—in the instant he opened his eyes to Christ's miracle of *grace*.

To someone walking by and glimpsing over at him, this masterpiece might be regarded only as a lonely soul sitting by a river and nothing more; yet with the knowledge of his story, it was so much more than that. It was a life saved tonight, brought back from the brink of despair and given a second chance at renewal. A beautiful butterfly emerging from its cocoon that previously had enclosed a broken and tired caterpillar.

As the night lingered on, the statue stood firm and proud with palms lifted high, fettered to the spot its creator had erected it in during 1974, the very same year John had been brought into this world on a hot and humid Labor Day weekend. The quietest and easiest birth ever as recalled by his mother many times with a smile and wink to him.

***

It was 2 a.m. when John opened the door to his hotel room. The emotional ride that he had taken today would soon come to a very different close than he had imagined just hours before. After a warm shower, John crawled into bed with the evening still reeling in his head.

He knew deep within that God had indeed fulfilled his promise of taking care of him tonight. He had pulled him from the mire and saved him from himself. Even though he had strayed far and almost from reach. God had lovingly drawn him back to safety like a shepherd pulls his lamb to sanctuary with his staff.

***

*You did not choose me, but I chose you and appointed you that you should go and bear fruit and that your fruit should abide, so that whatever you ask the Father in my name, he may give it to you. John 15:16*

***

John laid there knowing that he had been spared this night. God was not done with him nor had he cast him from his attention and care. John remembered the moment he had heard his phone ring and looking up and seeing the twin shooting stars fall before him. He thought to himself and wondered what the significance could be—a star perhaps in memory for each of the two Jasons that were lost? Or maybe this was because of the two recent times he had fallen from grace? The first when he had stood outside cursing God for taking his son and the second for sinning against God by attempting to end his own life? It didn't matter except for the fact that they had gotten his attention, and that moment would be etched in his memory forever. He had felt truly connected with God at that very instant as if the Lord was touching him and directing him with His will. Then he thought about the Lord's Prayer. 'Thy Will be Done on earth as it is in heaven.'

\*\*\*

*Jesus replied, "Truly I tell you, if you have faith and do not doubt, not only can you do what was done to the fig tree, but also you can say to this mountain, 'Go, throw yourself into the sea,' and it will be done. If you believe, you will receive whatever you ask for in prayer."*   Matthew   21:21-22

\*\*\*

John fell asleep feeling the comfort in knowing that all things in God's time will be done. He was in awe of just how significant God's miracle tonight for his benefit truly had been. He would still struggle with his loss of his son and his childhood best friend, but he now had a renewed will to seek forgiveness from the pain he had caused his wife—the one treasure he had let slip from his grasp by his own hand. He had no one to blame for that tragedy but himself.

As John's eyes entered the rem stages moving from left to right and back, over and over in sequence, he fell into the most comforting sleep he had ever experienced. No torment, no premonitions, no painful memories relived. Only happy dreams filled with flashes of the possible future he would have missed had God's divine grace not intervened in the final moments of his fall. John quite possibly was the most fortunate human alive at that moment, he may also have been the only human that had witnessed the astrological masterpiece of colorful beauty unfold as two stars fell in unison, standing out brighter than all the rest in the star-filled darkness that had enveloped above his head. *Had it quite possibly been only for his benefit?*

# Chapter 16

*Wednesday Morning, a Quick Stop and Home*
**Fresh from the Cocoon**

S o a new day with a new outlook on life had begun for John as he checked out of his hotel room with one last stop to be made on his journey of reconciliation before heading back home to Ash Grove, Missouri. *Meet Miss Carissa.*

John had awoken refreshed, renewed, and noticeably changed. Even the clerk that had checked him in Monday evening remarked how rejuvenated he looked this morning. "Wow, Mr. Austin, I believe you have gotten the best sleep and relaxation of any guest I've checked in and out!"

John smiled and quipped back, "It must be the water in your indoor pool or possibly the coffee!"

"Yes, sir! That *could* be the reason—or perhaps the warm and delightful greeting from the Hotel clerk instilling that feeling of comfort from the check-in!" They both smiled and laughed in unison.

As John got seated in his truck, he quickly realized, after looking over at his console box between the seats, that the handgun he had purchased and almost ended his life with was still sitting loaded in that spot he had placed it earlier this morning. It was locked up, but he felt an urgency to get rid of it. He no longer had any compulsion to own it or even have it in his presence.

He didn't want to give it to Bob or anyone else because of the guilt he felt for buying it to begin with. He imagined everyone would be able to read the reason on his face and what he had almost succeeded in using it for under his possession. Much like touching a hot burner on the stove in his youth, he didn't want to touch it again because of the pain seared into the skin, and his memory seemed quite lasting.

Then the thought entered his mind that he would like to go back by the Keeper of the Plains one last time to see what he looked like in the new light of day and take a snapshot on his phone. He also thought that his place of rebirth may be just the site to cast the steel stone of sorts into the murky waters of the Arkansas River. A final resting place for the tool that had come so close to making it his final resting place. John opened the console and looked at the revolver lying there before he finally picked it up and flipped the cylinder open that encased the cartridges, pushing the rod back that emptied the bullets into the palm of his hand. He packed them back neatly into the cardboard box they had come in and laid the now unloaded revolver back where it was and shut the console before starting his truck and steering it back to the place he had just left roughly six hours earlier, but a past lifetime ago in essence.

He thought of Jordy and Mariah, and of course Miss Carissa, as he wound through the streets of Wichita on his drive back to the statue that had since become a friend of sorts. As he rounded the corner of West 2nd Street North, which became Central Avenue, he peered out of his window to see the old Chief still maintaining his same stance proudly and unshaken from the previous evening's dramatic event. Possibly, he stood ready to be a part of changing someone else's life by being an instrument of God's?

John turned onto Seneca and then into the parking lot of the Mid-American All-Indian Center. He parked and reached into the console, quickly tucking the cold metal revolver into his jacket pocket once again. *Deja vu.*

This time, John was walking up to the statue from a different point of view that did not afford him walking across a footbridge but instead walking around the Indian Center's pathway, leading up to the back of the statue. As he climbed the few stairs up to the base of the statue's perch, there was a plaque titled 'Circle of Life' with a symbol that he had not noticed last night.

He paused and read it quietly aloud to himself, *"For the Plains Indian, the sacred hoop was the all-encompassing symbol of the entire world, with one half of the circle representing the physical realm, the other the spiritual. Equally significant was the number four. The four quadrants of the hoop were symbolic of the four seasons, four directions, four times of the day, and the four elements. Water, Fire, Air, and Earth. At the center of the hoop, distinct from the four quadrants, is a smaller circle in the shape of a turtle. The Plains people believed we are all floating on a primordial sea on the back of the turtle. Each quadrant, when placed to correlate with a specific direction, is represented by a unique color, animal, element, and planet.*

John studied the symbol and took out his cellphone to photograph it. The image spoke to him, and he wanted to remember what it looked like as he would later want to research it more. As he looked both left and right from where he stood at the plaque he was reading, he was dead center between the footbridges. Each leading a different direction away from the statue. The one he had entered from last night was to the right over the Arkansas River; the opposing side would be the Little Arkansas River. Today, he had returned to the site from a totally different direction. He felt as if it was a gentle reminder that he was in a different frame of mind, and upon leaving, he would not be returning by the path that had brought him here when he was distressed. A new adventure down a brand-new path that was now led by the light of his savior once again. He was now well on his journey to *renewal*. Life could now be *relived* under the grace and guidance of his master and father from his rebirth.

John made his way around the trail to the rock ledge he had sat on last night. He looked up at the chief still holding up his cupped hands. John imagined if he could see the face up close, the chief would smile and wink at him in recognition of the spiritual blessing he had witnessed with John the previous night. John looked out over the rocks to the river and spied what looked like a deep and murky spot not more than a good stone's throw. He scanned for any other people in the area, and upon not seeing any close by, he quickly pulled the revolver out, drew back, and in one quick move tossed it with perfect aim to where he wanted it placed. He watched as the water rippled away and quickly dissipated back into the calm, flowing waters from where the revolver had entered its final resting place. John bowed his head in reverence and prayed thanksgiving for the miracle he had received and that the item he had just deposited in the river's depths would never be found again.

He looked upward saying, "Farewell, Chief," as he drove away leaving the chief behind him as he headed southeast to Winfield, Kansas on his continuing journey toward Miss Caris—um, *Carissa*, on his way back home.

***

Winfield was fifty-two minutes down South Kansas Hwy 15 to 77 then straight into town according to his Google map. He turned on the radio and hit scan to find a channel. It stopped on 97.9 or B98, older mellow rock. Jason would have hated it, but he left it there to help direct his thoughts elsewhere.

Carissa had told John in one of their conversations that she had moved to Winfield with her sister almost immediately after Jason had passed. She had told John that her sister had begged her to come earlier and let Jason fend for himself after he had turned to regular drinking, like his father. A hard suggestion for an aunt to make about her nephew, but she knew it was what her sister needed to do.

Carissa hadn't gone into much detail about Jason last night as her focus had been more on him. She had pressed John to tell her what had been bothering him. She knew minute details about him being upset and passing out in Jordy and Mariah's home. She revealed to John that Mariah had indeed called her to see if he had reached out to her after he'd left their home. When Mariah had explained a little of what John had told them, Carissa asked for John's number so she could reach out if he didn't call her. Carissa's interest had of course peaked when John's name had come up because she had always seen 'Johnny' as a good influence and friend to her boy's early years, just when he had needed it. It had brought great sorrow to both her and Jason when they moved so quickly to Hays, Kansas and back in with her sister and mother after Ray Dean, her estranged husband, had been incarcerated for assault and battery. They had lived there all together in Hays until her sister moved to Winfield after getting a teaching job at Southwestern College.

Later, she and Jason moved to Wichita to start over on their own. Jason would have been about seventeen when they ventured out away from Carissa's mom in Hays, Kansas. Carissa's sister Katrina had chosen a much different life plan than her. Katrina had always been pretty much Carissa's polar-opposite.

Carissa and Jason had both struggled living in the home brimming with memories of drunken rages filled with both verbal and physical assaults on them by Ray. She wanted as far from Knob Noster, Missouri as she could get once Ray had been convicted and sent to the Tipton Correctional Center. It happened to be where John and Jason had met and become best friends. Once they left, Carissa never once visited the town again or answered a single letter she received from Ray. She had let the attorney that her sister retained for her file the divorce and finalize all ties with Ray. She knew by this time that Ray was a 'no-good waste of a man and was never going to change.' When he had turned his anger to their thirteen-year-old son, she knew the bottle had poisoned him to the core.

Jason Dean had understood as much as a young teen could mentally comprehend, but he also suffered as much or more as Carissa, because when they moved, he lost his very best friends in Johnny and Tommy. Jason wasn't given much time to say goodbye, and after moving, he never really interacted the same with any other kids no matter how hard they pressed him. Jason would write Johnny and Johnny wrote back, but the day came when Jason saw no point in it. He wasn't going to get to see him anyway. It wasn't like they lived a half mile from each other like before.

The pain grew too deep in Jason, and he cut things off quick like a splinter that was deep in your foot. If you wiggled it and messed around too much, it made the pain more agonizing. It was better just to take the pliers and yank it out like his daddy would say, "Boy, you got to just man up and rip it out. Quit crying like you was a baby, like your momma is." Yes, Jason had more of his father's traits inside him than he ever really understood or wanted for that matter. But it took years for them to begin to manifest in him.

Johnny had been his best friend from the day they first met. Johnny seemed to understand him and liked Jason even despite his dad's temper and the squalor they lived in. Jason's mother had tried to keep the home clean and food on the table, but between being poor, Jason away anytime he could be to avoid the trouble his father brought, and Ray picking a fight with her whenever he stumbled in—it had been too much for such a young mother.

She and Ray had tied their paths together much too soon and at entirely too young an age. Carissa had met Ray at the local soda shop when she was only fifteen, a sophomore. Ray had already been a drop-out for five years, but she loved that bad-boy image he exuded. His image was the total opposite of how she viewed her dad, but she liked that.

She had found herself pregnant only a couple of months after they'd met. She married Ray, so her momma and daddy wouldn't lecture or berate her, and she also thought she loved Ray. He was the only boyfriend she'd had up to that point as her parents were strict about dating. They didn't really know about Ray until the day she confessed about her predicament.

It didn't take long after Jason was born for Ray to start disappearing throughout the day and early evening. He would show up just before dinner time with just enough groceries to make them whatever meal he craved and wanted served that night. He would sit in front of the television eating then return to playing cards with his buddies and drinking. The next night would be a repeat of the night before. He worked at times for the local cab company, or sometimes he would repo cars for the bank from others just like him that chose not to pay for the obligations they'd made. Ray's early bouts of car stealing had at least been useful in teaching him a trade to put money on the table in a more legitimate way now. He would bring home winnings from his poker games occasionally. It usually was cash or jewelry he could pawn. Once it was an old Chrysler New Yorker he'd won on a lucky hand. He drove it into the dirt, never properly licensing or insuring it. Ray said that was just a way the government tried to keep track of people and keep them poor with fees. It was always the world against him personally.

Carissa quickly realized that she had made a huge mistake, but for the sake of her son, she stayed and endured years of a loveless marriage to a man who cheated on her regularly. At one time, Ray had two separate family lives going on at once: one with her and the other with a brunette who danced at a club. Ray had robbed her of her self-esteem, but she knew no pain she couldn't handle. She was strong both mentally and physically. Carissa seemed to be made of steel wrapped in a package of internal and external beauty and determination.

It was as Jason started to enter his teens that Ray would begin to verbally attack his son, calling him a lazy loser among other self-esteem robbing names. Ray was more than likely looking at Jason as if he were staring into the mirror. He surely looked at his boy and saw a reflection of himself before he had become the loser he now was and took those personal feelings of self-loathing out on his son. The more frequently his drinking became, the more his meanness grew exponentially.

Jason was growing into a good-looking boy with a chiseled physique and piercing green eyes just like his father's. The two were very different from each other up to this point, but given more time, Jason would begin to assimilate more than just his father's physical traits. Carissa always tried to second guess if she'd left Ray earlier, would it have made a difference in Jason?

Or was it more of genetics that eventually cloned Jason into his father?

Carissa would absorb the physical blows and as much of the verbal ones as she could, pushing Jason to stay out with Johnny and Tommy as much as possible as to avoid his father's wrath. It was a terrible position to put Jason in, but with her self-worth at an all-time low, she knew no other solution. That of course changed the night Ray turned the slapping and hitting onto Jason. She would have killed Ray that night had she the means to do it. She knew at that point she had to act quickly.

Everyone in the small town quietly knew what the situation was out at the Dean house, so it was no surprise when the deputy had finally hauled him in and charged him with domestic abuse and assault and battery.

When Ray finally looked deep inside, he realized the monster he had become and agreed to plead guilty, giving Carissa and Jason the chance for escape that they desperately needed.

Jason had a hard time acknowledging the fact his father was in prison. He felt it was partially because of him. Maybe he should have been tougher and stood up and defended his father even though his momma had said there was no defense for a child and wife beater. He knew he should be happy like his momma was about getting away. But with it went the refuge and camaraderie of his blood brothers and everything he'd grown up being comfortable with. The cave, the secret treehouse his friends and he had built from scraps found lying around throughout the town and outskirts. *All gone in an instant.*

Jason later had even missed his favorite teacher and confidant at school, Mr. Anderson, the math teacher. He had been graced with super math skills from an early age. His teacher had nurtured it and spent many hours after school tutoring him. Jason seemed to find solace in math problems. It had been a way of forgetting about his father being a drunk. He saw Mr. Anderson as his surrogate father, even though he had no idea what that meant at the time. He too now had been taken from his life by his moving from town.

Jason had one thing that he had kept and was never without, no matter where he moved or ended up. It was even found in his pocket the day he tumbled over the railing and lay dying in the hospital. It was really the only thing that the hospital had given his momma from his personal contents after they had pronounced him deceased. The nurse handed her a small, plastic baggy with his wallet containing one five and three ones, an expired driver's license, a small tattered picture of Johnny and Tommy with him in the middle from the seventh grade, and a small, banged-up Case pocketknife with two folding blades and larger folding serrated blade. That was it. Not much to show from a forty-three-year-old grown man's life accumulation of possessions. Jason's possessions were always more of a mental collection. He had never been one to keep a lot of physical things.

John had remembered one day when Jason had brought three or four items to school in his pocket.

Jason had come up to him wanting 'Johnny' to pick one of the items to keep. He said he would throw them away if Johnny wouldn't pick one. It seemed Jason didn't want to be mentally troubled by keeping track of more than one item. He said, 'It would drive him frigging nuts. It'd send me to the crazy house—pick one Johnny—for the love of God, just do it!'

It was one of Jason's quirks that John would carry with him in his recollection of him forever, only to be brought out when conversation would turn to his childhood memories. Those memories had grown very rare. It was, however, a window into Jason's soul which had been well-hidden growing up with him. John couldn't imagine the torment he must have endured and how it must have affected him in so many different ways. It was just one of the memories he had shared with Carissa on the phone when he was able to steer the conversation away from him and his troubles to other topics that night. He had also asked her if she still had the pocket knife because he would like to see it again, just for old time's sake.

***

John pulled into the town of Winfield and quickly searched for a place to park so he could call Carissa. Again, mentally, he had to correct himself from adding the 'Miss' in front of her name. He didn't want to be the reason for making her feel aged by calling her Miss Carissa, a term that apparently annoyed her a bit as she had called him on it several times during their late night, early morning chat.

The phone only rang once before Carissa answered in a cheery and upbeat voice. It was almost was as if she were holding her phone waiting for it to ring so she could spring into action with anticipation.

"Carissa! Good morning! I made it. I'm at the Dillon's Fuel Center on the far side of Main. Of course, probably the only Dillon's Fuel Center!" John laughed.

"And you would be right Johnny! But the question being—how many 'fuel centers' in Ash Grove have a pharmacy in them, huh?" she quipped quickly.

"Well—Carissa, you do have me on that question, especially since we don't even have a Dillon's Fuel Center. I hereby abdicate my argument over to you, Ma'am."

"Look at you trying to impress an old lady by using such big and stupefying words!" If Carissa had of been talking on a wall phone with a cord, she surely would have been twirling it in her fingers like a school girl of the past.

"Miss Carissa, I can tell it's going to be an interesting time meeting you today. I can tell I'm going to like you even more if I don't trip and fall and make a fool of myself before I get my first word out!"

"Now, Johnny, I would expect a warm and Brobdingnagian hug from you before you ever would attempt to enunciate a single thing to me."

"Do you have your phone Googling these rebuttals? I said I concede! And yes, I will give you a huge hug the very first thing if you promise me right now that this competitive side of you is not the predominate one!" They both laughed out loud, and if you could see each of their faces, you would see blushing and true joy as if they were school kids playing on the schoolyard at recess.

They decided to first meet at the Tunnel Mill Park because Carissa thought it would be a fitting place becoming of the scenery John was looking at when they first talked last night on the phone. John smiled as he realized that a woman would think things out this deeply as to where the most appropriate spot to meet would be due to a past place of conversation. Carissa quickly followed by stating she'd be there in thirty to forty minutes because she had overslept. Afterall, he'd 'kept her out' so late the evening before. That would make it roughly 11:30 a.m.

John Google mapped the park and easily found the entrance as it was only a couple of minutes away. Literally across a couple of streets from where he was, although when he crossed the railroad tracks and the road became gravel leading out through a field toward a tree-line—he couldn't help but wonder if Carissa was playing a final, mean-spirited joke on him. It looked like it led to nowhere. He snickered to himself. But he dared to drive on until he saw that it was indeed a park with a large circle drive that led back to the road he had entered on.

He found a place to park his truck just off the road onto the grass. A thought came to his mind. It wasn't a thought that he would let get out of control like in his recent past but a curious thought all the same. Water had become somewhat of a predominant factor in his life ever since his float trip with the Pierces. He mentally listed them beside a number after each one: Jason's death in a river—one, the little shack he now resided in was beside a small creek—two, the Arkansas River where he most recently had visited and not only almost ended his life but had re-engaged with Carissa, who quite clearly had been instrumental in saving him—three, and now here he was beside a river again where he was about to meet Carissa face to face after thirty some years—four. He then thought back to the symbol on the plaque that was just behind the Keeper of the Plains. It mentioned the four elements, water being one.

It was just odd, he thought. He'd never really thought about water other than to drink it or bathe in it before, and now, it seemed to have more significance. Maybe he was putting too much thought into it. He looked up at the sky and saw some dark grey clouds making their way closer. John quickly added rain—5 to his running list and smiled. He pulled his phone out and opened his picture gallery up. There was the last picture he took. A close-up of the Plains Indians symbol. He really liked the way it looked. It was well thought out and had not only physical but spiritual meaning as well. It now had a special meaning to him. He had never really thought about getting a tattoo, but now he tried to picture this symbol on his forearm. He thought surely God wouldn't think it was sacrilegious for him to bear this symbol that was present in the spot Jesus had saved him from himself? He quickly wondered what Shelly would think if he came home with it? He then remembered that when he got home, Shelly would most definitely not be there waiting for him. He had made sure of that before he had left.

The guilt-demons tried to push their way back into his mind and make him squirm under their control again, but John shut that down quickly.

"Lord, thank you for all you have graced me with. Please watch over me and my family and friends and keep us under your protection and love. Your will to always be done, with that in mind, please help maintain my strength and faith in you. Amen." John smiled in assurance and did not begin to falter as in his recent past.

John continued to walk toward the dam area where he noticed a few fishermen tasking their luck and skills. He himself was never a fan of fishing, but his son had always wanted to take a tackle box and rod when they would go camping. He, like his son, would rarely touch it when they arrived at the lake, but it was there if he wanted it or even remembered it. Again, he smiled to himself. The memories now seemed to be beginning to bring comfort instead of pain. He was certain he would still experience setbacks of suffering, but he now had stockpiled ammunition of the spiritual kind and not the other to fight back.

He knew he had a lot people back home that needed his attention. People he had put on the back burner of his life while he wallowed in his own self-pity. When he accepted his calling, he had known that it meant putting others ahead of himself. He'd somehow lost sight of all of that in the quagmire of pain and confusion that his personal loss had brought him. John now felt renewed in his abilities and responsibilities. He was hoping that after meeting with Carissa, his four to five-hour drive home would give him time to be inspired for a message to give Sunday that would show the congregation they could trust and count on him again.

John looked up to notice a dust cloud heading his way. It was as if the cavalry had crested the hill and were rushing toward him to save the day. The dust plume was preceded by a silver Subaru SUV that came to an abrupt stop beside his truck only to be quickly engulfed by the following cloud of white. He saw an aged but familiar face through the window just before the veil of dust encircled them.

"And *THAT* must be the melodramatic arrival of Miss Carissa!" John laughed as he covered both his eyes and face while walking toward the vehicle before the mixture of air and dirt had a chance to dissipate. He began to wonder if every entrance she made was as theatrical as this and the one last night was. "She seems to be a real showstopper," he quietly said aloud with a chuckle to himself.

The door to the Subaru flew open almost before it had ceased sliding in the grass and gravel, and out jumped a smiling woman with auburn-colored hair hiding hints of grey streaking throughout. As she moved in close to him quickly with arms held wide open, John stepped into her hugging arms that surrounded him and pulled him in tight. John reciprocated by putting his arms around her waist and reaching up toward her shoulder blades, his safe sanctuary training kicking in. Emotions came flooding in, leftover from the night before, as he squeezed tightly the woman that had broken through his mindset so timely, just as the curtain had begun to draw closed

on his world. He released the tightness of his grip
several times, but Carissa was having *no part* of it. As his
muscles would release, it was as if she sensed it and
counteracted with increased tension in her arms.

They finally stepped back a bit from one another,
looking each other over as if they were inspecting the
other for signs of change. John noticed in her face
small brown specs of the freckles scattered throughout
her mild complexion he now remembered Miss Carissa
having. Her skin showed some age with small crow's
feet in the corners of her eyes, but the green still bore
the sparkle of youth that Jason's eyes had always had.
Carissa reached for John's hands and grasped them,
pulling him to her just a bit closer saying, "Johnny—it
is absolutely a serendipity seeing you. You are all grown
up, but you still have that teenage gleam and hint of
social discomfort in you!"

"And you, Miss Carissa, seemed to have foiled the
aging process altogether yourself! You look wonderful
and as beautiful as I remember! And buried in that
mess of a sentence somewhere—is an absolute honest
compliment."

There was some awkward silence between them as
they each looked into the other's eyes and shared some
smiles, each searching for the mixture of words to
respond back to one other. Each quietly pondering
what the other was thinking at this moment.

For John, the reality of this whole situation was a
culmination brought on from a deep pain that dreams
from his past had stirred due to the greatest loss he'd
ever endured. And for Carissa, it was a chance call from
a past neighbor, merely mentioning John's name, and

that he was asking about her son, that had brought this moment to her. They had both suffered the loss of a child, a son. They both looked as if they were simultaneously realizing the common ties that had climaxed in this specific moment. What were the odds that this small window in time could be coincidence? It felt more like the careful weaving of circumstance from only an artist that knew the entirety of these two mere strangers but for a moment in their lives shared over three decades ago. Only the creator could weave this kind of a moment together so beautifully and seamlessly. A tapestry of threads from different worlds woven together to create a story merged between two travelers from two entirely different lives shared in the same macrocosm.

One can only imagine how boring it would be as a non-believer, calling every unforeseen miracle both huge and small a *mere coincidence* or trying to scientifically explain it away. John and Carissa both seemed to know the importance of accepting these things as gifts from God and to give thanks of gratitude for these special *snapshots* in time.

When the distant thoughts that each had just experienced returned to smiles, the sliver of awkwardness had vanished. They shared conversation as they walked around the circle drive in the park and reminisced again of the past as old friends would. Just as they rounded the half-way point of the circle for the fifth or sixth time, a sudden crack of thunder warned them of the impending rainstorm to follow. The grey clouds passing overhead were bringing a curtain of rain toward them in the close distance as they walked more quickly toward their vehicles. They were about five minutes too slow by the time they reached John's truck and climbed in soaked to the bone but still laughing like teenagers.

As their time was winding down before John needed to head back home, he struggled with how much of last night he should share with Carissa. How close he was to ending his own life. He wanted her to know just how important her part was in saving him, but he didn't know how to broach the subject. She had just shared the fact that Jason really hadn't died from only the fall, but that he had been slowly *drowning* himself in the bottle long before the day he had tumbled over the second-floor balcony to the ground.

John heard Carissa say the word *drowning,* and he immediately remembered what he had seen spelled out on the game board so many years ago.

John looked into her eyes, his own tearing up with guilt as he began to tell her his story of the Ouija board and the question that he'd asked of it one childhood night long ago. The culpability was something he'd carried since the night his dream about the incident had made him aware of his possible role in Jason's demise by toying with imaginable spirits.

He expected her to pull back from him in anger and rebuke, but instead she pulled him in close and whispered, "Jason's father had given him his death sentence. It had nothing to do with you or that silly childhood game." She kissed him on his cheek close to the ear she had whispered in and then pulled back to looked into his tear-filled eyes. "John, you are a good man of faith, a child of God, and were the best friend to my son that he'd ever had. You can't possibly think that I, or God, or *you* should hold yourself accountable for him dying. I held myself responsible for not leaving Ray soon enough—for weeks and weeks until I begged God to take my life in exchange for my Jason's. I knew he couldn't or wouldn't be able to do that. But he finally did answer my prayers. Not the answer I thought I was looking for, and it wasn't as soon as I wanted it, but he answered it in his time. Do you know what that answer was or when he gave it to me?" she inquired with tearing eyes as she tried to turn his face back toward hers.

John looked away again through the blurred window of his truck that was covered with raindrops sliding from the top down in unison with his heartbeat and the beads of salt water that raced down his cheeks and then looking back at Carissa he said, "I have no idea."

Carissa moved in close again, so close he could feel her warm breath, and whispered in his ear, "It was when you answered the phone last night and said my name. He brought you back into my life because it wasn't possible to bring Jason back to me; you were his answer to me. You are the closest person to me like the son I lost." She laid her head on his shoulder and reached around his neck and hugged him close and spoke quietly, "God brought us both together so we can reconcile our demons and move forward with the lives he created us to follow. He didn't create us to be miserable with blame and pain. He wants each of us to be happy in this life until we again see our boys at the end of this one—in *His* time. So you drive home safely tonight Johnny Austin, knowing that all is well in our worlds, our souls, and that we are forever connected in a way that no other living person could ever imagine." She then reached into her pocket and handed John the pocketknife he had asked to see.

John looked at it, studied it carefully as he turned it over in his hand, squeezing it tightly, and said, "Do you know what's so special about this knife that Jason kept it with him?"

Carissa looked at it in John's open palm and said, "I have no idea Johnny."

"It was the blade that he, Tommy, and I cut open our palms with to become blood brothers so many, many years ago," John said quietly as he looked up from it and back into her eyes.

Carissa closed his palm around it and told him, "Looks like it found its way home."

John hugged Carissa close and sobbed. He softly repeated the words, "I am so sorry," several times before she covered his mouth with her finger as if to say stop—then she smiled with her lip quivering and turned to open the door to step out. She turned and held her hand up to her ear signaling for him to stay in touch, to call her. He smiled back with a nod and then started the diesel motor with a twist of the key.

As John pulled away, he glanced in the rearview mirror through the back window to see the water-blurred outline of Miss Carissa waving at him as the rain began to slow its downpour. By the time he hit the highway, a beautiful rainbow stretched from one end of the sky to the other. John's four-and-a-half-hour drive home was quiet and reflective and without event.

# Chapter 17

*About 7:30 p.m. Wednesday Evening*
## From One World to the Next

As John's truck rolled into the garage, he quickly killed the ignition and doused the lights. He was tired and didn't want to draw any attention to the fact he was now back home. He let his head fall back onto the headrest; he forced himself to release the tension that his shoulders carried from the long drive home. He might have craved a beer to unwind, but after thinking how Jason's world had ended, he suddenly felt no thirst for alcohol.

John made his way to his back door of the shack, past the porch swing that barely swayed in the light breeze, and he let himself in. He knew he had promised to call Bob when he got back, but he just didn't have the strength to go through all the talk that would be expected of him. He would do it first thing tomorrow morning. Maybe an early call and meet up for coffee at the Copper Grill. He could use a good breakfast to break the tension, thinking about the conversation Bob had shared with him earlier.

*** 

A woman always seems to be more forgiving to another woman than she does a man. When Julie had picked up Mary and Shelly from the hospital on Monday, Julie heard the story of how John had responded to her after almost literally bumping into him downtown. Never once did she blame Julie about her and John's circumstances as she had Bob. Her memory was still on the fuzzy side, but Shelly most definitely remembered John telling her to go to Hell and that he would meet her there. All three women were still left in the dark as to why John would have unleashed on her. None had yet heard the nasty rumor that was still being passed around town.

***

Wayne was the first who was directly involved in the rumor to hear the growing story of his 'passionate love affair' with Shelly. The news had smacked him in the face almost first thing Monday morning as he opened the doors to the hardware store, letting Mrs. Snodgrass in to make a plumbing purchase. He thought it odd that she would be making this kind of purchase and at this early hour.

As she was at the counter checking out, she was on her phone and said those three words aloud in a questioning way, "Passionate love affair?" Then she turned and looked Wayne up and down as she handed him her check. "Now, Wayne," she cracked a condemning grin, "I'm sure you know I don't care much for John and his family, but you devil you— schtupping the man's wife when he's already as down on his luck as he can possibly be? And people think I'm the cruel bitch in this town." She turned and walked out as abruptly as she'd entered, her painted lips turned upward in a smile like the Cheshire cat.

Wayne stood there in shock holding the check in his hand that was hovering above the cash till as he tried to make sense out of what had just transpired. "What the . . ." fell from his mouth, before he dropped the check in the register drawer and turned to see if any employees were standing behind him. "Where in the world did that come from?"

***

Where or how does one begin to explain a human being such as Beverly Snodgrass? She had decided after witnessing John's latest message on Sunday that she needed to step up her game and personally put more effort in. Apparently, trusting others to take the ball and run was getting her game plan nowhere. John's message last week was not only current but it was pertinent, and she realized it. She had let her hatred and anger cloud over the fact that John really was a good man deep down and could be a strong, positive influence in her town and church again. But her jealousy of whatever leadership qualities and power he had inside him ate at her and drove her to attempt to destroy it. After all, this was her town, her church, and her birthright.

Beverly had lived in Ash Grove her entire life, never venturing out any further than Springfield. She saw the town as her fortress because her family had been instrumental generations ago in building it, and as the true last living heir of her family, she wasn't going to be the one to lose it all to an outsider, a 'move in,' no matter what gifts he had to offer it.

Her family's wealth had bred her to feel privileged. She had never had to want for anything. Her only real struggle through life was to live up to the image her mother and father had expected. Beverly's youth had really been sad if you had been able to sit back on the sidelines and watch as she grew from a content baby into a young girl being pushed to be something she wasn't born to be. God creates us all in his image, but her family had made certain to transform her image to mirror theirs.

Wayne had grown up beside her literally, from the day he had shared a crib with her at the church nursery until minutes ago as she accused him of cheating with the wife of someone who had become a best friend to him.

Wayne was the one person who had seen her from not only the sideline of the game but from inside the game as well. He had tried to be that one kid in school that reached out when others would poke fun or ignore her. She was the kid that lived in the town mansion that every girl dreamed of being in but had no chance in the small rural community filled with families struggling to pay the bills on time and put food on their plates.

Wayne had always wanted to do the right thing, but today, he had no other cheek to turn. Beverly had crossed the line for the last time. He knew she was up to something, and whatever it was, it would be designed to benefit no one other than herself or her interests. Wayne would not be her pawn any longer.

***

Ash Grove was a fine small town. It was a very welcoming and loving town for the most part, with a long history of prosperity since being incorporated back in 1871. Thirty-five years before that, one of the town's most famous first residents had been Nathan Boone, the son of frontiersman Daniel Boone. Nathan and his wife raised fourteen children there. The town really started its growth just after the conclusion of the civil war, when churches, hotels, flour mills, and even an opera house were built.

Quiet rumors of Beverly's family having ties with another famous resident and possible bloodlines was that of Arizona Donnie Clark, born in Ash Grove on October 8, 1873. Otherwise known later in her life as 'Ma Barker.' The rumors of a possible affair at one time with Beverly's mother and one of Donnie's sons, Lloyd Barker, when she went on a short trip to Denver, Colorado had never been proven nor dismissed. It was furthered fueled by the fact that as Beverly aged, she had taken on strong visual attributes when compared to photos of Ma Barker and her son Lloyd Barker. That could also explain her being so subjugated to evil. The blood that ran through the Barker family seemed thick with nefariousness, a trait that seemed to come biologically natural to Beverly Snodgrass.

***

Wayne all the sudden felt sick to his stomach minutes later after Beverly had left that early Monday morning. If this rumor was being spread around town, he feared that Shelly may be the next to suffer its consequences if she hadn't already. He knew he had to give her warning, and he gave her cellphone a call.

Wayne felt relief when Shelly answered. He asked if she was still in town and said he needed to talk to her, and she told him she was staying at Mary's, and he was welcome to come later that afternoon when they got back. Shelly thought it was odd when Wayne asked her not to wander around town until he had talked to her, not that she was planning anything since she was supposed to remain resting in bed. She didn't feel compelled to share with him that part on the phone since he was coming over later anyway.

Shelly turned to Mary and Julie and told them that it had been Wayne on the phone, and he was sounding kind of weird. As soon as she was to be released, they would head back to Ash Grove, getting Shelly settled in and return to girl chat.

*** 

By the time Wayne was able to meet up with Mary, Julie, and Shelly later in the afternoon, the rumor had gone full blown throughout town. He had noticed condemning stares from customers coming in to shop that obviously believed what they had heard, yet were not brave enough to say anything to his face. Wayne had never been fond of cowards who talked behind people's backs, but as a businessman in a small town, he knew that it was best to let the anger pass with a hardy smile and hello and go about his business.

When he greeted Shelly at the door, Wayne almost felt as if he should check over his shoulder before giving her a hug. He noticed she looked rather pale as Mary invited him in.

Mary smiled and then asked Wayne, "There is kind of an odd air in the Grove today—don't you think? I don't know what it is, but it just felt different pulling in."

Wayne immediately stated that they sit down, that he had some 'not so good news' to share. "Shelly, first off, you don't look exactly well—are you okay? Anyone say anything hateful to you as you came into town?"

"What do you mean—hateful? We just got here from the hospital in Springfield; we haven't talked to anyone except each other. I had to get some staples in the back of my head from a fall I took Saturday," Shelly replied.

"Saturday? You've been in the hospital since Saturday? I don't remember getting any calls telling me that!" Wayne stated as he sent glares across the room to all three women. "Are you okay? What happened?"

After hearing the story about Shelly's fall, Wayne started putting things together and looked at each one as he said, "Well, ladies, I'm just going to have to let you know that all of Ash Grove will now accuse me of having affairs with the three of you since I'm sure someone saw me come into your house today Mary, I'm sorry, but all of your reputations are more than likely being tarnished as we speak!"

And so, Wayne explained what had transpired earlier this morning and the frowns and look of dismay he had received all day long up until now. They all

185

quickly surmised that John must have somehow gotten the news before each of them and that would explain John's horrible reaction to Shelly. Wayne stated that he was almost certain who the root of the rumor was, and that he would be confronting that person very soon.

Shelly felt somewhat relieved, but at the same time angry that the rumor had been started and even more perplexed that John wouldn't have asked her about it instead of just reacting like he did. They all at once started filling Shelly in on the dark turn John had taken after Shelly left once Jason's funeral was over. Shelly broke down in tears and with her head injury; she quickly had to lie down and rest. *Exhaustion!*

Mary got a cool, damp cloth and lovingly laid it over Shelly's forehead and told her it would all work out in the end. "Hang in there, sweet Shelly, it's going to be okay. I know you two will work things out. You were made for each other. You two are a blessing to our community and to each other. It's going to be okay," she assured as Shelly gently nodded off to sleep from the stress and medication.

Julie called her husband, and Bob told her he'd talked to John and that he was in Wichita seeing an old friend and should be back by Wednesday or Thursday at the latest. They compared rumor notes and agreed that was what had set John off, more than likely stumbling into someone who shared the gossip with him. He surely had no idea that Shelly had fallen and gotten hurt. Bob said that John was supposed to call as soon as he got into town, and they were going to talk.

"I hope this mess is on its way to being mended and things can get back to where they were. This couple's lives are devastated and when it seems like hope is on the horizon—*bam*!" Julie said. "Wayne seems to know who is at the bottom of this as if we don't already have a stinking idea!"

"Now Julie, don't you and Wayne go jumping to conclusions. That's why I say you could never be a cop, which is why you married one!"

The next three days had some in town on eggshells, some looking for answers, some lay in healing, and one still plotting the next step.

\*\*\*

Henry had been checking at least once a day since Monday afternoon on the pastor's place, wondering where John could be. He too had heard the rumor, and it had him on edge. He knew it couldn't be true, but the fact that John's truck was gone with no word really worked on him. Henry had shared with Molly what he had heard, and the news had sickened her. Henry knew he should have just kept it to himself, but he figured she was bound to hear it from someone, and it might as well be him.

Molly's health had started to decline even more since her incident with Henry's handgun at the festival. The energy expelled that night and then the following embarrassment of having to meet with the chief of police was just one more thing than her body and mind couldn't deal with. She felt deep inside that maybe God was beginning the call home to her. She wasn't ready to confide that to Henry. He was mentally slipping, and he really needed her to be his rock.

Molly had horrible scenarios playing through her mind about what would happen with Henry when she was gone. He was taking care of them both physically, but she was the mental anchor that kept them stable and grounded. Without her mooring, Henry would surely drift out to sea, so to speak, and be dangerously lost in the currents. Her hopes that John would be his stability in her absence had been dashed after he lost his son and Shelly.

Molly spent the hours trapped in her worries like she was trapped in her electric wheelchair. The tracks worn in her home's carpet from circling through the house day and night mimicked the tracks in her mind that had been worn from the repeated thoughts that circled through her brain. Molly spent many hours in prayer, presenting her requests in every different term she could think of to get an answer of relief knowing Henry would be cared for. Then, and only then, could she have the courage to let go. She was tired, yet at the same time felt so cumbersome to her husband, whom she knew would give the world to her if he could.

The two of them, both Henry and Molly, had been such a stable part of the Ash Grove community. They were known around town for being loving and giving people who were deeply committed to each other. They had been humbling in every way, never boastful about anything. Mary had always promised Molly that she would always be there to help Henry if need be, but her 'fear of leaving' her home would never allow her. They didn't live in the circle of comfort that Mary had around her house. They were about three blocks outside of Mary's mental limitation.

"What will I do? What will Henry do? I just don't know how much longer I can hold out," she quietly told herself. And with a sigh of frustration, she circled back around and out to her front porch where she watched her small world go by as it shrunk evermore day by day.

Life in Ash Grove had seemed like such a Mayberry town at one time. That aspect was changing lately. The world was getting more and more angry with itself. People were turning inward instead of reaching out in a neighborly way. The kids seldom played outdoors anymore, too busy with their electronic gadgets. The parents all entered their houses through their garage doors at the press of a button, rarely even waving to their neighbors. That's what homes had become—houses.

The family unit was crumbling. Both parents working, kids left raising themselves, and the family-run businesses being snuffed out by corporate America. Molly would sit feeling like a product that wasn't needed anymore. Replaced by the newer version. She felt broken. Her only real purpose now was to keep her husband safe from the world that was turning its back on them. She wondered, as she sat on the porch watching what little happened outside, if she was the only one that had noticed. She thought for a moment, if we could take it all back, where our brilliance had brought us to at this stage in the world . . . would people even go back? Did people now even realize what they had missed and what they had become?

And then she smiled for a moment. The sparkle in her eye gleamed brightly the moment she saw her 'walking reverend' making his way down the sidewalk toward home, yes she thought to herself, thank God our *home* is still a *home*—not just another house on the block.

# Chapter 18

*Thursday Morning Back in Town*
**Getting Re-acclimated**

J ohn woke up before his alarm went off. He looked around, and for the first time since he had been staying in the little shack behind the church, he noticed it just didn't feel right. He had gone from his home with his family to being disheveled, spending most of his time on the back porch and rarely inside. He suddenly felt out of place. This didn't feel like home anymore, not that it ever had. What was strange was how quick the feeling came over him. He had gone to bed feeling nothing unusual. Yet, he woke up, and as his eyes opened, he could feel it. Awkwardness. Out of his element. It was almost unnerving.

John looked up at the clock on the wall and saw that it was six a.m. His first thought was he had better text Bob to let him know that he was back in town. He picked up his cellphone and messaged Bob, 'Back in town, breakfast at the Copper at 7:45? Anxious to talk.' *Send.*

John heard the knock on his door. He wondered if Bob had realized he was home. He got up from his bed and threw some shorts and a t-shirt on then stumbled out toward the front door. Once he rounded the doorway from the bedroom, he could see the tall outline of Henry's frame through the door's glass window. As John swung the door open, he said, "Henry! Good morning, sir!"

"Pastor John, where in the world have you been? I've been checking every day sometimes three or four times a day! I've been worried because of the talk in town."

"Now, Henry, you don't believe everything you hear, do you? I hear there are some doozies going around. Hey, I'm hoping to meet Bob for some breakfast over at the Copper—would you want to tag along? I'd buy your breakfast as long as I can afford you, big guy!"

"I would hate to barge in, but I'd love to go . . . Are you sure it wouldn't be a problem?"

"Henry, I owe it to you. We've missed several of those evening walks I've been promising. I think it would be good for all of us. Hang out in the living room a minute while I throw some water on my face and change clothes. I still haven't heard back from Bob, but I just reached out a minute ago to him." John walked back to his bedroom and changed then went to the bathroom and washed his face as he hollered out to Henry, "I just got back from Wichita. I went there to track down an old friend from my childhood. Unfortunately, I was about a year too late—but I was surprised to bump into his mother, quite a time, quite a time."

"Well, Pastor, you do seem different this morning. What happened to your friend? Did he move?"

John folded the washcloth and while drying his face off continued, "No, Henry, he left this world in a sad and long, painful way I'm sorry to say. But running into his mom seemed to help her out, and she *certainly* set me back on a positive path. God works in his own mysterious ways, Henry, no doubt about that—in his own time, yes sir, his own time. So how have you been feeling buddy?"

"That is a hard question to answer Pastor John . . ."

"Henry, my good friend, call me John! You and I don't have to be formal. Friends, that's what you and I are, just John from now on please." John peeked around the doorway at Henry and smiled.

Henry started to answer, but just as he did, John's cellphone made a whistle signaling a new text message had arrived. "Hang on just a sec, Henry, I bet this is Bob answering about that breakfast!" John picked up his phone and read 'Sounds great, lots to talk about, and you got the check!' John laughed out loud. "Looks like he can make it, and he says I get the tab!" John typed back, 'Of course I'm buying, Henry is here, and I'm buying his too, see ya there!'

"You know your wife is still in town, don't you?" asked Henry.

John suddenly felt different for a second. Almost like he walked from one world to another, running parallel to each other. "You don't say—Where is she staying?"

"She's over at Ma . . ."

"Mary James?" John interrupted. "Do you know how long she is planning on staying?"

"I think that is up to the doc from Springfield," answered Henry.

"What? What doctor, Henry?" John walked back around the corner into the living room and looked into Henry's eyes with anticipation.

"Pastor John, I've opened my big mouth, and I apologize. I'm going to let Chief Bob talk to you, and I'm going to skip out on breakfast this time. It's not my place to say anymore. I'm sorry," Henry stated as he hurriedly walked toward the front door to leave.

"*Henry!*" John hollered as the front door swung shut. John was working himself into a panicked state as he ran back into his bathroom to grab his phone. He quickly dialed Bob's number and paced as it rang once, twice, three . . .

"Hey there, John. I'm about ready to head to the Copper . . . Whatcha need?"

John answered back almost before Bob finished his question. "*What I need* is to know exactly what is going on with my wife Shelly. Henry just told me she was here until a doctor said otherwise! What happened while I was away, and why did nobody call me and fill me in?"

There was a short pause before Bob responded. "John, you remember when we talked the other day— right? And you said you weren't in the right frame of mind to talk. Shelly is okay. She had a fall, but she is fine. Let's meet at the Copper now, and I'll tell you everything I know. Okay?"

"I feel like I should go to Mary's and see her! I spoke horribly to her and now this . . ."

"John—let's talk at the Copper Grill first so you don't just bombard your way in at Mary's without knowing the background. You and Shelly have been on eggshells or not even talking to each other for months. Don't you think you could wait an hour before you possibly muck up a chance to get some resolution?" Bob asked.

John's heart was pounding, but he knew Bob was right. "I'm headed to the Copper now. See you in *five minutes*." Click.

# Chapter 19

*Thursday Morning at Mary's Home*
**Shelly and Mary**

Mary was a story worth reading. She was such a loving, caring, and vibrant woman once upon a time. She still was, once you got past the oddness of her disability. It's not exactly normal being held captive within a circle of comfort that one builds around a geological area close to home.

Mary was thirty-five and was a beautiful and vivacious woman. There had been many single men who tried to break through and form a relationship with her but had always given up with the impossible task not being able to circumvent the circle of comfort equation.

Mary had never really felt the need to have a man around to make herself complete. Even as a teenage girl, she had little interest in boys as far as a relational one. Mary was more about feelings of deep encouragement for whomever she was with. She truly loved everyone and wanted them to feel love and contentment no matter where they were on their journey.

She had suffered her greatest losses when her mother and brother had passed. Her mother's car had washed off a low-water bridge in flood state, and her brother had the boating accident. Those two separate losses were within a couple of months apart, and they had a profound effect on her. She had lost almost her entire family except for her father, and he moved away after her brother drowned.

She hurt but was too strong to let it show. Few in town had asked much about her after she began staying at home so much. Maybe fear of saying the wrong thing or maybe fear she had become the town crazy lady. Those that did come visit knew the depth of her caring soul for anyone in pain. She was by far the most innocent soul that ever existed in Ash Grove. She never had nor ever would conceive an idea of hurting anyone no matter the circumstance.

Shelly had grown very fond of Mary and missed her most of all, other than her son and husband, when she moved back home to Tularosa. Mary had given Shelly a strength she had struggled for after moving to the Grove and taking a new job along with the struggles of being a new 'pastor's wife' and, of course, mother of an upcoming teenage boy.

Mary had prayed many nights when Shelly had lost her son. She, out of all, could understand the pain of how he was lost and the fear he had surely felt the moments before he perished. Water had become a painful memory to her, except for the memory of being submersed as a child when she accepted Jesus as her savior.

Rainy days now affected her mood more than any other thing in this world. The rain always seemed to swallow her joy and turn it to gloom. She hated that fact, because before her losses, the rain had always made her feel renewed and refreshed. Before her mother and brother perished, she would spend hours on her porch, rocking on the swing watching the drops come down and trickle to the ground and puddle. Book in hand, rocking back and forth, page after page. But now, when the rains came, her porch was always empty, those that truly knew her well—saw those raindrops as Mary's tears crying for her family that were no longer with her.

Shelly had begun to feel the same way about the rain, which was probably one of the subconscious reasons she moved back to Tularosa, New Mexico. To run from the loss of her son, the ominous chasm between her and her husband, and the rain—back into the comfort of her mom and dad's support in the dry comfort of her distant desert home of the past.

Shelly should have realized that running from her problems would only exacerbate them. She suffered as much as John apparently had been; the only difference was the way they were each handling themselves. She had started out angry that John couldn't save their son only later to feel the guilt of never reaching out to him. The longer the time apart became, the wider the gorge eroded that separated them. Her world had felt devastated and then left undone. Uncared for. That hurt almost as much as waking every morning knowing Jason wouldn't come in to hug her or be there later to tuck into bed. She felt like she imagined a tree would feel if it could after a tornado had come through and stripped it of all its limbs and leaves, leaving only a trunk struggling with the loss of being able to reach for the sun or feel the wind blow through its appendages.

It had been a hard decision to make, but she knew it was the only choice she really had.

Being back in Ash Grove was something Shelly felt called to do. She knew she couldn't hide forever without facing the things that had sent her running those months back. She could announce the exact months, days, and hours, but there was no point. Jason was never coming back, but she had prayed there may still be saving her love with John. She had spent too much time not knowing where they stood in this limbo or holding pattern of 'what ifs.'

Mary was a comfort from the moment Shelly had stepped back into her home. She felt the glow of her warmth and the tenderness of her soul. Shelly had always felt as if Mary were from some distant world or an angel from heaven. She was like no other—genuine, open arms always drawing you in, filled with love and understanding. Almost as she would imagine Jesus being in the flesh.

\*\*\*

Shelly had slept well through the night with little stirring. Mary had sat in a rocking chair beside her, watching until she could hold her eyes open no longer. The distant thunder had awoken her and began to stir her inner thoughts. She hadn't realized that it was likely going to rain today. She glanced over at Shelly's face still calm and restful.

Mary began to let her mind drift to questions she'd let linger in her back thoughts. How would Shelly and John's first time seeing each other again go? What could she do or say to help ease them into being cautious of each other's feelings? She knew that Shelly wanted her marriage back but was fearful how she and John would react together now that they shared the loss of Jason. Shelly had told her how hurt she was that John would quickly assume the worst of her when he'd heard the rumor of her and Wayne. So much damage between two of the sweetest people she had grown to love so much.

A louder crack of thunder made Shelly's face wince, and then the sprinkles on the window pane began to be heard. It was surely going to be gloomy today.

Shelly shifted around in the bed before her eyes opened and focused on the figure sitting next to her. She first called out John's name and then realized she was still at Mary's and that it was Mary sitting beside her.

"Did you stay here all night?" she asked. "I'm okay . . . You really didn't need to."

"Shelly, it was not a bother at all. I love having you here. I just don't want to miss a minute!" Mary smiled. "Could you use some coffee? It seems it's going to be a rainy grey morning today."

"I think I could use some. It might perk me up a bit. I was having some sad dreams of John and myself. He was telling me that he was leaving me for good. I just don't know how I feel about all of this. My mind is all mixed up. The minute I think I know what I want, I suddenly feel like it's a mistake. Will it ever be clear like it used to be—*one way or the other*—Mary?"

"All I can say, sweetie, is that you don't have to make any rash decisions. You and John just need to talk and see where you both are. You still have a lot worth saving, looking in from the outside, but you two need to figure out where to go from here. It's good that you came back to see where you both stand. Avoiding each other was never going to resolve anything. It just gives room for doubt to grow. I'm going to go put some coffee on and let you move around and wake up, okay?" Mary reached over and squeezed Shelly's shoulder affectionately.

"I hope John gets back today. I don't want to put this off any longer. I need to start thinking about getting back to Tularosa and my folks—and my dogs! They are probably going crazy!" Shelly smiled for a moment. "I'm going to shower, and then I'll be out, fresh and new!" Shelly looked out toward the blurred window and the drops streaking downward. She sat up still facing the window and then folded her hands together, bowing her head she began praying for strength and wisdom and for a personal miracle to happen between her and John.

Mary quietly walked out and pulled the door to a hushed close. As soon as she was down the hall, her cellphone rang and she quickly answered it.

"Hey Mary, Bob here, I just talked to John. We are meeting at the Copper in just a few minutes. Henry let it slip about Shelly's hospital visit, and John was going to come straight over to see Shelly, but I convinced him to talk to me first and get some background of the situation. I thought you might want to give Shelly a heads up so she's not caught off guard."

"Shelly was hoping she could see John today. She's anxious and nervous and scared but ready to see where they stand. I'm glad you gave me a warning though. While she looks good this morning, I think it will be a physical and mental strain on her, probably for them both."

"I'll call you after he heads your way."

"Shelly is getting up and around. Give us an hour."

"You got it Mary. Talk to you in an hour or so."

***

When Shelly came into the kitchen, Mary poured her a cup of coffee, and they sat down at the table. "Shelly, I just got a call from Bob. He is meeting with John as we speak. They're at the Copper Grill, and Bob is filling him in about your accident. He found out from Henry, and he was ready to rush right over, but Bob convinced him to talk to him first."

"So he is coming over here afterward? Fairly soon?" asked Shelly.

"Yes, probably in about an hour. Are you okay?"

Shelly's hand holding her coffee began to tremble. Mary could tell that her nerves were suddenly weakening and seeking refuse somewhere inside her mind. Her confidence was beginning to wane. "Do I look all right?" Shelly asked. "Maybe I should go put makeup on?"

"Shelly Rose Austin! You look incredible! You look vivacious! You don't need to do a thing to yourself except gather up your self-confidence that I saw just ten minutes ago. This is the same man that fell madly in love with you eighteen years ago. The same man that I know for a fact has missed being with you. You both have suffered mutually and are both the same two people that walked around this town holding hands just a few months ago!"

"I know, but—*what if . . .*"

"Shelly, look at me honey, look into my eyes and listen! You got this girl; you are going to be fine. Give yourself some credit. Follow me in here . . ." Mary led Shelly back to the bedroom she had just walked out of a minute ago and over to the mirror. "Look at those piercing blue and entrancing eyes, that incredible blonde hair, and those cheekbones. Now look deeper past that exterior beauty and look inside. You have the soul of an angel. You have the heart of a beautiful goddess who beams with the radiance of love! What man could ever have a chance if you put your focus on them? Mary put her hands on Shelly's shoulders and drew her in, giving her a comforting hug.

"It's going to be all right, Shelly. You two have a strong foundation you share. Yes, you both lost an important and irreplaceable, very valuable, part of that foundation. But you have the Lord, the Creator that helped give you two the strength and stamina to build that foundation together, and he is still right there holding you up and giving you strength. Pray to Him, thank Him, praise Him and tell Him what you need. He listens, girl. He answers—and He loves you more than you will ever possibly understand." Shelly was struggling, trying to figure out how to own what Mary was telling her. She knew that God had plans for her, but in this part of her journey, she couldn't find any way to understand why. Mary continued trying to comfort her and build her up for the moment that was nearing.

"He didn't create a one-of-a-kind special woman like you just to have you fail and wither. Spread those wings with courage and speak honestly and openly to John. You respect him; he respects you. Now do what you came to do, say what you need to say, and get that path lined up again where the Lord is pointing you." And with those words, Shelly's eyes became bluer, her glow became brighter, and her shoulders lifted with confidence.

"I'm ready, Mary. Thank you for being you. I love you so much. I do have this." The two hugged tightly and then walked back into the kitchen and sat back down to their coffee. And now the wait for the sound of a door knock . . .

\*\*\*

John was already seated when Bob walked into the Copper Grill. Becky had already greeted 'Pastor J,' and when she saw Bob walk in, she put her hands on her waist and said, "Now look at this, Pastor J *AND* Chief Bob? The two best of Ash Grove's minds sharing breakfast on a rainy, gloomy morning? Must be a save 'em or shoot 'em meeting . . ." Becky said with a grin.

"Hello, Miss Becky, obviously this kind of a day has no negative effect on your sunshiny disposition," Bob quipped back.

"You two look like the only thing you're missing is a large cup of coffee and a stack of pancakes each!"

John quickly answered back, "Coffee only for me, Becky, and whatever the chief wants. It's on me today."

"Well, that sounds good. You still have that mindreading trick in your apron I see. Thank you, Miss Becky." Bob replied. Turning his attention to John, he said, "John, you look good. You look nervous and perplexed, but you look like the getaway did some real good. Julie and I have been praying for you, especially while you were gone."

"What happened, Bob? Is Shelly okay? Does she even want to see me?" John fired question after question with no room for any answers. He just kept stacking them one after another. "Do I have a chance to fix things? She hates me, doesn't she?" he continued.

"I have to be honest, John . . ." Bob hesitated for a moment. "I'm just not sure that you really need that coffee." Bob couldn't resist smiling. "Settle down, John! Shelly is fine, I don't believe she hates you, and yes, she is very much wanting to see you. She didn't come all the way over from New Mexico to see me or Julie, I don't believe. If she hates anyone, I believe it would be me!"

John quickly questioned what he meant by that statement, and then he and Bob talked as they waited for their coffee and Bob's pancakes. John's demeanor seemed to revert to a less nervous mode, and Bob quickly could tell that something super good must have happened while he was in Wichita; he was much like the pastor Bob knew and had grown to care about so much before his life had changed so dramatically.

Becky brought the coffees and told the chief that the cakes would be out shortly. She looked over at the smile on John and Bob's faces and asked them, "So you two guys look so happy today! Could I get a hug from you so the happiness will spread? I'll pass it on, I promise! These grey and gloomy days need all the happiness we can get!"

John was really enjoying the feeling of being 'normal' again, but as much as he wanted to sit and chat, he really wanted to go see Shelly. Bob could sense it in John's expressions and mannerisms. John swilled his first coffee down quickly, but Becky filled it up as soon as he set the cup down.

"John, do you remember how Shelly was the Saturday you ran into her and said the thing you said you wish you hadn't of? Did she look pale or heat-stroked?"

"Honestly, Bob, I was in so much shock from what I had heard a group of ladies say, right here in this restaurant, that I don't remember much. I walked out, down and around the corner, and almost bumped into her. The last person I expected to see and especially after hearing that she was seeing Wayne. I didn't even know she was back in town. We looked at each other, and I told her to go to hell, that I'd see her there someday, and I walked off. I felt horrible after I said it, but pride wouldn't let me go back. I never really even considered that the rumor was true when I truly thought it over."

"Well, at some point, she passed out and landed on her head there on the concrete. No one knows exactly how long she was there, but I got the call when the ambulance was leaving. Mary came with me and . . ."

"Mary? *She left her neighborhood?*" John questioned.

"She sure did—never said a word about home until she called me to see about a ride Monday for her and Shelly. She was sounding anxious and nervous at that time, and Julie was on her way to see Shelly. Julie took them to Mary's house and stayed late Monday night with them," Bob answered.

"Well, I'll be, some things you just never expect! So, Bob—you see now that I'm acting more myself, I'm no danger, nor in danger. Is it okay if I head over to Mary's to see Shelly? Does she really want me to come visit her?"

"Sit back for just a few more minutes; I told them you'd be headed there in about an hour and that was only thirty minutes ago. You don't want to rush this! You're kind of starting over, aren't you? Almost like dating each other again—like you just asked her out. Don't scare her off, buddy!"

John sat drinking coffee and nervously tapping his feet underneath the table. Bob sat talking to him like he was his high-school wingman, giving him mission advice and encouragement.

The other customers enjoying their breakfast were surely watching the two as if they were back in high school and two buddies on the football team were 'hanging out' at the malt shop. John never looked more at ease for someone so nervous to visit his girl for the 'first date.'

Twenty minutes later, Bob was telling Mary he was on his way and nervous as a schoolboy. They both shared a giggle when Mary conceded that Shelly was in the same frame of mind. "Things are going to turn out fine, I can feel it Bob." And with that, they agreed she should just stay low, back in her bedroom; if she was needed, she'd be close. Bob was available and close by if she called.

# Chapter 20

*Rainy Thursday Morning in Ash Grove*
**John and Shelly . . . Like a First Date**

J ohn walked up Mary's steps to her front door as the rain sprinkled down on him, soaking his head until he stepped up onto the covered porch. He fidgeted a bit like a teenager would before knocking on his new girlfriend's parents' door. He started to knock but hesitated a moment, and in that mere second, the door swung slowly open, and in the doorway stood a beautiful blonde-haired woman with the bluest eyes he'd ever seen. Her eyes weren't just blue—they were several shades of blue like brilliant faceted sapphires that sparkled even though the rain-filled clouds obscured them from any light source.

He must have looked like a soaked puppy standing at the door, but he was so lost in her eyes he didn't feel the drops of rain draining from his hair down onto his face. John was more mesmerized by Shelly's beautiful face; it was as if he'd seen her for the first time ever. Her skin looked velvety soft, and she absolutely glowed.

Shelly slowly smiled, looking into John's eyes and softly questioned, "Hello John, maybe you should come inside out of the rain?" And her beautiful natural lips parted slightly as she nervously ran her tongue between them. Both hearts were pounding as John and

Shelly each searched for words to form in their
thoughts as she turned to lead him in toward the living
room.

The room was dimly lit with the curtains open to
the darkened sky, and a table in the corner had several
scented candles burning with the faint fragrance of
tuberose oil. That scent had always been one of John's
favorite since they met in Hawaii. John's confidence
level rose as he felt like Shelly had gone to some effort
to set a mood of remembering their distant past. It was
instant infatuation for John when they had first met
each other. He had really put some effort into the chase
way back then as she took some convincing at first.

She sat down on the couch looking up toward him
and gave a couple of pats on the cushion beside her,
inviting him to sit next to her.

John looked around the room and saw no hint of
Mary and wondered where she could be. He turned his
attention back to Shelly and sat next to her searching
again for words to break the pleasant but awkward
moments of silence.

Shelly looked up and spoke softly, "I'll be right
back; don't run off."

"It took a long road to get here, Shelly. I'm not
going anywhere." John smiled and tried to sit back and
at least appear more relaxed. The truth was he had
butterflies in his stomach, and his mouth was becoming
dryer by the second as Shelly left the room.

John got up a second or two later and walked
around studying the various framed photos of desert
scenes. Some appeared to be Army photos from the
Middle East. He remembered Shelly telling him that

Mary had an interest in desert climate because of her brother's service in the Middle East. The brother she had lost in a boating accident at one of the area lakes close by. As John was circling the room, studying the photos, he suddenly heard a familiar song that he'd not heard in quite a while. The mellow sounds of Gary Jules. Shelly came around the corner with a CD case in her hand. She placed it on the coffee table and then walked over beside John who was still standing beside some of the pictures hanging on the wall.

"Have you wondered where your CD went to?" Shelly asked. "I found it under my car seat on my drive up here from Tularosa. It gave me comfort—yet it made me sad in a way. Some of the songs are haunting to me and some draw me close to you and of course one makes me think of Jason."

John turned immediately to Shelly putting his hands on her shoulders for a second before starting to pull her into himself. Shelly tucked her arms in close to herself and pushed toward John's chest, nestling in tightly, before laying her head on his shoulder. John could feel her warm breath on his neck as he surrounded her body with his arms.

The rain began to come down harder, and the sound of it began to compete with the sound of the music in the background. The moment they were sharing was intoxicating to them both. The sound of the rain, the smell of tuberose surrounding them, the faint sound of the music trying to eek its way into the blend of senses, that they were encased by was, at the least, *Overwhelming.*

John couldn't hear the quiet sniffs as Shelly fought back the tears, but he could feel the wetness they created as they slowly seeped through the cloth of his shirt and onto his skin. A single, warm tear ran down his neck that had somehow slipped past his collar, causing goosebumps to form on his neck as it slid downward until it dissipated into his skin.

John closed his eyes tightly as he let the warmth of Shelly's body, the heat from her breath on his neck, and the scent of tuberose take hold of the moment. He didn't want it to end. He didn't realize just how much he had missed his soulmate. He never could have imagined that what he was feeling could ever duplicate itself again like the feeling they'd both felt standing on that beach up on the North Shore of Oahu. In his mind, at this moment, he was back in that memory reliving the moment of holding Shelly much in the same way he was holding her right now.

The only thing that could possibly be missing at this moment were the waves creeping up and splashing their calves then surrounding their legs as they rushed past them and then receded back to where they had come. John didn't want to move. He feared if he did, the moment would end, and he'd wake up to the reality he had grown to know. An empty bed, an empty little shack and a heart full of guilt. He told himself over and over in his head to just hang on and remain still. Let this moment be his existence from now until the end.

Shelly was beginning to sob more uncontrollably. She tried to hold it back and draw it back into her shell. The shelter she had made herself into since all this tragedy and pain began. She wasn't ready to share this part of herself with anyone yet. She didn't want John to see this part of her that was still unhealed. Her wounds had begun to scab over, but the smallest bump would open them up again. Her arms began to lose their tension, and her shoulders began to drop, causing the chain reaction of their bodies beginning to pull apart. The bond they shared seconds ago was beginning to melt away, all without intention from either one. It was as if the earth began shaking, causing the welds to break and the seams to lose their bondage as the threads sheared and loosened.

John immediately felt the process even before it began. It was like there was a slow vacuum removing the air from the room, causing each of them to grasp for their own survival out of instinct.

Shelly looked up into John's eyes as their clutches reached the moment where they were no longer intertwined, and they separated. "John, I'm—I'm so sorry, I just can't . . ." she sobbed, trying to regain self-control. "I can't do this yet—I love you; I know that in my heart, but I'm still so broken. I'm so worthless to myself. I'm too broken to face you. I see you and as much as I want to just see you—to be with you, I see Jason. I hear him crying out. My heart is just too broken. You seem to be on your way to being healed while I—I'm just not . . ."

"Shelly—you'll get there. Hang on to your faith. I was just where you are. Don't give up. Don't blame, don't blame God, please don't blame me. Bad things happen to the most faith-filled followers." As John continued to speak, he reached out and put his hands back on Shelly's shoulders. He tried to ease back into a physical connection to her.

"We did nothing wrong. It's not punishment. It's just a horrible accident that can't be undone. But we *can* be healed. In God's time with your faith and hope— you *will* be healed, just keep asking for his guidance. I—I love you, Shelly Rose. I don't want to lose you. I want to be there for you. I wish I could push the magic button and cure you myself. I don't have that power though, but I will be there to help in any way I can." Tears began to slip from John's eyes as he tried to convince his wife of her importance to him.

"I *need* you Shelly. It's been such a hard journey in such a short time. Don't give up! I almost did. I never imagined that I would ever be here with you again. I have no one other than you, Shelly; I *need* you so *I can be whole again.*" John gently squeezed her tighter and then let his hands follow her shoulders and arms down to her hands as his fingers searched to slide in between hers and tighten his grasp.

The song 'Mad World' began to play. It was such a haunting song, and when it ended, the silence was deadening. The rain stopped as if it were a sign for John to leave. John knew this special moment had drawn to a close, but in his heart, he felt there would be another to follow soon. Shelly's eyes were tear-filled, but she thanked John for understanding. She told him she wouldn't give up but needed some more time. She would be heading back to Tularosa soon but would talk to him before she left.

This moment had taken so long to navigate its way to the present, yet it ended so quickly. John had

214

climbed out of the darkness he had fallen into with a miracle from God. He knew that Shelly was more than likely in a darkness like his, and it hurt. Seeing her up close and peering into her sadness was hard to do and then to have to walk away with her standing on the edge of her chasm brought him a fear of possibilities.

As John turned to watch Shelly slowly close the door to Mary's home, he climbed into his truck. He bowed his head humbly and began to beg for the Lord to save his wife from the agony and despair that she was trapped in and help the two of them be able to rebuild the love and trust that they once knew only months ago. "*Amen,*" John said aloud as he backed out of the drive and turned his truck back toward the place he called home for now.

He felt the comfort and familiarity of the porch swing out back calling his name on this rainy afternoon. Only this time it was to reflect on hope instead of despair. His hope was believing in the saying he had learned back in his home church before his calling, 'God is good all the time—all the time God is good.'

# Chapter 21

*Through the Months*
## Life's Journey Keeps Moving Forward

The next couple of days went by quickly, and before John knew, it was Saturday morning. He hadn't realized it when he woke up, but this would be a day to dread. He would find out why shortly as he soaked in the morning sun in the open air of his outside office. John had been sitting out on his back porch on the swing with his bible in hand and his tablet on his lap, finishing last minute tunings on his message for Sunday's service.

John had been thinking a lot about personal suffering. The suffering that he had been through, the suffering that his son had gone through, the suffering that he had just witnessed with his wife just days before, and the suffering that would surely continue to come in his future. It was a hard task not to resent those afflictions that fell on him. It was even harder to see them in his wife's beautiful but hurting eyes.

"Hello, John," a voice spoke out as a shadowed figure peeked around from the corner of the porch. With the sun backlighting the silhouette, it was hard to make out the figure, but her voice made his heart jump. She stepped into the shadow of the trees; her blonde hair stood out, and he quickly focused on her smile.

"Shell! What a perfect morning surprise! I was hoping you would come by and visit me. Step into my office! I'm just finishing up some work for Sunday." He quickly stood up from the swing as he walked toward the screen door. "I wanted to call or drop by Mary's, but I didn't want to push or make you feel uncomfortable. I have been thinking about you and  when we saw each other last . . ."

"I know, John, I—I just wanted to come by and see you before—well, before I headed back to Tularosa. My folks are wondering and you know, a couple of dogs are missing me . . ." Shelly smiled awkwardly, her arms just dangling by her side not knowing what to do with her hands, before continuing. "You know I need some time to sort all this out. I'm not just running away this time. I, um, I think—I think I know or have an idea of where we both may want to be eventually, and . . ."

"Shelly, I know exactly where I want you to be, but I want you to be ready. You have so much value in my world! You are worth waiting for." John reached with his hands out to hers with his focus solely on his wife's face as he continued, "I'm thinking of moving back, back into—our home. I know by myself, I'll find it difficult, but I'm at that point where life is moving on without me if I don't grab on and not let go of the past. I want to remember Jason—but I can't let his leaving us define me any longer. I know he is looking down on us from heaven begging me to— begging *US* to move forward with him as a happy memory of what he gave us. He's *still* in our hearts. John looked into Shelly's eyes as if to seek her permission to move back into their home they had shared as a family with Jason.

"I know you aren't quite where I am yet. God *moved* me, Shelly. He moved me and saved me through the works of another person. I sought answers to the point I went searching for an old friend in Wichita, and God sent me an angel just in time to *save* me from myself—someday I want to share my story with you. He looked down to the porch's wooden floor and then back upward to where their eyes met again.

"I just pray that you don't let your journey take you where mine was taking me, Shelly. I've never been to such a dark place. I almost got lost. I could have very easily been lost. *Forever!* Please don't let yourself fall like that." John felt like he was slipping into a sermon, but his heart was so steadfast on making sure the love of his life was listening and letting his words soak in deep.

"Reach out to someone that can make a difference, Shell. Just remember that I'm here for you. I'm yours still, if you choose a different path that doesn't lead you back—and Lord I hope that doesn't happen. I won't blame or hate you. I truly want you to be able to find the happiness we shared before we lost Jason. I know we got busy, we drifted—if there was one thing I learned from losing Jason is that, I need to hang onto the ones that mean the most to me. They can be taken from us in an instant, that love can be stolen from us. No blame or reason, but gone nonetheless in a flash or glimpse.

"I will always love you, Shell. You are the most incredible blessing God has ever given me along with

Jason, and there are reasons why we are here—right now, this instant. I can't tell you why. I just know we have to trust in hope." John fought back the tears as he felt like he was pleading his case before unseen judges watching to see how genuine his words were. He spoke directly from his heart. *Unrehearsed.*

The pain was swiftly feeling like it was being injected directly into his bloodstream. He was hurt that Shelly was going back, and he agonized giving her un-indicting permission to move on without him if it meant happiness in the end for her. He was so engulfed by his own suffering and thoughts that he realized he was looking past her and not at her. He stopped talking and focused on Shelly's face. Tears were streaming uncontrollably from her eyes. If the brilliant blue in her eyes were able to mix with her salty tears, there would have been blueish waves rolling out like on the beach they fell in love at.

The only sound Shelly was able to force out was too garbled by her emotion to be legible. She covered her mouth with both hands as she moved forward toward John who had begun to move closer when he noticed the agony she was trying to hold back.

John reached for her waist and drew Shelly in as if he were given just one shot at saving her life. He tucked his head in close to her ear and kept repeating, "I'm so sorry. I'm so sorry . . ." Her body shook violently with each deep breath she drew in. John thought to himself had he done or said the *wrong* things? How could he take a perfectly happy surprise moment and turn it around 180 degrees into this in just a matter of minutes? Or were the emotions they shared destined to metamorphosis into this state no matter what was said?

Was it just bad timing, or was it designed from the Creator that Henry would walk around the corner of John's shack to disrupt the emotional calamity they were engulfed in?

"Oh, I am so sorry John and Shelly? I—I didn't mean to, I should have called." Henry responded the moment he realized he had walked into something that he wasn't supposed to be a part of. He started backing awkwardly up. "I'll let you call me later, Pastor. I'm sorry . . ."

Shelly turned toward the screen door where Henry was backtracking and spoke, "That's okay, Henry; it's just some emotions we got caught up in. I'm leaving so you don't have to run off. John and I were just saying good-bye before I headed back to Tularosa . . ." Shelly turned back toward John as she backed away. "I'll call you John—as soon as I get home, back to Tularosa I mean . . ."

"Please, Shell, call me when you pull in for the night so I know where you're staying and that you're safe for the night."

"Okay, I will." She gave John a quick peck on his cheek as she backed away and turned to open the screen door. When she glanced back at John one last time before she walked out of sight around the corner, she touched her fingers to her mouth and lightly kissed them and waved as if to blow him one last kiss, secretly. John gave her his boyish wink that she had always said was flirtatious with a hint of danger.

"I'm sorry, Pastor . . ." Henry said once Shelly was out of site.

"It's okay Henry. I'm good. I think God has a plan that I can live with. It's going to take patience on my part, but it's a plan," John replied as he gave Henry a smile.

"You look like a new person, Pastor! I'm happy for you."

"Henry, let's you and I take one of those walks together and see what's ticking in each other's lives, what do you say? You in?"

"You know I am Pastor. But I must tell you, my life isn't ticking as well as yours seems to be."

John moved his bible and tablet to a little side table that stood near his porch swing and said, "Let's go walk and talk . . . Looks like the perfect day for it; I can finish up here later." And they took off toward the park where the paved circle had led them through many topics in the past, both good and not so good.

***

Life seemed to move slowly through the next few weeks in Ash Grove. It was almost back to a rhythm that seemed to hum throughout the town. There were still occasional troubles but nothing that really stood out.

Politics continued to add some fear, frustration, and division among the people even within the smallest of communities. No one seemed immune. The 'talking heads' continued to paint the news with the twists that praised their points and condemned the other. The country, now in the second year of the new administration, continued to make decisions that led to more division and controversy. One couldn't blame all the problems on the politics, but it did appear to many that the country would never be the same.

John continued to persevere with his messages staying positive and hope-filled. Many of the congregation would offer compliments to him as they shook his hand on the way out after service. They would thank him for showing that there was still hope to hold onto and there were still people hurting that needed us to reach out to. Love is easier than hate and so much healthier for a person. The town's people seemed to have simmered down about the gossip involving Shelly and Wayne also. It at least lay deep enough under the surface where there were no longer condemning stares or artificial smiles.

The district superintendent never did call on John for disciplinary actions because of his unruly struggles. No one ever had brought anything of dire need to her attention. It appeared that even Beverly had not yet attempted to use her persuasion in that way, as of yet. People seemed happy with his performance at the church and throughout the community. The congregation was starting to grow from the influx of families moving into town as the housing market began to increase. Word of mouth around town was that Deliver was the place to go to get connected with God and mission to those in need.

There were of course many conversations that had John reliving some of his dark moments as he bumped into different people around the town. People always wanted to hear John's story of his climb out of the mire. He would tell a good portion of it, but he never opened up about the entire 'Keeper of the Plains' encounter. Maybe someday he could tell Shelly first. He wondered if he could reach people that would normally never listen to a 'God filled story' should he ever write about it, maybe in fiction form?

John enjoyed his phone calls from Shelly when she would call, and of course he and Henry had returned to their regular walks in the evenings and afternoons. John had noticed more of a mental decline in Henry, as well as his constant agitation with a certain town troublemaker. Henry had become more and more worried about Molly's health and the speed at which her health and even attitude toward life was failing.

Mary would call John sometimes and hint for him to come over and share what was going on at the church and how Shelly and he were doing. Her excitement went back to a normal lull after Shelly left for New Mexico.

Life had begun to erase the difficult past John had fought through and replaced it with the rigors of his work. A shepherd leading his flock the way a pastor should takes up a lot of time. It had been one of the reasons he and Shelly had pulled away from each other to begin with. John had, however, taken the lessons his past had taught him and begun practicing at doling his personal time and shepherd time out proportionately.

John had told Shelly he was thinking about moving back into their house just before she had left, and two weeks later, he cleared it with the church board and moved back into the parsonage. John had one request, though, to move the porch swing from the back porch of the rental over to the front porch of the parsonage. He had become rather attached to it as it felt almost like family. It also had been a source of comfort along with some pain he felt he shouldn't forget. He wanted to be able to see it daily to remind himself of the struggles he had overcome. The 'dream swing' had taken him to places from his past, but he had survived those trips and learned valuable lessons from them. In a way, that swing had brought Carissa to him . . . the one extra special person that God had worked directly through to help set him free of his demons. Thank the Lord for Miss Carissa.

John had kept in touch with Carissa and had hoped he could talk her into visiting one day soon. When he would think back of their short time together, he would admittedly struggle with the out-of-the-ordinary feelings he had. They weren't sexual at all, but there had been some shared, mental, divine intimacy between them. He had quietly thought of her as his 'spiritual crush.' When someone literally 'saves' you— you maintain special feelings for them. Especially when you know the hand of God was the part of the equation that made it all possible. He'd never had a close friend that was female, like the friendship he shared with Carissa. A closeness on a shared devotional plane that was hard if not impossible to explain.

John made the move back to his home he had shared with Shelly and Jason. The feelings that overcame him as he walked throughout the house the first time were difficult, but nothing like they would be from time to time when he'd walk by Jason's room.

The house sat the same, the furniture unmoved, yet it felt slightly changed from the time it had remained empty and abandoned. As John walked up the front stairs that led to the covered porch, the front door beckoned him in as it squeaked from lack of use and oil on the hinges. The entryway opened directly to a stairwell on the left that wound around the corner landing to the upstairs bedrooms. To the right was the living room with a 'Ben Franklin' iron stove sitting several feet from the outside wall. His reading chair still sat lonely in the corner behind it, next to the lamp he had used to light his Bible well into the nights. The wooden floors throughout the home creaked from age but had been music to his ears once he'd gotten acclimated to it. The sound meant there was life in the home. Now the only sound the floors played was through John as he walked across the empty rooms. The life that had once made the floor perform full concertos through the movements of Jason had now fallen to the short, slowly played notes of John as he maneuvered around, much like the sounds of the off-key instrumental sounds played by the orchestra as they tuned up.

The kitchen lay straight ahead from the front door through an archway with shutters that swung open when you entered. Western style as if you would imagine walking through them into a smoky cowboy bar. The doors swung back and forth until the momentum died. Just past the kitchen was a small, informal breakfast nook where they had put a picnic style table with benches. To the right of the kitchen was a doorway that led to the formal dining room, and

on to the right, you circled through a large opening
with cylindrical pillars on each side back to the living
room near the stove. It was a wonderful home set up to
host groups of people that could circulate from the
front door around through the kitchen, formal dining,
living room, and back to the entryway. Shelly had loved
having groups of church families over before life
changed for them. Jason and his friends would run up
and down the stairwell and through the crowds then
down to the basement, which was his game room, and
back up, creating full symphonies of sound on the
creaking oak floors to the point conversations among
the adults would be strained.

As John looked around again, the first time he
entered since the float trip day, all of his memories
came flooding back to him. Some painful, yet even
through the tears, John now smiled in his reflection. He
was *home*. He was alone, but he was finally home.

Jason's room had remained unchanged from the
day they left to go on their float trip, like the rest of the
house. John knew many families never touched the
rooms of lost loved ones, and often, they were shrines
left with doors closed unless visited. John felt much the
same way, but Jason had always left his door wide
open, and so he chose to leave it open also. Many
times, he would feel overwhelmed with Jason's
presence. Sometimes it would be wonderful feelings
that filled his entire mind with memories, yet other
times the sadness would begin to overtake him, and he
would have to retreat to his front porch to the swing
that sat waiting for him, surrounding him like a

fortress, protecting his psyche from regressing back to darkness.

It had taken some time for Henry to get used to the fact that John resided back in the parsonage again instead of the tiny shack behind the church. Henry was a man of routine, and when that routine changed, it threw his entire world out of whack until the new routine could be formed. That took time. The time it had taken for Henry to accept the new norm of Molly being in a mobile wheelchair had been extremely difficult. It had caused Henry to fall into a depressed and somewhat combative demeanor. Those had been the era Beverly and he had clashed the most. Some of the locals were surprised Henry hadn't crossed the line in some of their tiffs and become physical. He had been known during some of those situations to make idle threats because of her meddling with rumors and innuendos.

Henry had been a good-natured man whom was just a little off the scale of normal in the time that John had known him. He had, however, heard rumors of a more volatile time in Henry's past, yet he'd never witnessed that side. Molly had always been his anchor and kept him calm in times when stress overtook his good nature. Henry often joked that he only suffered one thorn in his side and it was NOT his Molly! The meaning was always left open-ended, but those in town knew exactly whom he was alluding to. Even in the calmness amongst the country's turmoil, Henry was not naïve enough to believe that Ash Grove's viper was hibernating. He would be willing to bet his life's savings on that, which was quite a certain bet for him. Henry was counting on every penny of his life's savings going to take care of his Molly after he was called home to be with his creator.

\*\*\*

Mary started on many a Sunday morning with the best intentions to make her way to Deliver UMC to hear Pastor John's message. But every time she would get a few yards past her safe zone, she would feel the urge to turn and make her way back within her boundary. She never complained though, not internally or outwardly. She would be frustrated though as she really wanted not only the human contact with others but also to show support to her best friend's husband John. She wanted so much to be able to tell Shelly that she had finally gotten to see John in person delivering God's word. Several times, Henry had offered to record John's sermons and bring them to her, but she never wanted to stack another chore on him. He had plenty on his plate taking care of Molly. Her goal was to see him for herself, in person, a bucket list of sorts. She knew one day she would succeed.

Shelly had told Mary that the next time she came to Ash Grove, she was going to convince her to come to the church with her. They had shared some quiet conversations along with some secrets during Shelly's recovery. The two had grown even closer as friends before Shelly left to go back to New Mexico. They called each other on a regular basis to keep that closeness.

\*\*\*

Henry and John were on a walk early one evening when Henry turned to John and confided in him. "Molly will hardly get out of bed these last several days. She looks like she's aged a decade, and she tells me that she won't go to the doctor. She says it's nothing he can fix. She's told me I need to start getting ready to be alone."

As Henry looked down, John could see the tears dripping down his cheeks and landing on his shirt. "She's given up Pastor John. There has been something different in her look and the way she's acted for a couple of months, but lately, it's become worse. I don't know what to do anymore."

John asked if he wanted him to come visit. "You know I have missed seeing her on Sundays, and maybe I could see if she would open up to me."

Henry agreed that a visit from John might be just the thing. "I don't know if I can make it without her, Pastor. She's my rock. She keeps a lid on my nerves and from letting my temper get away from me. She knows when to tell me to shut the news off on the TV and sit back and relax. I've tried to be a God-fearing Christian my whole life, and it hasn't been easy, but without Molly, well—I wouldn't be the person of faith I am today. It seems these days I'm ready to explode at the drop of a hat."

"I know, Henry; my personality and traits have undergone some major changes since Shelly has been gone. I'll talk to Molly, but you remember anytime you feel like things are piling on top of you I'm here. I love you, brother, and I'm here for you day or night." John reached out and gave a loving hug to Henry.

John at that moment came to the realization that Henry and Molly were truly undergoing hard struggles, and it was having effects on them. This summer had been a hard summer for several others that were on his peripheral vision while he was dealing with his own personal demons. Some of the old guilt tried to start creeping back into his head. Had he ignored those that he was called to watch over to the point it could be irreparable?

As the two started to walk back to their homes, John started compiling a mental list of failures to friends during these past months. On the top of the list was Wayne Renfroe. After stopping off at Henry and Molly's, he would to head over to the 'Man Cave' and pay a friendly visit to his close buddy, Wayne.

# Chapter 22

*Seasons Begin their Change*

## John Visits with Friends and Finds a New One

J ohn had made his rounds visiting with the Tanners and later that evening headed over to see Wayne. There were hard topics covered with Henry and Molly. Tears were shed as each faced some changes that were happening in their lives. John comforted them both, assuring that God would help them transition with their future, no matter what it held. "God isn't going to abandon you. You also have a community of great friends through your faith in Christ, myself included. We are here for you."

Molly sighed in relief. "This old world is falling apart, Pastor John. It feels like it is forgetting a couple of old people like us. You're a blessing to this community, and I'm sorry you have had such a rough summer. My prayers have been with you and your wife. I hope you know that." Molly reached her arms out and squeezed John tightly as she sobbed.

"Why Molly, I just don't know how I would have made it without those prayers of yours *and* the walks I share with your husband! You two have been wonderful to my family." And with that, John assured them again that he was a stone's throw away anytime they needed him.

John was walking down toward Wayne's 'Man Cave' when he heard a strange sound. At first, he thought it was Wayne's sign swinging in the wind above his front door. It was kind of a whine or squeaking sound. John knelt a little lower and concentrated on where the sound was coming from. There was a rustle in some bushes just past Wayne's building toward the railroad tracks.

As John walked cautiously to the corner of the old lumberyard fence adjacent to the tracks, he slowed to a stop. "Aw girl, what's the matter there?" He talked in a soft caring voice as he slowly eased toward the dog that was tangled in some rolled up barbed wire fencing. The poor girl was so knotted up she could barely do more than whimper and shake.

John moved closer as he softly consoled her and began slowly holding his hand out toward her muzzle. "It's okay girl, if you let me, I'll get you out of there." With each slight tug, the entrapped dog winced in pain and yelped. John quickly realized he was going to need some wire cutters before his attempts would change the dog's predicament. He looked back toward Wayne's place and said, "It's okay girl, I'll be back with some help. I'll get you out soon; hang in there, girl."

Wayne answered on the second knock and cheerfully reached out for John's hand to shake. "John, good to see you out and about! I've been wanting to get together with you."

"Hey Wayne, I'm sorry, but I have a bit of a problem happening. Do you have some wire cutters handy?"

"Sure, but that's not really something I was expecting first thing! This doesn't have anything to do with the crazy talk around town, does it?"

John smiled and laughed out loud. "No Wayne, nothing to do with that! I was on my way over to see you, and I've found a pup in distress. She's caught up in some wire just around the corner by the tracks behind your place."

Wayne grabbed his tool bag and the two quickly headed back to where John had found the dog. "See girl, I told you I'd be back with some help."

The two quickly snipped some wires and got her freed, expecting for her to bolt when she was able to. Instead, she just sat staring over at John and pawing at his hand. He quickly pulled her muzzle toward his chest and stroked her head softly. "Other than the wounds from the barbed wire, she looks pretty good. Dirty as can be for someone's pet, don't you think?"

Wayne replied. "I've not seen her around here before. She looks like she has some Shepherd in her along with maybe white Labrador. I bet she'd clean up to be a beauty!"

"Um, I don't think so Wayne. I got her free, and that's where my job ends!" They both laughed as they headed back to Wayne's. John looked back at her as they rounded the corner toward the front door. "See, she's not interested anyway." And they headed inside.

Wayne and John talked for a couple of hours, both enjoying the company. They both assured each other of what they already knew. Wayne was certain who had started the rumor. "Ninety percent of all the nasty rumors can be traced back. She has it out for you, John.

I'm not sure why she sees you as a threat but watch yourself. I have a feeling she's not done yet."

John looked at his watch and decided he'd better call it an evening. "Don't get up Wayne! I can see myself out. See you Sunday?"

"You know you will John!"

As John pulled the door closed, he looked up the street, and there by the four-way stop looking back at him—was the dog he had helped earlier. John walked by not saying much, hoping she wouldn't follow him. But immediately after passing her, he heard the pit-pat of feet against the pavement keeping up with his steps. John turned around to look as he stopped.

"It's not going to work girl. I won't keep you. You don't want a messed-up guy like me, I'd forget to feed you, no time to play. You can do better than me!" Yet, as he turned to proceed home, the quiet footsteps followed.

As John cleared the last step on his porch, he turned to see the dog sitting at the end of his short sidewalk. Her head was tilted slightly downward in a humble stature. John thought how Jason would be begging by now to keep her if he was still here. He would be saying, 'See dad, she's our dog! She picked us. We can't just *not* love her. We should *adopt* her into our family!' He looked at her again but this time attempting to see her through the eyes of his son's.

John opened the front door then turned to the dog still sitting patiently at the end of the walk. "Oh, come on girl let's get you cleaned up, but I'm telling you, you made a poor choice!" The moment he motioned to her, she stood up and calmly trotted up the steps and through the door as if she'd lived there all along. John had found a new friend to keep him company. But in all actuality, John realized his new friend had found him. He seemed okay with that.

# Chapter 23

*Late September in Ash Grove*
**A Man and his Dog**

I t hadn't taken long for John to accept 'Barbie,' named after the predicament he had found her in, as his newfound companion. She had stolen his heart quickly. John's heart had vacancies that needed to be filled as time away from Shelly lingered on. From the first morning he found Barbie lying in Jason's doorway, he knew she was meant to be with him. Barbie went everywhere he went. Walks around town, walks with Henry, visits to congregation members, and she even had started sitting beside his altar chair during Sunday service. Something even most of the members were okay with and enjoyed seeing.

Barbie loved front porch time with John. She would either lay at the top step observing the world from her perch or nestle closely to John's leg as he rocked back and forth on the swing with his laptop and bible in tow. The two of them were rarely seen apart from each other. The new joke around town when he was seen walking with Barbie was, 'There goes the Pastor and his other woman.'

The fact was that John was lonely. He had recovered rather well after his near-fatal end in Wichita, but the loneliness started to sink in again. He talked to Shelly regularly, but it wasn't the way he wanted their lives to be, and he felt he was stuck in limbo. His psyche would be stable after his Sunday message, and then as the week would transpire, John would begin to regress slightly within himself.

Bob, Julie, and Wayne had all been amazed at how quickly and differently he had changed once he had returned from his trip, but as time passed, they discussed how they were noticing his subtle withdraw from the outside world again. One night, when the three were visiting Mary, Julie spoke out. "I'm afraid we could be losing him bit by bit, and he's come too far for this to happen."

"I know Shelly is hoping they are working things out. She has a lot riding on it. She has told me she needs to be sure before she makes the move back." Mary's response sounded almost a little defensive.

Julie answered, "I don't understand how she could ever determine 'if it will work' by being a thousand miles away?" She had used quotation marks with her fingers up by her head as she had said 'if it will work.' "Good golly, John is so lonely he has picked up a stray dog! She's a sweet and smart dog, but it's a sign that the man needs his wife back!" Her look was directed to Mary.

"Julie, there are extenuating circumstances that Shelly has shared with me . . ." Mary said looking sheepishly back at Julie.

"She's my friend too, Mary! I'm worried about her all the way out there and away from her husband, living with her parents. I know her dad isn't keen on her coming back to John or Ash Grove, though I have no idea why. What other 'extenuating circumstances' can there be if I may ask?" Julie started to get up from the couch, pulling on Bob's arm, a signal that it was time to go.

Bob reacted quickly, "Whoa, whoa, whoa here friends! *Julie*! There is no call to take this out on Mary. We all care about John and Shelly. We all feel like we're watching a freight train slowly speed toward a bridge that's out. Let's try and help . . . not hurt each other in the process." Bob always seemed to know how to steal the heat from a possible fire before it raged. It was a gift, especially in the profession he was in.

Mary looked very frazzled and panicked. "Shelly confided some things to me that I just can't share. She will have to let whoever she wants to know when she's ready. I can't, I'm sorry. It's a bad spot I'm in, and I'm sorry. I wish I hadn't said anything. The tension in this town and in this world is getting out of control. Everyone is dancing around all the issues that are on the fringe and . . ."

Wayne who was sitting there watching quietly was finally prodded into the conversation. "Not with the politics now. We are all too good of friends to let this turn to the political BS that this could too easily become. Let's refocus on how we can convince Shelly to come to a decision and let her know how important a timely one is for our good friend John. Anyone up for a trip out west?" he said with a mischievous wink.

Bob was the first to pipe up. "I would love to take a trip with all of you, but tensions around this town keep me here, so I'll be staying close to the man and his dog!"

Mary cleared her throat, "Well, I guess you all know where I stand on leaving town."

238

Julie looked over at Wayne. "I love you, Wayne, but I'm not sure I can travel that far with you and still have the same feelings I have now!" She winked at Wayne, followed by a friendly scowl ending in a smile.

They all laughed out loud, and the previous tension that was swelling quickly dissipated as Julie nestled back into her husband's shoulder on the couch. It was obvious it was going to take more planning and another bottle of fine wine between friends to get this dilemma of John and Shelly resolved.

The good news was that John and Shelly had great friends that were now all on the same page of trying to nurse them back together. Before John had returned from Wichita, his friends had no idea how to broach the subject. Now, it just took formulating a plan and implementing it. Bob was all about a good plan. Years of police training mixed with experience!

Just as Wayne was about to uncork another bottle of wine, there was a knock at Mary's front door. As Mary opened the door, she turned to the rest and said, "It's the Pastor and his other woman!" They continued to laugh as they greeted John and Barbie.

John cracked a smile and replied, "I feel like the town jester! Now, I know where all of these crazy rumors get cooked up at!"

"Were your ears burning, John?" Julie laughed.

"Well, as a matter of fact, Wayne's should have been burning! Were they, buddy?"

Wayne looked over at John and said, "Hey now, let's not let this turn into a pick on me conversation when it was clearly headed to a pick on you!"

The group continued to laugh, and they all turned to John with questions of why Wayne's ears would be burning.

Pastor John turned to Wayne and asked, "Are you still looking for dates these days? I may have just the person to interest you. I have visitors coming in a couple of weeks. They want to hear my preaching and see where I rest my head and call home! I'll warn you right now though, she's a spitfire, auburn-haired, fun-loving lady, Wayne!"

Wayne smiled a devilish grin and answered, "You know I sit out in your congregation every week, John; you really don't have to farm women here to coax me into the fold! But from your description, she sounds right up my alley!"

The rest of group broke into uncontrollable laughter. In unison, the others all said, "Any alley will do!" Even Wayne had to crack a smile with that funny, slightly barbed comment. A comment that again—they had all delivered in unison!

"Just who is this auburn spitfire, Pastor John? And where in the world did you meet such an interesting sounding gal?" asked Mary with a hint of concern.

"All I can say at this point is that she is a special part of the equation that helped bring me back into the world of the living. There is definitely something divine and magical about this woman, Wayne." He then looked over at Mary and said, "There is nothing to worry about Mary; her divine magic was spiritual and nothing else!"

"Well, you have my attention . . ." Wayne rebutted.

He had Mary's attention also, even if he had attempted to reassure her, she was mixed with a little *worry* as well. Maybe Shelly should head back here quick before it was too late?

Pastor John sat down on the couch and told them a little about Miss Carissa and his connection to her. He of course left out some of the major details of what had transpired between them the night they shared together over the phone at the 'Keeper of the Plains.' John also told them she would be bringing along some other newfound friends from Wichita, Jordy and Mariah Wells. He told them what a wonderful and animated older couple they were.

John kept them all intrigued with the tale of his trip to Wichita in search of his old friend Jason. He was careful in what he let them know because he still felt vulnerable of the circumstance he had been in at the time he had met the friends he was talking about. The truth was he wanted to be forthcoming about the whole story; he felt very comfortable with this group of friends. But he knew that Shelly deserved to be the first to hear of his journey he had survived from the beginning to the outcome.

John suddenly pictured Shelly in his mind and immediately felt the emptiness of her absence. He fought internally to keep up a joyful appearance, but his pain was deeply felt. Barbie nudged in close to his legs and glanced upward to his eyes as if she sensed the change in his mood. It is amazing the sixth sense that a faithful furry friend can acquire in time with their masters.

Mary caught the interaction between John and his dog and suddenly seemed to feel the same sorrow that wove its way into the room and around John. She deeply wished that Shelly were here with him, and that she was ready to move forward in coming back and starting fresh confiding in John all the things she had been feeling.

Julie came back into the room with a freshly opened bottle of Malbec, and after pouring everyone's glass again, she held her glass up high and said, "'There are good ships and there are wood ships, the ships that sail the sea. But the best ships are friendships, and may they always be!'"

And with that, the friends toasted, hugged one another, and continued into the evening enjoying each other's company.

***

Off in another house at a party of one, there was a different kind of planning. Things were going too smoothly and trouble-free at the parsonage for her liking. It was time to turn up the heat.

If truth be told, Beverly wasn't even sure why she felt like she did. It was an inherent evil inside her. She recalled the conversation she'd had when her mother became so sick, just before she died so many years ago. Her father had died the year before her mother's affliction. He'd had a long illness and was bedridden for his last year and a half. It was a story her mother told her the night before she passed that would stick with Beverly in the back of her mind *always*. It was a story of shame and fortune. A story her mother made her promise to never reveal. It changed young Beverly after it had settled in for a time. She knew it; she felt it. She was only nineteen when her mother passed and left the remainder of her fortune to her. Her mother started the story off by informing her upon her passing, that she would be the last living heir to 'Ma Barker.' *The rumors had been true.*

Beverly had grown up as one of the wealthier in Ash Grove. Her parents had brought her up in Deliver UMC and rarely missed a Sunday service. Her mother always knelt at the altar during prayer time as Beverly sat with her father in the pew. Her mother would almost always return with tears in her eyes. Beverly had long concluded that her mother cried for Jesus every Sunday.

She never really saw her mother and father affectionate with each other. Beverly grew up consequently not showing much affection in her life either. The word love didn't show up in conversations among her family very often, so the word never really had grown a lot of meaning to her. Love was more of a description of how she felt about *something* instead of someone. She loved candy as a child, and she loved shopping for new clothes at Sears and Roebuck in Springfield as she grew older, but that was the extent her real knowledge of love. Her grandparents on both sides of her family either passed when she was too young to remember, or they just didn't come around. They didn't exist in her world growing up. She never got detailed answers when she would ask about them.

243

The only friend she could really recall growing up was Wayne, and she treated him very poorly and was surprised as she became closer to adulthood that he would even acknowledge her. She realized she was mean to people, so she did have a conscience, yet she didn't really think about any consequences to her actions. The things Beverly cared about were possessions. She cared about her immaculate home, especially her bedroom, where she spent a great deal of time. She cared about her clothes and toys. As she grew older, she cared about her books she read, and she knew she should care about her mother and father. After all, they provided all the nice things she was surrounded by. It really shouldn't be a surprise that Beverly had ended up the bitter, evil person she had become. Her husband, Billy, seemed to avoid as much contact with her as possible, and she seemed perfectly content with that.

But after that last conversation with her mother, things started to make sense to her, and the questions that had laid quietly in the back of her mind began to become more obvious to the answers that she had never intentionally sought. She was the last of the 'Ma Barker' bloodline. A public enemy number one of the country's law enforcement in her day and all because she was a cold-blooded and evil-to-the-bone mother who had raised four likewise evil, money-hungry, bank-robbing sons that seemed to enjoy killing for sport.

As she thought back to the conversation with her mother, it felt as if she were not only telling her of her past and her roots for mere conversation but also as a form of confession for her sin of cheating on Beverly's father that week she had gone to Denver, Colorado some twenty years back. As she told Beverly about how she had met Lloyd Barker, the son of Donnie (Ma Barker), a tear had slowly filled each eye. Possibly a visual remnant of the pain of her sin she had committed or maybe the loss of a passionate love she had briefly shared. Her mother seemed intent on sharing only the facts of the story and not the feelings.

She continued telling her about how Lloyd had hated his wife and children who were sucking the life out of him and spending the money he and his brothers had worked so hard to steal and stash away.

She looked up at Beverly and said, "The money we've been living on—that gave us these luxuries." She continued on, "Lloyd's wife was crazy and jealous and ended up shooting him not long after our affair. Jenni was her name. She had found out about us and was so furious she shot and killed him when he walked unknowingly through their front door." A single tear began to poke out of her mother's tear duct as she struggled to lean closer into her daughter, continuing with her story, "Later, after she was found guilty and sentenced to life in a state insane asylum, I convinced her to tell me where all the money was so I could make sure her kids were taken care of. She believed me, and I took it. All of it. The money is the only reason your father stayed with me."

"Mother, whatever happened to their children?" Beverly had asked her.

"Why would you even ask that Bev? Why would you care? I took care of my own, and believe me, I've paid a price. I doubt the Lord can forgive someone

245

enough to allow an evil woman like me into his kingdom. And I'm practically knocking on his door now."

Beverly's mother died in her sleep later that night. Beverly realized after her conversation why her mother kneeled every Sunday at the altar and came back with tears in her eyes. She also realized why there was such a cold chill that surrounded her and her father all the years she was growing up.

But that was then, she thought to herself. On her way to her office, she noticed the back of Billy's head and quietly guffawed. There sat her husband watching the television as usual, never a care of keeping things in this town in order. How in the world she had ever tied herself down to a loser like him, she wondered. She then thought of the similarities of her mother's life and what she herself had come to be. Even their husbands were similar. The bright-red lipstick accentuated the frown that the thought of the recollection brought to her face. It was her signature Avon color, 'Revenge.' She had known it was her color the moment she saw it. Once she'd seen its name, it sealed the deal. She never went out in public without it.

# Chapter 24

*First of October*

## An Early Fall Surprise

Mary could hardly wait to give Shelly a call and tell her how great Pastor John was doing. She was also still a little concerned of this new friend Carissa that he had talked about. She had put it on the back burner, though, because he was trying to set her up with Wayne; however they had met, he must not be attracted to her himself.

She also wanted to see how things had been progressing for her—and the surprise that the doctor and she had revealed during her hospital stay from her head injury several months back. The two sounded like high-school girls catching up on what had happened to each other over the summer.

"Shelly, Pastor John has a dog! I think I heard him say it was a Labrador and Shepherd mix. She's very pretty and so well behaved. She follows him everywhere and lays by his feet snuggled up to him."

"A dog? Doesn't he remember he already has two? What are we going to do with three?"

"So you're coming back?" Mary asked excitedly.

"Well, I mean—it just makes me feel like maybe he is moving on. He's already got a new dog. Next, you'll tell me he's seeing someone new," Shelly answered sounding rather hurt and frustrated. Mary decided right then that she would not mention Carissa.

"Why Mrs. Shelly Rose Austin, you get yourself back to Ash Grove immediately if you're finally getting worried about losing your man and the father of that *baby growing inside of you!*"

And there it was. It was finally said aloud where it echoed through each of their minds abruptly as it echoed through the room she was sitting in when she spoke it. Now it could sink into the two of them during an awkward moment. There were several seconds of silence between them, each one searching how to continue the conversation, when Mary asked the question. "So honey, just how big is your baby bump showing?"

"There will be no missing it. None of my clothes fit, and my skin is itching me like crazy! Now I'm wondering what he will do when he sees me. I should have told him all along. Mary, I've got plans to be there in two weeks! Please keep it a secret. I may tell Julie—*I want to tell Julie!* But we all know that Julie can't keep a secret. Can I stay at your house again for a day or two?" Shelly's giddiness could be seen even over a cellphone in digital bytes.

"I'd be upset if you didn't!" The two spent more than an hour talking and laying out plans. Mary was going to have a hard time maintaining her own silence, especially around Julie. At one point, Mary had asked about when the conception had taken place. She had curiously done the math in her mind, and it had to be close to the time they had lost Jason.

Shelly had told her the story of the night in the camper before they went floating on the river the next day. How John had pursued her that evening, but she had turned him away fearing Jason may wake up and hear them. Later in the evening, she had awoken with stirred urges and snuggled closely into John while stroking the back of his neck as he slept. She was surprised when he had woken up still with desire after her turning him away. It had been a wonderful and much-needed moment of passion after all the stress-filled months. It seemed to be the beginning of renewing their relationship, and they were both on board, full steam. Then the next day happened and robbed them of their son and then the dream of being close again. Shelly said that neither of them could even look at each other, they were so devastated. In the weeks to come when she suspected something was happening internally, she decided to come test the waters with John. She herself didn't know for sure that she was pregnant until the doctor informed her after the general blood tests he had run. Mary had been the first and only to know from that night on until her mom had sensed it.

Shelly had hoped that John and she would hit it off again and both realize their love could remain strong, but then she met him downtown and he spoke the way he did; she withheld her news, not knowing where it would all lead. She and John had remained in closer contact after they talked at Mary's, and then when she stopped in to say goodbye before heading back to New Mexico. That was the most difficult goodbye she had ever experienced other than saying goodbye to Jason when she'd found out that he was truly gone. She told Mary she practically talked to Jesus aloud in her car as if he were a passenger sitting next to her the whole two days of driving back to her parents' house.

She spent many nights crying on her mom's shoulder, begging for an answer of what to do, when her father came in and listened to her story. Shelly had dreaded letting her father know anything negative about John because she was sure he would tell her to forget him. Her daddy gave her advice that she never expected to hear from him.

She said, "Mary, my daddy looked straight into my eyes and said, 'Shelly, you've always been my treasure. I've taught you every way I know how to give you the confidence in pursuing the important things in life. I also know that you've been John's treasure since the very day he met you in Hawaii, and he has always shown you love and compassion. This horrible loss you've both suffered shouldn't keep you from loving this new treasure you've both created. This baby is a special gift from God. You two should grow old together loving this child and teaching it that same confidence.' So my answer is a resounding yes! I'm coming back to Ash Grove where the man I love is, and we are going share and raise this gift from God together."

After Mary hung up the phone with Shelly, she was too filled with excitement not to jump up and down in the air like a child. "Thank you, Jesus!" Mary repeated over and over. Life was coming back together.

Healing was taking place among the friends she loved and adored.

If only a person as broken as Beverly could receive some healing, she thought. Stranger things in this world have happened, for that she was certain.

# Chapter 25

*Later in the Afternoon*
## How Could She?

**B**everly stepped out into the late afternoon, hoping she would run into Henry the 'walking reverend.' She was spoiling for a fight, and he would be an easy target. She knew his wife, 'Wheels' as she now referred to her, was not up to snuff lately, and she could set Henry off by some derogatory comment about her. She was feeling a charge through her veins just thinking about an interaction.

She hadn't really counted on a quick drive-by, but up ahead and moving toward her was Wayne. Just a quick practice quip could get her juices primed. She quickly ran a fresh coat of her red lipstick across her lips and then blotted them on a tissue just as she came up to Wayne.

Wayne's good nature forced him to be cordial as he said, "Good afternoon, Ms. Beverly. It's starting to get chilly out already, don't you think?"

"Well now Wayne—not as chilly as I imagine the preacher felt about your house call to his wife when she was in town."

"Just what is wrong with you, Beverly? If you don't like this town, why don't you go and buy a different one?" As she passed by him, he stood there watching to see if there would be any response at all from her, but she just continued down the sidewalk as if she'd never heard him. But inside her thoughts were the words, 'because I already own the town I want; it just needs the vermin eradicated from it.'

Wayne walked away shaking his head in dismay that there could be a person so needy of kindness in their life but would continually deny any attempt to receive it.

Beverly briskly moved along with her next plan of motivating John to leaving the area. She had heard so much about this new dog that he had rescued, renewing happiness in him. As she turned the corner by the church and walked past the parsonage that sat quietly with an empty porch and no visible witnesses around, she reached into her purse and opened a baggy, pulling out a meaty turkey leg and quickly tossed it by the edge of the bushes near the front step of the porch. She didn't even give a second thought as she kept walking down the sidewalk, smiling as she breathed in the cool fall air.

Beverly had researched what things were poisonous to dogs and then mixed a concoction together, soaking the turkey leg in it. It would be an early Thanksgiving dinner for John's dog. The only real disappointment she seemed to feel was that so far, she hadn't seen Henry. Oh well, she thought to herself. There would always be tomorrow.

# Chapter 26

*A Day or Two Later*
**A Chain of Events**

J
ohn woke up and glanced toward Jason's
room. He'd had to get up in the middle of
the night to let Barbie outside, and then she
never came back in like she usually did.

He'd woken up to the sound of her
whimpering in his ear. He imagined she was wanting
some porch time since the night wasn't as cold as it had
been a day or two earlier. Missouri weather was so
unpredictable.

John decided to get up and get around early.
Barbie had kind of taken over the doorway to Jason's
room for some reason. He didn't understand why, but
he felt comfort in seeing her lie there in the evenings.
He'd been having some tough times at night with
dreams and nightmares about the river again.

He was counting the days until Miss Carissa would
be coming to Ash Grove to see him. She seemed to
have a magic aura that gave him comfort in his painful
times. As he made his way to the front door, he
thought he heard Barbie whimper. He swung the door
open, expecting her nose to be pressed against the door
to push in and greet him, but the porch was empty.
John stepped out onto the porch and walked to the
edge of the rail, surveying the yard.

The leaves sparkled in the morning sun from the cool dew that the evening had brought. He heard a slight whimper from out in front of the bushes below his porch.

"Barbie, come here girl . . ." John walked down the steps and looked first right and then left. That's when he saw her lying close to the bushes and looking up toward him but not really moving. "Hey girl—whatcha doing?" As he knelt beside her, she winced, and that's when he noticed the blood-red substance coming from her nostrils and mouth. There was a large puddle in the grass underneath her muzzle.

"Oh, Barbie girl, what did you get into?" John petted her head and Barbie whimpered again. Her breathing started to become labored as she looked like she was starting to convulse. *Panic!* John immediately reached in his robe and pulled out his cell phone. He quickly dialed Doc Edwards, the vet that attended Deliver UMC. After giving him the specifics of what was happening, Doc Edwards said he could be there in ten minutes.

Tears began to well up in John's eyes as he tried to comfort Barbie. He quickly ran in and got some wet towels to clean her head and muzzle. As he tried to lift her head, she winced in pain. John had a feeling that she may not have long to live. He had no idea what she'd gotten into, but he was scared for her. He had quickly grown so attached to her; he didn't know what he'd do without her.

He looked up toward the sky and called out, "Lord, please! I can't take another loss." And with that, John laid down in the cool wet grass alongside Barbie and stroked her head and side and calmly spoke in a soothing voice, assuring her what a wonderful friend she was and that he was there with her and wouldn't leave.

"I love you girl, it's okay. I'm here with you. You are such a good friend."

She was gone by the time Doc Edwards arrived, and John was inconsolable.

Doc Edwards called Wayne knowing they were good friends. After Wayne arrived and convinced John to come inside, Doc was able to wrap Barbie in a black blanket and load her in his vehicle. He didn't mention to John his suspicions that she had been poisoned, but he was going to run some tests and find out.

*\*\**

Word travels fast in a small town. Beverly was walking tall down the sidewalk when she heard the familiar whine of a speeding electric wheelchair closing in on her from behind.

"*Oh, this should be dandy!*" She said aloud to herself as she turned to see Molly barreling down on her. Had Beverly not looked to see Molly coming, she might just have gotten run over as Beverly slid to the side just in time for Molly to pass her and quickly hit the brakes and turned to face her square on.

"I know what you did, Beverly Snodgrass! I had no idea you could sink so low as to poison someone's pet!"

"Why, Molly Tanner, I have no idea what you are ranting about," Beverly quipped back. She then either out of habit or act of defiance pulled her trademark lipstick out and started applying a bright revenge-red coat on her lips before blotting her lips and dropping the lipstick back in the top of her purse.

"I've never seen such arrogance in my life! The nastiness that you spread around this town, the downright meanness that you've done to the people, including my husband! But this takes the cake. I don't know what makes you hate Pastor John so much. But putting one of God's creatures through a painful death so you can make a suffering man even more miserable is beyond reprehensible. It's *disgusting*, and he will know exactly what I witnessed the other night."

Beverly turned and started marching on, leaving Molly talking to herself. She made it about thirty feet until she heard the whir and hum of Molly's wheelchair headed her way from behind, again. This time as Molly came up quick, Beverly clutched her purse tightly, and as she turned to face her, she swung her black leather purse hard and fast. It contacted Molly's forehead with such a force it caused her to whip the steering wheel abruptly to the left, and the chair veered off the sidewalk, through some grass, and over the curb, toppling end over end. When the movement had stopped, there was the most eerie silence that remained hanging over them both. Nothing but a high hum winding down steadily as the shiny wheel slowly squeaked to a stop. Beverly stood in shock as she stared motionless at the pile of wheelchair and parts strewn on top of Molly as she lay inert in the middle of the street. When what had just happened finally settled into her consciousness, the panic soon set in.

Beverly turned 360 degrees, scanning for anyone that might have witnessed what just happened. She quickly looked for movement from Molly, and after not seeing so much as a tremor, she briskly slithered away without looking back again. Walking as fast as she could, her mind went into self-defense mode. She had to be seen somewhere far from here for an alibi. She thought to herself, what had she done?

# Chapter 27

*October Fifth, 2018*
**What Just Happened?**

P astor John laid the last shovel of dirt over the newly dug grave and bowed his head. He silently prayed to his Master to help him through the rest of this day to come. He questioned why a faithful servant should have to bury two friends in a single day. Granted Barbie wasn't in the same realm as Molly was, but it was too much for him to face after the summer of pain and loss he'd already endured.

He couldn't imagine how Henry was taking the awful news of Molly's accident and sudden passing. To lie dying in the street of your hometown just mere blocks from your home was difficult to picture. John felt horrible that she had passed alone without her faithful husband Henry with her. He knew Henry was beating himself up for not being there. All of this had happened so quickly. He wished he could see the whole picture at once so he could have a better understanding of why. He then thought to himself that the little bits he witnessed at a time were hard to swallow; maybe it was in God's wisdom that we couldn't view the whole reasoning at once.

John looked down at Barbie's fresh grave and hammered the small teak cross that had been given to him by one of his congregation into the ground as a headstone. He wiped away the tears in his eyes as he glanced up toward the clouds that were darkening quickly overhead. At least the rain had held off for his first heart-wrenching task to be completed. Now if only they could lay Molly to rest before the storm set in.

\*\*\*

Beverly was uneasy about going to Molly's funeral service and for good reason, but Billy had insisted as a member of Deliver UMC and a long-standing family of the Ash Grove community that they attend. She reached into her purse for her lipstick, but it seemed to be missing. She looked down and dug throughout her purse to no avail. She didn't really believe signs of destiny, but she decided that maybe 'Revenge' red wasn't appropriate to wear today anyway. It would be the first time she could remember going out in public without covering her lips with it.

\*\*\*

As John walked out to survey the sanctuary and make sure all the necessary arrangements were taken care of, he caught a glimpse of Henry sitting on the front pew with his head dropped down, his chin nearly resting on his chest. Friends were talking and resting their hands on his shoulders in attempts of comfort. He looked like he was trying to acknowledge them but was unable to lift his head up. John walked quickly over and sat down next to him putting his arm around him and drawing close to share a private word.

"This too shall pass, my dear friend. Molly is with the Lord now—no wheelchair and no pain. Hang in there, Henry; you are surrounded by a town who loves you. I love you, brother, more than you know."

Henry reached up and placed his hand on John's and squeezed tightly. "I know Pastor, but I wasn't there for her when she needed me most. I'm ashamed." His breath sucked in with loud, short breaths as his shoulders heaved up and down.

John squeezed him tighter and softly whispered, "Henry, you failed no one—most of all Molly. Just like I didn't fail my son Jason. This world isn't the world we belong to. Eventually, you and I will see our loved ones in the world we do belong to. Failure isn't even in the vocabulary there. They know, both Molly and Jason, right this moment, how much we love them and how much pain we are feeling because it's hard to let go. This too shall pass. Be strong, my good friend."

The music had begun, and so Pastor John had to give Henry one more squeeze on his shoulder before getting up and heading over to the pulpit. Once John reached his spot behind the altar, he looked up and surveyed all the seats filled in the pews. Standing room only. Practically the entire town was here. All denominations, all walks of life, and all ages from infant to elder. As he started to speak, the door opened wide, and a backlit silhouette of a last couple entered the sanctuary. All eyes turned in curiosity to witness Billy and Beverly Snodgrass tiptoe in.

Pastor John continued to speak, "What a sign of how truly loved Molly Tanner has been in this town. I believe she was friend to almost all of you and touched your life in some special way through her days here in Ash Grove. She was such a warm-hearted woman whose smile filled the room much as we have filled this room in her honor and remembrance." John's face showed the pain of what this day had brought so far. His eyes were grey, and his hands that usually gripped the sides of the pulpit firmly, were shaking.

"This will be a time we gather to remember and share some special memories—a time to reflect how we were blessed by knowing Molly, and a time to reiterate our love and support to the wonderful man that she has left behind with us. Please let us bow our heads together as we pray for guidance and give thanks to the Lord for all he has given us through the blessing of Molly."

\*\*\*

It was the hardest service John had ever been called to give. It was the first funeral for someone he truly knew and felt so close to. He fought constantly to keep the tears from flooding or his voice from stuttering. He was also told, as people filed out, that it was one of the warmest and touching dedications of someone's life they had ever witnessed. Words from people he knew and some from people he'd never seen before.

He looked over and saw that Henry was being taken care of, surrounded by a group of loving townspeople, and he suddenly felt as if his body would give out completely. The day's sad events had ended, and now he needed to sit back in his own home alone and soak it all in to be filed away in the different parts of his mind. Jason, Shelly, Molly, Barbie. All recent losses in one form or another. Worries about Henry too. He was ready for Miss Carissa to be here and work her mental magic on him. Saturday October thirteenth couldn't get here quick enough.

He had a lot of prepping for company to do, but that would start tomorrow, today was a chance to fall back on the couch and let it all gel. As he laid back and kicked his shoes off—they had barely hit the floor before he was out like a light. His eyes hit REM cycle quickly as his mind began to unload its content into dreams.

# Chapter 28

*The Evening of October Fifth into Early Morning*
## Was That for Real?

A s John tossed and turned, calmness suddenly swept over him, and his body became motionless. Shiny rings seemed to radiate out from around his view. He was encircled by the rings, and they glittered brightly as each one rolled away after the other and then faded into the infinity until all was engulfed by the darkness. He quickly noticed that it was so silent it was almost maddening. A small beam of light began dropping from above his head and seemed to be targeted for the center of the rings that still were generated in a rhythm around his body. He tried to stand upright, but suddenly felt like he was floating in a mass of liquid. *Unstable floatation.*

He felt captivated by the entire uniqueness of the experience. He wondered if he was being prepared to enter another world. Way off on the horizon was another bright light that seemed to be making its way toward him, and he quickly surmised that the two beams, the one above him and the one before him, were heading toward the intersecting rings that surrounded him. He felt like he was part of a metamorphosis of some kind.

John suddenly felt overwhelmed with warmth, his core radiating outward. And as the beams drew closer to him, the brightness became almost blinding until he was caught in the middle of a strobe effect. He began to focus on the fluttering light and could see that there were thousands of beautiful monarch butterflies encompassing him, causing a turbulence that began to lift him out of the blueness. Instantly, the two beams collided causing a kaleidoscopic event that culminated into the most beautiful palette of colors and swirls that he had ever witnessed.

This had to be heaven; this was the only thought he could comprehend. His cheeks began aching from the smile he was uncontrollably grinning. He managed to push the word 'beautiful' from his mouth before a vacuum sucked the entire atmosphere from around him, leaving him standing on a small island of pearl essence.

As John tried to make sense of what had just happened, he felt the light brush of flesh touch each arm. Goosebumps quickly rose from his skin as soft fingers trailed down from his shoulders to his wrists. He quickly turned and was met by the vision of his wife; she was so angelic in appearance. Her body shimmered, and her eyes were even bluer than the last memory of them that was still ingrained in his thought. She smiled at him with an incredibly intriguing look, emanating the most vibrant spark of life that he had ever seen. He looked into her eyes, but she motioned his eyes toward her midsection. John's eyes followed the lead of Shell's downward, and his hands followed from her neck down to her waist.

That's when he saw her miracle. He looked back into her eyes in amazement and then back down at her tummy. He could see through her transparent skin and the electrical sparks and colors moving around inside her, a small silhouette of a lifeform. As he leaned in closer, he could see the pulse of its soul flowing in and out throughout its tiny body within the confines of Shell's body.

Words could not be spoken, no matter how hard he tried, yet he seemed to relate to Shelly telepathically, and words were not needed. He understood, yet he didn't comprehend how all of this was happening. They had tried for so long to conceive with no success. They had both come to accept that a biological baby between them would never be possible. God had worked a miracle around that difficulty by placing them in precisely the specific spot and time for them to find Jason. They knew immediately he was a gift from God. It was part of what pulled John down so hard when he couldn't save him. He felt he had failed God somehow and as punishment had been responsible for Jason, a true gift from God, being taken away from them, causing a cataclysmic effect on their relationship. Had they possibly been unworthy of the gift he had bestowed up them?

But he had now come to terms with what had happened and seen it was never about punishment but now, what was all this that was happening to him?

That question still lingered as John suddenly snapped back to reality in the present time. When he finally realized where he was and started to reacquire his bearings, all he could spit out again and again was, "How would that even be possible?"

John got up from the couch and was slightly off balance at first, almost tumbling onto the coffee table before regaining his balance. He headed into the kitchen to make a strong cup of coffee expecting at first for Barbie to come trotting around the corner to his feet.

John had always had the most vivid dreams. Even in his youth. He would wake up and run into his parent's bedroom and swear to them he had just returned from another world. He would retell what he had seen in such elaborate detail that occasionally his mother would falter for a moment with the possibility that quite possibly, he had been elsewhere.

It had been a long and difficult day. John was ready for it to be over, but it was ten o'clock p.m., and he was wide awake now.

He was missing Shelly more than ever and feeling like he'd experienced an out of body moment with her. It seemed so real . . . but so impossible. Dare he call and share it with her? A resounding *NO* came to mind immediately. He should instill no pressure to Shelly. He had to let her make all the moves so she would truly make her own choice.

\*\*\*

John walked by Jason's room when it hit him that the doorway was empty as was the bed inside. Empty seemed to be his new normal. He reached for his cellphone, contemplating again to call Shelly. He so wanted to share his dream but realized she wasn't ready to hear about babies or children. He walked through the doorway and sat on Jason's bed. His eyes scanned the shelves and dresser top at all his possessions. He missed him so much.

The dream had awoken his desire to sit next to him and listen to his stories and dreams. He pictured Mr. Wiggles and Dozer running and plopping on the bed beside Jason. He hadn't thought about them in a while either. He had pushed those thoughts of the past back to the farthest corners of his memories.

It's funny how a bizarre dream can wake the repressed memories you thought you had hidden away. They started flooding into his mind as if he were turning the pages of an old photo album. As the memories began coming back to John while he sat on Jason's bed—he suddenly felt like he had no sense of permanency in his life other than his faith. Everything else seemed to come and go. Was life supposed to be like this? Each day just a memory that you tuck away and pull out when your life is void of new memories in the making?

John knew he needed to do something to busy his mind. His dream had awoken his thoughts to search and make more out of things than needn't be. He had a habit of overanalyzing things when he let himself get into this state of mind. He stood up, scanned Jason's room once again, and quietly said aloud, "I miss you Jason; I love you so much—I hope you know I did my best."

And for the first time since he'd moved back in, he quietly pulled the door closed as he stepped out.

# Chapter 29

T he day was finally here! The previous
week had been a difficult one for many
in Ash Grove. John had a hard time
delivering his sermon on Sunday. He
had already written it before he had the
challenge of giving a funeral to such a
close friend. His message was on Hope and
Reconciliation. It can be a difficult message to begin
with, but to have a loving husband who has just lost
the love of his life sitting out on the front pew as you
tell him that God doesn't want you to lose hope, well, *it
wasn't easy.* John could tell Henry was listening intently
but struggling. Again, God uses us and circumstance to
weave appropriateness and encouragement into the
fabrics of our needs. Henry seemed to be more stable
after the service. He was still surrounded by a support
group of loving friends and believers.

John's week after he got past Sunday was filled
with excitement and nervousness of his impending
guests. He had decided to Give Jordy and Marissa his
bedroom and Carissa the spare room/office. He would
take Jason's room. He needed to feel the closeness of
family again—maybe God's unspoken plan?

John had gotten a call from Jim, his pastor and
mentor whom had just gotten back from his summer-

long trip to Botswana, South Africa. Jim had said he'd heard of what had happened and was so sorry he hadn't been there for him. He was going to be in the Springfield area to give a talk about his project and would love to come see him this next Sunday. John had of course told him to come, that he had quite a group of visitors that would also be there, and he'd love to introduce them all to him. It was set! Sunday would be quite a day!

***

There was a knock at the door. John quickly made his way from the kitchen and swung the door open to see three smiling faces. He reached to shake Jordy's hand, but Carissa quickly swept around Jordy and Mariah and threw her arms around John's neck, pulling him in close with a tight grip.

She leaned in close and quietly whispered, "I've missed you, Johnny boy, and I am so sorry for what's happened lately." She pulled back to survey his appearance. John smiled back with a quick wink as he opened his arms for Mariah who was heading in for her hug also. Everyone was laughing and talking over each other and John's front porch was filled with joy for the first time in a long while. He soaked it in before inviting everyone inside to get out of the brisk fall wind.

Jordy and Mariah were seated on the couch in the living room, and Carissa followed John into the kitchen to help fetch drinks for all.

"So how are you Johnny? And, of course I want honesty," asked Carissa.

"Honestly . . ." John paused a bit. "It's been a rough minute for me. I got re-attached to my wife when I got back from Wichita, and she had to head back to Tularosa to make sure she was ready to face our relationship. I rescued a dog who stole my heart and she got poisoned by someone, who for unknown reasons hates me. I buried one of my best friends from my congregation and now am worried what will happen to her husband. Yeah, it's been a rough minute or two. To top all of that, I had the most mesmerizing and out of nowhere dream that has me wondering if I'm two steps from requiring a padded room." John smiled a semi-sarcastic grin as he handed filled glasses for Carissa to deliver to the living room.

"Honestly, Carissa, I have been looking forward to seeing those brilliant green eyes and that rascal smile of yours for quite some time. I need an evening of conversation from a female who seems to know what buttons to push to turn me back into a normal person. The funny thing is, is that I don't understand exactly how that can be you. I don't mean to make that sound bad, but I really don't even know you—but I feel like you are a soulmate on some cosmic level. Jesus inserted you into my life in perfect timing to save me from myself. Now I seem to question if I can maintain that sanity on my own with Jesus when you are missing from that equation. Does that even make sense? I have a plan though with a semi-ulterior motive!" John raised his eyebrow suspiciously.

"Well, now Johnny—you have my undivided attention!"

"And you will just have to wait, Miss Carissa, because there are thirsty guests sitting in the next room that wouldn't even begin to understand our new relationship! We will talk later over coffee and a fire in the fireplace. I promise."

\*\*\*

Mary's phone rang, and her smile grew three times larger when she realized it was Shelly. It widened even more when she heard the words she would be hitting Ash Grove late Friday evening, on the *down-low*! Mary could hardly contain her excitement. She was so excited for both Shelly and John. Such a much-deserved time for them. She promised to keep the secret, although it wasn't going to be an easy task even if it was only three days!

"Shelly, you have to promise to tell Julie when she finds out that it's your fault I couldn't share the news!"

Shelly replied, "I swear I'll tell her it is really her own fault that she can't keep secrets!" The two laughed and giggled together. "You be working on doing whatever it takes to be able to go to church Sunday morning with me! I can't do this alone! You're my cornerstone, my rock and strength Mary!"

"Oh my, I had forgotten that I had told you I'd do that."

"Mary, you made it a couple of days at the hospital with me—you can make it five blocks out of your comfort zone! I need you! Also, while I'm

272

thinking of it, could you see if Wayne knows of any place that I can keep Mr. Wiggles and Dozer for several days?"

"That's a task I can complete, Shelly. No problem. And I will mentally work on the other one. You drive careful and give me some calls while you're traveling, check in with me—okay?"

"Mary, I may just have you on speakerphone the entire trip!"

"That works for me; I'll just be here at the house anyway!"

***

Carissa and John sat down and began enjoying a conversation with Jordy and Mariah. They were such an animated couple. John had almost forgotten how quickly he had felt comfortable with them. John promised to show them around Ash Grove in the morning. He told them how wonderful the food was at the local restaurant called the Copper Grill. He warned them about the waitress Becky and how he wasn't responsible what she verbally served them!

"She is a firecracker!" John laughed.

"I'm wantin' to see that church of yours too, Pastor J," Jordy interjected.

"That's funny, Jordy, because that is exactly how Becky refers to me!"

"Smart minds think alike is what I always say!" replied Jordy.

"Yez sir, Jordy, smart something, just not so sure I'd have put minds after it," laughed Mariah.

The evening continued with pleasant conversation, and John showed off his cooking skills to them by ordering pizza. He laughed saying Shelly had never allowed him to cook because she wanted control of the ingredients. She was never adventuresome in the culinary ways.

John could tell that his statement about ulterior motives had been eating at Carissa the entire evening. He took comfort in being able to secretly smile and wink throughout the evening at her, keeping the intrigue just at the outer edge of her reach.

There was a knock at the door just about the time they opened the pizza boxes up. As John opened the door, he suddenly realized he would find out sooner than later if there was going to be any kind of connection of intrigue between Wayne and Carissa.

"Wayne, buddy, come on in. I knew there was a reason I ordered an extra thin crust pepperoni and sausage! Folks, this is the friend I was telling you about that can smell pizza every time I have it delivered! The cooks know to always add an extra when I call it in, just because of this man's nasal reputation!"

"What? I'm surely not interrupting dinner at this hour, am I?" Wayne asked.

John introduced him to everyone as Wayne quickly slid into his usual chair and shook everyone's hand. During the rest of the meal, John tried to covertly watch the glances between Carissa and Wayne trying to judge if there was chemistry. He thought several times that he'd seen a small spark of curiosity between the two! He would question Carissa later after the evening wound down.

John told Wayne that Jim was going to be visiting church Sunday morning. He stated he was getting a little nervous with the way the congregation was growing for this Sunday. "I'm going to need some polish time before then! My old boss and mentor, three very special new guests—no pressure, right?" He laughed.

Wayne said, "Well, maybe you will luck out and the power will go out! Storms are in the forecast for late Saturday evening and most of the day Sunday. At least it's rain and not an early snow! Of course, in Missouri, one never really can trust a forecast!"

"As a man of the cloth, I should make it known that," John interjected, "oftentimes, the Lord seems to have other plans for us than the forecasters are led to know!" The table erupted in shared laughter.

\*\*\*

As the front door closed, the evening was also drawn down to closing. Jordy and Mariah Wells had retired to bed, and Wayne was heading down the front steps of John's front porch.

"Well Miss Carissa, I guess that leaves you and me to share some coffee, firelight, and conversation." John smiled before continuing. "Of course, if you're tired, we can continue this tomorrow."

"Johnny Austin, you've been ornery all evening long! There is no way you are getting off the hook that easy! I'm not sure which has my curiosity up more . . ."

"Yes? Please continue."

275

"I'm not sure if I want to find the answer behind your enigmatic statement of ulterior motive . . . or who in the world is Wayne Renfroe and was there some kind of ulterior motive in him showing up for dinner tonight?"

"I'd say first thing before I can answer those questions, Miss Carissa—is to define these big words like enigmatic!" John laughed before he continued. "Maybe, just maybe, they are one in the same? Why? Was there any spark of curiosity between you two?"

"I'd say there was some pleasant friction there that could possibly lead to some spark. How old is he?"

"Somehow, Carissa, I didn't see that as even a question! But I'm guessing now that he is just a tad bit younger than you maybe, but age is only a number in our mind to taunt and scare us. Then again, I see you as young at heart, full of energy, and spunk-filled until the day God calls you home kind of woman. I pictured you two hitting it off that day you roared up beside me in a cloud of white dust. My ulterior motive would be you two becoming such an item that you change your gypsy way of life and plant roots here—both for your sake and Wayne's. And okay, I would gain another friend here that understands me more than anyone else besides Shelly. And I see you and Shelly becoming incredibly close if I can ever convince her to come home again."

"Johnny, she will. I sense it. You know I'm a spiritual woman who also is in fine tune to the inner connections of the global energy field." Carissa smiled back at John with a devilish wink. "My senses are communicating with the atmospheric protons and

276

neutrons telling me that she is yearning for your love and companionship as much as yours is hers."

John laughed out loud. "Can you conjure up a voodoo mojo of mystical love for me?"

"Why Johnny, I'm serious!" Carissa playfully winked and took a drawn-out sip of her coffee, adding mystique to her statement as she continued looking John eye to eye with a mysterious flare through the steam rising from the cup. "She'd be a fool if she wasn't—and I don't see you falling for a fool. You just need to regain that belief in yourself again. I know you have faith in God. Use just a tiny bit of that faith and apply it to yourself. I'm certain he won't miss it with as much as you have for him. Magic stuff, I tell you." She looked back down into her coffee cup and the steam as it filled her face again, accentuating her green eyes with the reflection of the firelight.

John felt goosebumps immediately over almost every inch of his skin. "How did you do that?"

"Do what? Pass some self-confidence to you through my mystical atmospheric connection?" She devilishly smiled again. "I use my powers only for the good!" She laughed out loud to lighten the mood. "My answer is yes. I would be interested in getting to know Wayne—very interested."

"This is totally out of left field and crazy, but you seem to have somewhat of a relationship with mildly crazy, am I correct? I want to get a tattoo I've been thinking about. Want to go with me tomorrow to deface my forearm?" John looked at her inquisitively.

"Hmmm, did not see that coming, Johnny. Do you have virgin skin, or will this add to a collection?

Because if you don't—you do know you can't erase it if you change your mind, right? And they kind of hurt!"

"Um, yes and yes, and I don't act on the spur. I had this idea from my trip to Wichita. Kind of a commemorative slash memento kind of a thing. I'm gonna do it with or without you being there!"

"Wonder what Shelly will think? Some girls would be confused by a 'bad-boy' preacher man with ink on his arm!"

"I think she would understand—eventually." John sheepishly smiled. "But I've made my mind up, and I'm stubborn once that's done. I'm gonna set it up for tomorrow afternoon. I've got bad-boy friends you know that can help bring another member into the club!" John grabbed her hand and led past the kitchen to the spare room and study. "Better get some rest, Miss Carissa. Busy day tomorrow. I'd ask Wayne to go, but I kind of want this to be just our thing. I'll make sure he's around before dinner tomorrow this time!" He opened the door for her to enter and gave her a quick hug. "Thanks for coming. I really needed this. You are some kind of special. *Were you always this cool?* Even when Jason and I were kids?"

Carissa laughed. "Johnny, that was so long ago and so much life has happened since then that I don't even remember. I know I should be a broken mess from a lot of my past, but with God's grace—I'm *enthusiastically* happy. I refuse to let the darkness swallow me, and I try and bring a firelight wherever I go so others can know that in this sometimes dark and crazy world it's possible to be brightened up if we help each other out."

"Words to live for. Permission to paraphrase you this Sunday?" John smiled and touched her shoulder with a quick pat.

"Johnny, anything for you. You were my baby's brightness in his dark world before I was even aware there could be light. I love you for that. It makes me feel like Jason was able to at least experience a slice of happiness with you in his life back then; God knows his father snuffed out enough of the light around him."

They hugged in the doorway, and John enjoyed feeling the warmth of someone near him. He imagined for a moment it was Shelly before he let go and turned to head upstairs to his Jason's bedroom.

***

Before John turned the light out, he reached for his phone and texted his friend Wayne. '*Wayne. Carissa is interested in getting to know you. She is* **VERY** *special to me. If you don't have a real interest, please don't toy with her. If you do, you have a chance at a once in a lifetime life loving companion. Give it some serious thought, friend!*'

John turned off his phone and quickly fell asleep thinking of Shelly and the dream he had several nights back.

***

After everyone was awake, John took his guests to the Copper for some tasty breakfast. Becky was in rare form and kept his guests entertained throughout the meal. Jordy commented to the owner that it had been one of the most pleasurable dining experiences *ever*.

They later traveled over to Deliver UMC, and John showed them around. They even went back to the 'shack' he'd stayed in right after the accident. He shared some of his journey and shared that the porch swing that was on his porch now was the same that he'd practically lived on, where it was attached on the small screened-in, tin-roof covered porch just off the kitchen. You could see the small creek now that the leaves from the trees had fallen.

Jordy and Mariah were worn out from the trip down and the walking around Ash Grove. They got back, and Jordy found John's recliner. He and Carissa told them they were going to head out toward Springfield on some errands and would be back late afternoon.

"Make yourselves at home. Help yourselves to anything in the kitchen, and I left my number on the table. Enjoy some TV or napping." John handed the remote to Jordy. "I'm sure, like myself, you know how to work this baby!"

"I'm old, sonny, but I'm not dead!" Jordy quipped with a smile.

Off they went to get John inked. John turned to Carissa once they climbed into his truck and said, "I heard back from Wayne. He is very interested in you and stated that you had the most beautiful green eyes he'd ever seen. He asked why I'd kept you hidden."

Carissa laughed out loud and her drink sprayed out across John's windshield. "I'm sorry, Johnny. I'm out of practice hearing compliments from men or being told they are 'interested' in me." She leaned up and started wiping the liquid from his windshield with a tissue.

They both smiled at each other and then turned away. John looked over again and saw her smiling to herself with her hand covering her grin slightly as she gazed out the window. He felt like a high-school kid out with a friend and no worries at all.

Thirty-five minutes later, they were pulling into a little tattoo shop called Royal Ink in Republic, MO on the outskirts of Springfield.

"No crying, Johnny, when the pain starts," teased Carissa. Two hours later, John had new permanent artwork on his left forearm. "It's beautiful, Johnny! Nice job, Matt, you are quite the artist! And he didn't even shed a single tear!"

Suddenly, John wondered what the elders in his church would think. He smiled to himself and then didn't worry again. It was spiritual to him and that was all that mattered.

"Thanks Matt, I love it; who knows—I may become a regular!"

***

John and Carissa barely hit his front door before his cellphone started ringing Wayne's familiar ringtone. "Hey there, buddy, you must be calling to offer us all dinner tonight." John looked over at Carissa and smiled.

Jordy piped up from where he was sitting in the easy chair. "I sure enough hope his wallet is fat cuz I am one bear-hungry old man!"

Mariah let out a loud guffaw. "Ain't that the God's honest truth. When aren't you bear-hungry, you old coot?"

"Well, Wayne, sounds like you may lose a little of your wealth tonight." John winked at Jordy and Mariah. "Wayne wants to know if everyone is okay with Mexican cuisine tonight? We have a sweet little spot downtown." He looked to see everyone nodding in approval. "Mama Loca's Café it is, Wayne! Meet you there in thirty minutes?"

"Johnny, I'm nervous about what to wear now! I just brought some ole jeans and my hippie tops." Carissa was giving a sad frown. "I didn't realize when I was packing that I would be trying to impress a younger man!"

"Sweetheart child, you could make my old lady baggy britches look good. You ain't got nothing to worry about, Ms. Carissa!" Mariah shook her head and laughed after her remark.

"And I ain't sayin' a single word in that mess! I'm old enough to know when to keep my mouth resting for the eating part of evening!" Jordy was shaking his head back and forth in an overly animated way.

"I've known Wayne long enough, Miss Carissa, and believe me when I say this, the only problem you will have is throwing him off your trail now." John winked again and smiled. The room was filled with laughter as everyone headed to their different rooms to get ready.

\*\*\*

As they walked into the restaurant, John pointed back to the round table by the foosball game. Wayne stood up and waved at them. John turned to Jordy and Mariah and quietly said, "I hope I don't bore you tonight because I'm sure we will be left out of the quiet conversations between those two. I'll surely try my best to impress you with local lore! This was the birthplace of the legendary Ma Barker, you know."

"Hey, I think that woman still owes me some green-backs," Jordy fired back.

As they sat eating and sharing their meal, they all agreed what a great spot it was. John occasionally glanced at either Wayne or Carissa and noticed that they did seem enthralled in each other. He was happy as he smiled to himself. He would be thrilled to be a part of bringing together two special friends of his. He usually didn't play the matchmaker, which may be the reason it seemed to be working. *Beginner's luck!*

He quietly took the evening in, watching the happy expressions of friendship from all his friends and the little nuances of new romance between two of his favorite single people. He reflected on the message he was giving on Sunday. He also reflected how far he had come in a fairly short time from where he was. He hoped and prayed that Shelly was well on her road to recovery and acceptance. He quietly and internally spoke to his father. 'God, I miss her. I know you know everything about me even before I do. I'm asking that you please consider my prayers of bringing her back and giving me a chance to be the man I was made to be for her—Amen Father, God.'

"Let's get a closer look at that new ink on your arm, John." Wayne leaned across Carissa squeezing in close to her to get a closer look.

"You see that, Mariah? Remember when I was smooth like dat? That's a move now Wayne! I couldn't have taught you a better move than that. That, son, is an original 'Jordy Squeeze' right there! You ever been to Wichita? That's gotta be the only place you coulda picked that up!"

The table broke out in laughter at Wayne's expense. Carissa, in good sportsmanship, added to the move by snuggling in a little closer.

"That's right, Ms. Carissa! That there is full permission for a goodnight kiss later!" Afterward, she ended her quip with an, "Uh huh, girl! You remember the 'Mariah Move' don't ya, Mr. Jordy Wells? Because I sure do, mister; it's why I got you right here! There ain't no man can resist that!"

"Jordy—Mariah, I'd say since we stuck the bill with Wayne, the three of us ought to head back to my place and let these two kids finish off the evening without us third wheels! Carissa—I know you're a big girl! Wayne—you know when to have her home!"

After hugs around table and a few more comical innuendos, John, Jordy, and Mariah left the two to discover the warmth and excitement of feeling young and desirable to someone new.

# Chapter 30

*October Twelfth around Midnight*
**Shelly is Quietly Back in Town**

Hugs and giggles between two girlfriends when Shelly walked through Mary's door. "You get that coat off and let me see that baby bump!" Shelly could hardly move fast enough before Mary was tugging on buttons and pulling the opening wide enough to see. "You are huge! Lord, there is no hiding that! You look so good, Shelly. You are glowing!"

"I feel glowing Mary! I'm ready to be back and more than ready to surprise John and show him his gift from God!" Shelly was all smiles this trip.

"So can I ask or is it a secret?" asked Mary.

"Not until I tell John! Sorry Mary, but he should be the first to know."

"I'm just lucky to be a part of this secret right here, you, standing here in my house on the down-low! I feel like I'm part of a clandestine event! Did you get the dogs dropped off okay to Doc Edward's?"

"Yes, he said he could keep them as long as I need. Thank you so much Mary."

"So sit down, I have some other news to tell you. It seems John has some new friends in town from his trip to Wichita. I just know a little about them though. I haven't met them yet, but from what I hear, Wayne and a lady that brought an older couple with her are hitting it off well! I guess the woman and the couple are all staying at the house with John. They came to visit and hear him preach, so they'll all be there too."

"Interesting, I guess I'll just have to steal the show though! I'm happy for Wayne. He deserves to meet someone he likes, just hope he doesn't become too attached—Wichita is quite a drive to be making all the time with the hours he keeps at work."

The talk went on until Shelly finally admitted she was exhausted and needed to sleep. They could go through her outfits tomorrow and plan the grand surprise to a T.

***

John was burning the midnight oil working on his message for Sunday. He felt a little nervous with all the friends that were coming. He knew, though, that he had the ultimate power behind him. Look where he'd come from. He glanced down at his forearm and remembered just how he'd been saved by that power. He had been saved at the last minute and renewed to live life again. Awe . . . to be able to *relive life* again!

***

John woke up with his bible and laptop beside him. His cover and sheets were underneath him, and he still wore the clothes he had on the night before. He looked around as he re-acclimated himself to his surroundings. He was in Jason's room. He leaned over and buried his face in Jason's pillow, trying to inhale the scent of his son. He suddenly missed him terribly. These moments seemed to come from nowhere and would crash around him like a huge wave at Waimea Bay on the north shore of Oahu that had caught him off guard when he and Shelly first met.

He looked over at the gaming posters that hung on the walls and then over to the computer sitting on his small desk. He remembered how often he would use his computer as punishment and how many times he had unplugged the monitor and taken it from him. How frustrated he was with Jason that electronics were so important to him. He now would give anything to see him sitting there talking loudly to his gaming friends online. Just a moment to be sitting beside him watching and listening—*breathing him in and feeling his excitement.*

John lay back down and released a heavy, drawn-out sigh. He thought to himself and realized suddenly that he was no longer a parent. He really wasn't a husband either. He wasn't sure he ever would be again.

The message he was going to give on Sunday was how we are asked to lay our sorrows and burdens at the altar so we can continue without letting the past rob us from the future before us. But suddenly, John felt like a hypocrite. He hadn't really laid his burden down and truly left it for God. Sure, he had begun to lay it down and pray for help, but he always seemed to pick it back up as he got up from kneeling and then threw it back over his shoulder *only to grovel in it later*—like this morning.

There was a light knock on the door, and John turned instinctively to it and said, "Come on in; it's okay."

Carissa peeked around once a small crack appeared in the doorway. "Good morning, sunshine! Wow! You must have gotten up early to already be dressed—wait a minute, that's what you were wearing last night!"

"Yes, mam, I had a bit of a late night preparing for tomorrow. And before you ask, the answer is no, I was not waiting up for you! Although those clothes you have on look suspiciously like what you wore last night," John retorted.

"Things are not always as they appear, Johnny. Yes, they are my clothes, and yes, I am just getting in— but these clothes have not left my body since I put them on yesterday. Wayne and I literally talked all night! I feel so sorry for him because he had to open his store this morning, and I get to get a couple of hours of shuteye, I hope."

"Carissa, I have nothing planned today. Relax or sleep all you like. I should probably get some coffee going for myself and see if I can get anything for the Wells and then go over this message a couple of hundred more times! I'm feeling this morning that I need to practice what I am about to try and share." John smiled and gave a quick Johnny-famous wink to her.

"With that, I will leave you to your studies and ask you to please don't let me sleep the day totally away. Eleven a.m. would be just enough beauty sleep to give me something to work with so I don't lose all I gained last night with your wonderful friend! And I don't usually dive in head first, but—um, who knows? Ash Grove doesn't seem like a horrible place to plant some roots maybe, just maybe, if they have a pool to dive into?"

"Miss Carissa, you don't know how much that warms my heart to hear you say that. Wayne would be one of the luckiest men around if things keep progressing for you guys. He's a great guy and friend. I would feel honored to have been a part in introducing such a couple to each other, and yes, ma'am—Ash Grove has a great swimming pool! *Dive away!*"

\*\*\*

John barely got his sermon opened back up on his laptop before his cellphone rang. "Hello, Julie."

"Hey, John. I didn't wake you, did I?"

"Julie, what are the real chances of YOU waking me up? I'm surprised you have even stirred this early on a chilly Saturday morning! I can't believe you have even poked your head out from under your covers!"

"Don't go there, John; I'm calling offering to make dinner tonight for you and all of your guests! I was thinking of coming over and bringing all the supplies and using your place? That way your guests don't have to get back out after dinner, and we can all have a kind of a pre-Sunday party with you. We can invite Wayne and try to see if Mary would come. Your house isn't too far past the CZ (comfort zone)!"

"That sounds terrific, Julie! I'll run over to Mary's later this morning and ask her face to face so she will have a harder time saying no!"

"Perfect, with her and my family, Wayne, you and your house guests, I come up with a count of ten—sound, right?"

"That's quite a party! Are you sure you're up for doing that task on your own?"

"You have a special day tomorrow and some special guests—I'm sure I want to! Does six sound like a good time? That way, we have some together time before it gets too late for you old coots!" Julie laughed.

"Sounds perfect, Julie. I'll leave the door open so you can come over anytime you need to get things cooking!"

***

John knocked on Mary's front door. It usually only took one or two knocks before she answered, but he tried a couple of more. It was 11:30, so he was certain she would be up and around. Standing there, John remembered the evening he stood in the rain on her porch and reached to knock just before the door opened to Shelly's quiet and somewhat seductive smile. He wished he could repeat that evening now.

The door slowly started to open, and John looked down to step back a foot or two, and when he glanced up his heart skipped several beats, and he thought he was in one of his dreams that seemed to be so real but yet impossible to be true.

As the door swung wider, John got a full glimpse of Shelly as she stood leaning closely to the edge of the door. There was a very distinctive bulge in her stomach that fit awkwardly to the straight edge of the door. His eyes tracked back up to meet Shelly's bright blue eyes that were glimmering with strands of her blonde hair hanging just in front of them, like a veil on their wedding day at the altar.

The only words that John could form and press out of his mouth were, "Is this even possible?" His facial expressions bounced between *shock, awe,* and then *absolute joy.*

Before John could articulate another word or thought, Julie smiled and said a sentence that would change John instantly and give him the realization that the question he'd just asked the other morning—was now answered in an instant. As she took John's hands and placed them on her stomach, she spoke softly, "John, I want you to meet *your son.* He's been restless thinking about this day, just about as much as I have been . . ."

John bent down on his knees and pressed his head against Shelly's bulge and ran his hands around her searching for movements. He suddenly smiled and looked back up into her eyes.

"I think I felt him kick!" He stood up, and as he ran his hands back up her body, he pulled himself in close and leaned into her ear and whispered, "I love you Shelly Rose. Are you really here and is this really true?"

"We're here, it's real, and we're here to stay if you'll have us?"

John squeezed her even tighter and whispered, "You just try to leave—I'm never letting you go again. God has answered my prayers and given abundantly more than I can comprehend."

"I know you have tons of questions, John, and I will answer them all, every one of them, but today let's just be together and let everything soak in. It's a lot to take in, I know." She pulled back so she could look into his eyes more easily. "John, let me quash any thought that you could start questioning—I've been with no one. I would never do that. The night in the camper with you is the last time I've been with anyone. You are the only man for me in every way."

"Shell, I never really doubted you. I'm so sorry for the way I spoke to you that day. I was a broken man in almost every way. I'm healed now. I'm ready to devote myself to the two of you right here and now. Nothing could change my feelings and my God! We're going to have a boy? Another son?" John couldn't contain the smile as it grew back across his face. Yet for an instant, as he reflected on Jason's absence, a sadness moved over him. It seemed to sweep instantly over Shelly also.

"I know, John—there is no replacing Jason ever, but God gave us this boy for a reason. He knew how torn and destroyed we were. Jason will always be with us wherever we are. He would want us to remember him but move forward and love this boy as much as we love him."

A crack of thunder in the distance forewarned them of the impending storms that were heading toward Ash Grove. The forecast had been a bitter cold front with strong storms moving in overnight and into Sunday.

# Chapter 31

*Saturday Evening October Thirteenth*
## Better Add One and a Half for Dinner, Julie!

J ohn and Shelly had made their appearance later in the afternoon back at 'their' house after they both recovered from the unplanned encounter. Carissa had instantly sensed who this beautiful blonde woman had to be before any explanation had been given. She quickly moved in and pulled her in close in her usual Carissa 'love you to the core' hugs that John had now become accustomed to. Shelly seemed to embrace her with genuine appreciation and warmth.

"Such a beautiful baby bump, Shelly! I can't imagine how wonderful you are feeling right now. I am so happy for you and John!" Carissa loosened her hug and stepped back to admire the new life inside of Shelly.

"Lordy, that's a big bump for five months?" Mariah asked.

"Nineteen weeks and two days! And I know—he's going to be big like his daddy!" Shelly answered. She reached over for John's hand and he smiled the proudest father's smile possible.

Shelly was worried only about one thing. How would Julie take finding out this news at this late date, especially when she finds out that Mary was in on the knowledge from the day at the hospital when she suffered her head injury. She hoped Mary would be able to make it, and before Julie got here to work on dinner.

She leaned in and whispered a reminder for John to check in on picking Mary up. "Please tell her I'm desperate for her to be here. I can't face Julie alone!"

John assured her he would go pick her up and that he would be beside her to support the decisions she had made. He reminded her about what good friends they were, and it wouldn't be an issue.

\*\*\*

As the door to John and Shelly's house opened, Mary entered with the word 'brrrrr' as she shook and removed her jacket. "It feels like it could even snow out there!" Mary nervously looked around for Shelly as John entered and closed the door.

Shelly quickly moved toward Mary and held her arms open to greet her. "You got this, Mary, I'm so, so glad you made it." Shelly smiled as she hugged her tightly.

There was another knock on the door quickly, and Bob opened the door and stated, "Knock-knock we're here!"

"Come on in Chief!" John hollered. He briskly moved back to the living room as the Pierces filed in so he could start giving introductions to all. Wayne filtered in almost immediately, and John began introducing everyone until he pulled Shelly close to him and stated, "And an unexpected guest Shelly! And a MOST unexpected guest—our boy yet to be named!"

Julie's mouth almost made a thud as it came close to hitting the floor. Bob had somewhat of an 'ah hah' look on his face and his two kids both yelled, "Shelly!" in unison and ran to hug her. Julie barreled in with both hands covering her mouth.

"Well, I have to keep my hands here to keep the shock and possibility of bad words from popping out!" Everyone laughed, which promptly broke any anxiety that might have been in the room. Hugs and pleasant words of joy were shared by all. It was a most unexpected and joyful evening as it progressed. Stories and explanations abounded about each person in the room.

John and Shelly looked absolutely at ease and full of the happiness that both well deserved.

Julie smiled at her husband, Bob, and leaned in close to whisper, "God is good—life seems back to normal for everyone! John and Shelly look more in love than when they moved here! And Wayne, how giddy and lovesick is he? I really like Carissa, I hope she moves here, she would make a perfect member to our group!"

Bob said, "Slow down, Julie; it takes more than a day to get someone to move from another state! Let's let one woman get moved here first, then we'll concentrate on Carissa. I'm just glad their nightmare looks like it's on the mend and behind them! God IS good all of the time!"

To which Julie responded, "All of the time . . . God is good!"

Julie filled everyone's wine glass before she was going to announce dinner was ready. After topping the last glass off, she smiled, and Bob wondered what toast she'd come up with this time? She sure had a captive audience as she tinged the side of her glass and glanced across the room before locking eyes with Shelly. "'Here's to old friends and here's to the new . . . here's to eternity, may it all last forever plus a few! '"

John and Shelly's house had been re-christened with the love of familiar friends and new friends and fellowship that flooded the interior with joy, happiness, renewed love, and freshly found intrigue and romance. The wooden floor was performing a most lovely symphony of creaks and pops from all the movement of life going on again within the home's walls.

Shelly swallowed her wine glass of sparkling grape juice and cleared her throat before adding, "I want to thank you all for everything you have done for John and myself through the very difficult—side path that life took us on. We wouldn't be here tonight together if not for at least something that each one of you gave of yourself for us." Shelly began to tear up and tremble slightly. John pulled her close to his side and said he echoed her words to each one of their friends sitting there.

As they sat down to bless the food, John said he would keep it brief because he was feeling a little emotional . . . but added in his prayer those friends that were not with them and those that for whatever reason had yet to feel the comfort of God in their lives. He ended with an extra prayer for his friend Henry and the recent loss of his wife that he had suffered.

"Amen" rang out in unison from around the table. The rest of the evening returned to funny stories and hopes that the weather would somehow pass them by through the night. They all agreed that in Missouri, one never knew what kind of inclement weather could pop up from nowhere; you never knew until you woke up and looked out the window.

In usual Wayne fashion—the minute the food was being served, there was a knock at the door, but Wayne had the bowl of potatoes in his hand, so it had to be someone else this time. John got up and opened the door to greet Jim Whitley, to which he stated, "I followed the smell of wonderful food from the church to here!"

John smiled and welcomed him in. "Come on in, Jim, plenty of room and food at the table tonight! And of course, interesting conversation among new and old friends!"

Jim glanced over and saw Shelly, and then noticed her bulge and radiance. "Yes, interesting conversation indeed! It appears as if I have some catching up to do." He slid his chair up and reached for a plate of prime rib and said, "You leave the country for a few months, and you just don't know what you're going to have to catch up on!"

\*\*\*

When the evening had finally ended, and the guests had left, it was down to Wayne and Carissa sitting on the couch. Jordy and Mariah had headed to bed. Jim was staying the night over at Bob and Julie's. John lit a fire in the fireplace and dimmed the lights.

Shelly patted the seat of the loveseat, inviting John to sit next to her. He sat and leaned into her ear and said, "I hadn't mentioned it earlier, but our bedroom and the spare are taken. I've been sleeping in Jason's room, are you going to be okay with being in there—with me?"

Shelly snuggled in closer and took his hand in hers. "Tonight, I think that is just the perfect place for our family to be. Let's soak in some firelight and rekindle our own fire for a bit, then sneak upstairs, and you can remind me how much you love and adore me John Allen Austin."

John leaned his head back on Shelly's shoulder, closed his eyes for a minute, and reminisced of a daydream he'd had of a moment just like this one, on a crescent moon filled night not all that long ago, when he was certain a moment like this would never be possible. He thanked the Lord for all the miracles that had been performed in his benefit. He mentally put his pack of pain and burden on the altar and in prayer asked God to remind him to leave it there from now on. He opened his eyes and turned to see the woman of his dreams smiling at him as she reached to run her fingers through his hair. Her eyes reflected the flames from the fireplace and twinkled from the new life growing inside of her that they had miraculously made on an eve before their world fell apart. Tonight, that world was *healing*.

The rain began to fall a little harder as an occasional flash of lightning would cause shadows to mix with the ones dancing from flames. John looked over just as Carissa glanced his way, and they shared a quick smile. Life was new, and life was good again for both. It seemed life could be *relived*, even when you thought it was surely too dried up and withered.

# Chapter 32

*Sunday Early Morning October Fourteenth*
**Before She Wakes**

J ohn woke to the sounds of heavy raindrops hitting the windows and the roof. He glanced to his right, and there she was, her hair tossed around her head in disarray yet elegant. He reached over and softly touched the strands that were lying close to her chin. He wanted proof that she was really laying there next to him. She stirred and her nose scrunched up slightly and she wiggled her lips a little before she started to acclimate to where she was waking.

An instant later, a smile washed across her face, and she turned and looked John square in the eye asking inquisitively, "Mr. Austin, just how long have you been studying me?"

"Most recently, since yesterday at 11:30 p.m. I can't stop, Mrs. Austin."

"I know you think *you* woke me up but actually, he's kicking this morning, wanna feel him, Daddy?"

"Yes, I do Momma . . ."

"So John, what should we name our soon-to-enter-the-world little son?"

"I think we should think on that and find the perfect name. And as much as I would like to spend all day lying here beside such a beautiful lady . . ."

"I know, it's time to get ready for work—spoilsport!"

John leaned over and kissed Shelly's tummy and then moved upward and kissed Shelly on her cheek and then forehead. "Big day! I have a lot of explaining to do today! And hopefully some inspiring, Lord knows this world needs all it can get these days."

\*\*\*

Bob's radio went off just about the time his phone rang. Julie listened as his conversation went from inquisitive to serious. Bob was out of bed quickly and reaching for his uniform shirt and pants as he repeated directions.

He looked over at Julie as he hung up. "There's been a bad accident down on T and FR 17 on Scott's Corner by Hilltop Farms. Sounds bad Julie. I'm probably gonna be tied up through most of church. Please tell John I'm sorry, and make sure Rick video records it for prosperity sake, and so I can watch it later! Be careful too, the temperature must have gotten cold enough for this rain to cause black ice in places."

\*\*\*

John met everyone in the kitchen just before he was headed out the door. "Be careful coming in; I hear there was a bad wreck outside of town. The rain is really coming down, and it's cold enough it could be icing over in spots. Gotta love this Missouri weather!

Radio said tornadoes in and around our area are possible."

Shelly looked at John. "I'm going to call Mary and see if she would come today if I picked her up. She always said it would mean the world to her for you to look out and see her there in the front pew! I'm going to see if we can take that one off her bucket list today! Love you, John, you be careful yourself! No worries, it will all be golden! We've come this far, we can beat any weather they dish out!"

\*\*\*

John walked around the sanctuary, making sure everything was how it should be. He turned the heat up a little and listened a minute to the rain hitting the stain glass windows. He looked up at the dark shiplap wood ceiling and the old-style lamps hanging down. The predominant purples and blues with reds and greens of the stained glass mixed in against the dark stained-wood ceiling made you feel like you were truly in a room from the late eighteen hundreds. He had loved the ambiance of this sanctuary from the moment he had walked in.

He felt as if he were in the hull of an old ship leading the passengers spiritually while sailing across the pond. He looked around again. It felt perfect. He went back to his study for last minute prep . . . although he felt the tug of the Lord whispering to him in lingering thoughts that he would speak to him and possibly change his message up. John felt at ease with it. He felt truly connected to Jesus, and he had often strained to hear Jesus' answer when he asked questions.

Between his dreams and the way his life had always seemed to be led to the edge but drawn back to safety and redirected at the last moment, he would rarely hesitate now of late in believing he was in good favor with his maker. He had always believed in Christ. He had been raised from day one to believe, and while he grew older, he questioned and put to the side his faith, he had never walked away from it. John had always wanted that 'Come to Jesus moment' that others had talked about. He always felt like there was a plan of something special for him, but he hadn't truly put the effort in to prove himself worthy or pursue it.

God had given him his moment of extraordinaire though. Both in Wichita with a timely phone call out of nowhere that kept him from ending his life and then again most recently with the conception of a son after many years of not being able to conceive. Even after cursing him for taking his first son, the Lord had not forsaken him, as he had tried to convince himself. His faith had faltered so close to the brink, but Jesus had drawn him back and enclosed him in his love and favor. Yes, he believed something special was being given to him, yet also demanded from him. With this kind of faith, if he felt Jesus wanted to direct him on what to share or teach, he would never say no. He felt blessed more than he could ever repay, and he knew no matter what he had, Jesus would never expect repayment. He would always go the way of showing people he was a Christian believer by his acts of kindness to others rather than preach condemnation.

He had always been one that could let go of resentment and forgive and move forward. He knew that Beverly Snodgrass resented him horribly, to the point of trying to hurt his marriage and even taking his pet from him. She had cut him deep, but he wasn't ready to give up on her. Somewhere along her path, she had become terribly broken and was in dire need of love. Someday, he prayed, either himself or someone would surely eventually break through and reach her and the many others who turn away.

He heard chatter out in the sanctuary. Time was drawing near, and he wondered how many would brave the dark, cold, and rainy day to gather together.

***

As John entered the sanctuary and sat behind the pulpit, he quickly scanned the pews to see how many were there. He decided to break his tradition as he got up and walked down the stair and began shaking hands and talking beforehand. He never knew why he had been so formal before. It was time for a change. He noticed Beverly and Billy in their usual spots and decided to walk that way and put forth an effort. As he got closer, Billy stood up and reached out for his hand.

"Good morning, Pastor John. Hope we keep the power on this morning!" John looked over and smiled at Beverly, but she drew back as she said good morning and then turned away. He thought to himself—little by little, one day at a time.

John scanned the room and couldn't pick Henry out of the crowd, which was hard to do as big and tall as Henry was. He hoped he was doing okay and not withdrawing. He thought to himself that he mustn't forget to call him later if he didn't show up.

Each time the door opened, John scanned the area to see who it was, very anxious for Shelly to arrive, and yet nervous of how the reaction would be amongst the congregation. He almost wished they would have planned when she would arrive so he would be able to plan more how to respond.

"Aw, just let the chips fall." He said softly as he thought aloud, but Jerry who was sitting down next to where he was standing said—

"What was that you say, Pastor John?" John loved Jerry. He had helped him through some struggles when he and his family first arrived.

"Just practicing for when we get started Jerry! Pay no attention to my mumbling!" And then the door opened, and there she was. She looked incredible, even though she was dressed very casually. She was wearing a form-fitting sweater dress in light grey that just accentuated her baby bump. He smiled to himself, thinking, yes, that beautifully pregnant woman is my wife. Every sweet centimeter, and I am the luckiest man alive today! And, oh my, she had convinced Mary to come with her! John started making his way to them as they walked down the aisle toward him. John scanned the crowd and yes—they were focused 100 percent on a line from them to him. As they came together, John leaned in and hugged Shelly and then gave a hug to Mary. He scanned the faces, and there were shocked looks abounding. He quickly glanced at Beverly as he turned to help Shelly and Mary get seated.

The look on her face was unexplainable. It threw him for a loop momentarily. He couldn't read it. She almost looked like she'd swallowed a hornet's nest.

John never really wore the robe much. He liked to be a regular, everyday kind of person with his congregation. He had spent his life as a regular blue-collar guy, and he never felt comfortable appearing like anything other than that. Jim had told him that he would probably catch grief from the elders of the church but told him it was his call. He chose to wear suits occasionally but had dressed casually most of the time. He really hadn't heard any complaints.

Today though, he chose a blue sport coat and turtleneck. He and Shelly looked incredible together. He felt like a million bucks himself alongside her. He leaned in again to Mary and told her how grateful he was that she had tackled her circumstances in order to support Shelly and to see him give his message.

"Hopefully, Mary James, this will be the start of much more to come!" He winked at Shelly and mouthed 'love you' and turned to make his way back toward his place beside the pulpit.

***

As the piano music ended, John stepped up to begin with the morning greeting and call for needs and blessings.

"I know you all are seeing a face that has been missing for some time now and probably have some questions." John smiled a big grin. "If you don't have questions—I might suggest you check with your eye doctor as soon as you can get in!" The congregation broke into laughter. "I know you also have noticed that Henry and Molly are not here. We had Molly's funeral last week, and we will miss her terribly. Please keep Henry in your prayers as he is as one would expect having a difficult time.

You know, as a Methodist Pastor, we are taught to have a planned message, many times suggested from the lectionary and then things happen that make you feel like maybe God wants more control than you were ready to allow." He nervously smiled but looked completely at ease to Shelly. "I had a bit of a surprise this week; I'm here to tell you. But it was a blessing that I have been praying for and thought was surely not in the Lord's plan for me, but guess what? I was wrong. It seems that us pastors have no more powers of seeing the future than the people we try to reach out to and bring closer to God." John smiled and moved away from the pulpit and started moving toward the middle of stage.

"As many of you know my journey has not been a typical journey of late. Myself and my wife Shelly suffered a deep, deep loss. You can't lose a son and not suddenly realize that your world is completely different than you would expect it to be. Many of you know this loss of a loved one. John looked over across the congregation and then focused on his wife.

"The loss is usually followed first by sorrow, then there is doubt, there is question—and there is a good chance you can lose some faith over it." John began to fight the emotion he was feeling as he briefly relived the harshness of his recent past. "And to double down on that loss, my wife and I found ourselves in a place where we couldn't seem to face each other. I hear that can be common after losing a child, but if it is common, it makes it no easier a pill to swallow." John held his hands cupped together in front of him, trying to keep the nerves inside of him quelled as he continued to fight back tears. His voice began to fluctuate and tremble some. Shelly looked in admiration of his ability to continue even through his pain.

"Now, I'm not telling you this to seek your sympathy or put us up on display to show that we are special. We are only special in the Lord's eyes, as are each single one of you also. What I am here to tell you about is that we all live different lives and choose different paths, and many times, you and I meet back here each Sunday and occasionally elsewhere in town. In God's eyes, we are family. In my eyes, each one of you is a part of my family, and with that, a responsibility of mine because I know that my Savior wants that for me. He gave me a call that I answered to because I felt he was telling me I could be the kind of person who could love each one of you. John's voice began to strengthen as his resolve began to overpower his mind's will to trigger uncontrollable emotion.

"I was happy in my previous job. I made more money in my previous job. I'm not telling you that to make myself look like a martyr. I'm telling you that sometimes when you answer Jesus, there can be some sacrifice. Not only as a pastor or paid church worker but in general. When you are called, there can be a cost to yourself. My cost was that I let my family slide a little to the back shelf. I didn't mean to do it. Didn't even realize I was doing it." John moved back over toward the pulpit while he continued to look out across the congregation's faces.

"And then one day, in a complete and unexpected moment, we lost our son in a horrible accident." John moved his right hand over and placed it on the pulpit's side and squeezed. He then wiped a tear that began to form with his left hand. "It most definitely was NOT punishment from the end of the master's whip. It wasn't because I had put anyone in front of my family or my Lord. It was a horrible, incalculable accident. But it can shake you to your core when you lose your world." John slightly shook the pulpit with his hand, causing the congregation to snap to attention. "And in that process of trying to discover why my world collapsed—I let my responsibility to some," he moved his hand from the pulpit and began pointing his right finger slowly to each congregant in the sanctuary, "no—to all of you, slip through my grip momentarily. I dropped the ball. I continued down my path of mistakes and ignoring what my master was trying to teach me." John once again walked to the middle of stage and raised his voice slightly from the quiet volume he was talking with as he continued without pause.

"Our Lord did not create us to suffer or become mediocre. Can anyone here give me an amen for that?" Several responded to his call. "I don't want to get too crazy up here, but I believe that bears repeating. Our Lord did not create us to suffer or become mediocre or to ignore those who have become either one of those things. We are to look after one another. We are to reach out and give of ourselves to those that don't have. We are to put others above ourselves and our desires to a point that can cause discomfort, inconvenience, and yes, even pain. Not necessarily physical pain, but yes, pain. A few more amens were called out from the pews across the sanctuary.

"I am so fortunate. If I told you just how close I had come to losing everything that has been given to me, I'd be ashamed to face you. The one thing that it seemed I wanted to blame and be shed of after losing my son—was my faith in God. I cursed him. I'm sure many of you may have witnessed that in my lowest point. But what I can tell you now is that I am so thankful that God did not turn his head and walk away from me, even after I swore at him and kicked him to the dirt away from me. It shames me to admit that publicly, that I acted out this way, *but I did*. John let his head dip down toward the ground, letting his chin rest on his chest. The emotions his body was speaking was like riding a rollercoaster full of climbs and falls. Everyone in the room felt as if they were on the ride with him as his voice would tremble at times, and his body language would react in conjunction to his own words.

"Yet despite this seemingly unforgivable sin against him that I was committing, his actions through other people such as you showed me that I was horribly wrong in my blame of him. There is a person sitting out among you right now that was instrumental in saving me from myself. Even though I was hell-bent on self-destruction and punishing my savior for what I blamed him for, *He STILL*—used this person through their willingness to be used by their savior. My savior—Our savior." He glanced over at Carissa and smiled followed by a wink. "You can call me crazy right now, but if it weren't for them, you would be listening to a different pastor today." John looked around to survey the reactions his last statement caused. He saw some shocked expressions among some and tears from others. His hands fidgeted on either of his sides as they had dropped from exhaustion.

"If I tried to count how many different people that he used just to *grab my attention* and get me out of my self-destructive path I had careened off on, there would be too many to list. This is the love that He has for me. And He has that same love for you. He has that love for every human being out there, no matter what past they have, no matter what sin that you think is too great to seek Him, no matter who you have wronged." His hands rose again, and with a fist made in his right, he hit the palm of his left, emphasizing each statement as it was delivered. "If I never can give you any other words of wisdom for the time that I am fortunate enough to be blessed being here, it would be that God LOVES YOU no matter what wrong you've committed. You are *NEVER* too dirty to come to him for cleansing—healing cleansing! It doesn't mean life will be perfect from that point on. But he is with you and for you in every good and every hard time you encounter. *Beside you!*

"He loves me enough to give Shelly and myself a son. We knew we couldn't have children. We had tried for years, went through all the tests and prodding only to be told without in-vitro fertilization, our chances were slim to none. We accepted that.

"I don't know how many of you realized that our boy Jason was adopted. He was a true gift from God. The circumstances that we found him and were able to adopt him were so out of this world slim that there is no way that either of us could deny that he was a miracle and a gift. And we loved him like the miracle he was, and we will always love him as the miracle he was." John looked into his sweet wife's tear-filled eyes as they both nodded to each other in agreement about Jason being a miracle given to them.

"But God, the maker and giver of those miracles, deemed us worthy enough to bestow another miracle on us. He not only brought us from the brink of death and helped us get past our doubts and blame—but He doubled down with giving us the gift of life that is growing inside my beautiful wife's belly as she sits out there with nothing but undying love for a man like me, who was unworthy enough to shun her and curse the Father that gave all of this to us." The sanctuary was so quiet at this point that you could hear a tissue being pulled from a box by a woman who was so tearful her face was drenched with the streams pouring down.

"That's pure love, people. That's not anything but the purest form of love for what He created. And he wants that creation to have more than mere mediocrity or worse than that, pain and misery. He wants His creations to have more than to wake up with pain and suffering. There is a price to pay. But IS it even a price when it's helping someone else find what you've found as sure as your next breath—that we have a creator ready to love the least as He loves us?" The lightning began to flash more frequently as the stained-glass colors became more luminated, followed by cracks of thunder in the distance. The rain drops hitting the windows and roof became even louder.

"That's a price I'm willing to pay, and as a man of God, I can't help but believe it's a price you would pay too. I can't answer for you, brothers and sisters, but I plan on spending whatever time or effort it takes in my life to bring another creation back home so they can experience what I have experienced. Pay it forward friends like your life depended on it. A loud clap of thunder sounded as if God himself wanted to accentuate his last sentence.

"I wrote this down because a dear, close friend of mine gave me permission to pass it on. These are words to live by and so pertinent to the message I want you to receive today. It goes as follows:

'I know I should be a broken mess from a lot of my past, but with God's grace, I'm enthusiastically happy. I refuse to let the darkness swallow me up, and I try to bring a firelight wherever I go so others can know that in this sometimes dark and crazy world, it's possible to be brightened up if we help each other out.' John looked back again at Carissa, and anyone watching him would surely be able to put it together that these were not only her words but that she was surely the person whom he spoke earlier of that was used by God to save him from himself.

"Truer words couldn't be spoken, even if they had been carved in stone and passed through generations. These were unrehearsed thoughts by someone who was used by God to pull me from the depths of hell that I had dug myself into. God blessed the body of Christ, and you and I are that body! *WE* together—are that body made even stronger!

"And now, I'm going to embarrass a close friend of mine and tell you that those words came from the mouth of that beautiful auburn-haired woman sitting beside my wife. Her name is Miss—oops, she doesn't want me to put a prefix on her name anymore, my bad! Her name is Carissa Dean, and I'm so very lucky to have received her into my life. Thank you, Carissa, for those words of inspiration." John smiled and winked at her and Shelly. The sound of the congregation clapping overcame the sound of the rain and thunder for several seconds before another boom of thunder sounded almost immediately after a bright flash of lightning. The storm was upon Deliver UMC as John began wrapping up the message.

"Now to tie the message that was really spirit led and not the one I've been working on all week. I'd like to quote a couple of my favorite verses and ones that I feel are so pertinent to living life the way our creator intended. The first is so simple I don't know how we couldn't understand it and get it right daily, and yet we all struggle with it at times. It's from the book of John, chapter four, verse nineteen, I bet there are even some children that could quote this one for us all.

"'*We love because He first loved us.*' John smiled as he looked out and saw several children nodding in agreement that they knew the verse.

"Simple right? No way we can misinterpret such a boiled down and right to the core message. And the love that this verse is talking about is not the love that we say about our favorite food or activity or romantic love. This love is the love I was talking about that *He* has for each one of us, no matter what we do. He won't leave us. That is great information to know and hang on to. The second verse is longer, but it has some of the most important definitions of love; it gets used in weddings more than about any other bible verse. 1st Corinthians, chapter thirteen, verses four through eight. It goes as follows:

"'*Love is patient, love is kind. It does not envy, it does not boast, it is not proud. It does not dishonor others, it is not self-seeking, it is not easily angered, it keeps no record of wrongs. Love does not delight in evil but rejoices with the truth. It always protects, always trusts, always hopes, always perseveres. Love never fails. But where there are prophecies, they will cease; where there are tongues, they will be stilled; where there is knowledge, it will pass away.*'* The room was silent of thunder as he'd read the verse—it was as if the storm had ended in sync with his reading of what love really was by definition. Little did they realize they were in the eye of the storm and that the back wall of it would be soon upon them.

"Music to our ears and comfort for our souls is what this knowledge should be for us. I hope . . ."

The back door opened slowly from the darkened corner of the entrance. In unison with it opening was a slow squeaking sound that seemed extra loud in the silent moment between Pastor John's words. Out of instinct, most of the faces turned to see who would be coming in out of the rain so late as the service was winding down. A large, familiar man in a rain slicker emerged through the doorway just inside the sanctuary. He removed his rain-soaked hat, dropping it next to his side to the floor as he slowly scanned the back of some of the congregant's heads that remained facing forward toward John.

As they watched John's facial expression change, the ones who hadn't turned began twisting their necks around to view the latecomer. Most quickly recognized Henry's long, drawn, and wrinkled face, but the expression it exuded seemed intent, and nothing was familiar about it to those who knew him.

A short grunt exited Henry's throat as he began an intentional sentence that slowly emerged from his mouth. "I need to see Mrs. Beverly Snodgrass—Pastor John. I'm sorry to disturb this holy ceremony today, but it's important that I see her—*now*," he said calmly but with force.

The congregation that had remained facing forward toward John had now all started to turn toward Henry to determine what was going on. John motioned for Beverly to stay seated with his hand as he slowly stepped between the altar rails carefully edging toward Henry. John scanned the crowd looking for Chief Bob, but when his eyes met Julie's, she shook her head no. John saw a look on Henry's face and in his eyes that he'd never seen before. It was a look that brought instant caution and fear of what might be happening. He knew he needed to try to ease into control of the situation.

"Henry, my good friend, are you sure you shouldn't sit down and rest a minute? You look a little peeked. Are you okay?" He glanced over at Shelly,

Carissa, and Mary all seated together and between Henry and himself. John slowly hedged around, moving closer to the aisle that Beverly and Billy were on, hoping he could get in front of them before Henry started down the aisle toward her. John kept talking in a calming fashion. "Everybody, please stay seated, and we'll get back to our teaching God's desire of us loving one another shortly."

John remembered that Wayne had told him last night that he had to open his store and would be there as quick as he could. Jim was on the far aisle seat taking the whole scenario in and obviously trying to think of a quick plan without escalating the situation. As Jim slowly started to stand, he thought to himself, damn this setup of the sanctuary , the only way out was through the front entrance door where the troubled man was or around just in front of the altar and through a narrow and closed doorway off the side of the stage. It was unfortunately the perfect application for something horrible to happen if there were an active shooter. Thank God it hadn't progressed to that. Jim could see the tension in the tall man's shaky extremities and either rain or sweat pouring down his face. It didn't feel right, that much he knew for certain.

"I'd kindly ask you to sit yourself back down, sir," said Henry as he noticed Jim slowly getting up.

John continually moved slowly toward Henry who was standing at the back of the church near the entrance doors.

Henry started talking louder. "You all know the evil this woman has brought onto this town. I've been trying to catch her with proof of her toxic gossip for a long time—but now she has moved to committing heinous physical acts and must be dealt with."

"Henry, if that is true, we need to calm down and talk to the chief when he gets here. He has just finished with a car accident and is on his way to share the rest of the morning with us. We can all talk to him together. You would be okay with that, wouldn't you, Mrs. Snodgrass?" he said as he nodded up and down in a yes motion.

"She's an evil coward! She's a snake that will slither off before she gets her head cut off , I—I finally have proof of an evil deed she just committed . She killed my Molly, Pastor John. She caused my beautiful Molly to die alone in the street almost in front of our home." His voice was getting shakier, louder, and more agitated. "Please don't anyone move! Stop moving! I don't want to hurt any of you, but I need to show you," Henry started to reach in his left coat pocket, and as he did, people started to nervously squirm and look around as if they would take off running any moment. Men were beginning to calculate how to save their children and wives, and their actions were adding to Henry's paranoia.

"You haven't got the nerve, Henry!" retorted Beverly. "What proof could you have if I'm saying I've done nothing?"

John, again trying to be the voice of reason, calmly repeated, "Henry, listen to me, friend. Let's slow this down before someone gets hurt and just wait for the chief to get here. Let's think about how much you love God and all of these fellow believers. There are children in here with us that don't need to witness this,

Henry." John kept slowly maneuvering closer to where
Beverly was seated.

Henry began to stutter as confusion appeared on
his face before it again tightened and drew his dark eyes
deeper under his eyebrows. "I have to get to . . ." And
he struggled to reach deeper into his coat pocket.

That act of Henry reaching into his pocket
brought John quickly back to the night he reached into
his own pocket in a disheveled mental state. That night
he pulled his hand from his pocket, it contained a cold,
steel pistol that had nothing but the feel of hard finality
to its grip and trigger. He quickly prayed today wasn't
leading up to an act such as that.

The time this had taken up to now was mere
seconds, yet it felt like a slow-motion, stop-action
movie continuing minute after minute, frame by frame.

John looked instantaneously to different faces in
the crowd and quickly focused on details like fluid
coming from the tear ducts in Henry's eyes and then
over to Shelly's lower lip quivering in fear as she looked
down at the round belly that held their kicking son
inside. He glanced over at Mary and saw her eyes
darting back and forth between Henry and Pastor John
as the words shot out of each mouth and almost
seemed to tangle together somewhere in the middle.
He glanced over at Julie and saw her looking down at
her cellphone frantically texting someone, whom he
was sure was Bob. He prayed it was and that he would
show up instantly and remove the tension in the air
that he was so suited for.

As Henry's hand began to draw back out of his
pocket, there were hushed screams of 'no' from several

spots in the room. People began to lower themselves toward the floor as husbands reached for their wives and children to shove them downward under the wooden pews. Everyone knew what he was reaching for—*a gun.*

Henry looked from side to side in confusion and shouted, "No, it's just the evidence . . ." as he pulled his clenched fist out and hoisted it upward and began opening his hand out to reveal the item he had claimed as proof that Beverly was responsible for his wife's demise.

As John raised his hands and started speaking for everyone to '*calm down,*' all faces seemed to look his way for answers as Henry's loud voice battled for attention and control of the room. Henry held a small, silver cylinder between his thumb and pointing finger and continued in a fierce, enraged, and thunderous voice, "It's her damned lipstick! Avon Revenge! It's that vile red paint she wears everywhere she goes! No one else wears it, and I found it beside the curb where she killed my wife!" And he fell silent for an instant, much as a TV prosecutor would right before he would loudly announce, 'I rest my case!'

The silence was momentarily deafening before Beverly let out a laugh and said, "That's your proof that I killed your wife? You're not a walking reverend, you're an old fool."

And that's when John noticed Henry tighten his grip on the silver cylinder of lipstick as his scowl drew deeper within his skull, and then with his right hand, he began to force it deeply into his right-hand coat pocket. And this time, he drew it back out much quicker than he had his other hand. Henry made direct eye contact with Beverly and stared so hard and hot that Beverly surely felt the burning anger, like sizzling, orange-glowing irons being poked at her.

Julie had been cautiously texting Bob; her being the cop's wife, she seemed to know exactly what to do. He had texted her to FB Live what was happening so he could witness the event and radio what any first responders needed to do as he headed back as quick as he could, plus there would be a recording of it for evidence later. He texted her to '**pan surrounding area slowly, stay on the main threat**.'

And there it was in an instant. A dark, black, semi-automatic pistol gripped by a man who had just lost everything he lived for and was enraged by the thought that her life was ended by one of the members sitting in the congregation that was strewn out before him. He waved it back and forth in his shaky hand, unable to remain any form of rationale. The people started to panic even more as Beverly stood stunned facing her possible judge, juror, and executioner standing only twenty-five feet away. Her pastor, the one she had resented from day one, was between her and Henry but off to the side by a couple of feet in the aisle in front of her pew.

Almost everyone else was on the ground, either under pews or bent down below the backs of the seats—except for Beverly standing next to her seated husband, Billy, and Mary who sat just off to the side of Carissa who was seated by Shelly. Everyone else had taken cover of some sort as best they could. Henry's rage, mixed with his delusion, had come to a point where he knew no other path to take but end Beverly's ability to continue causing the pain as she had caused him and his Molly.

"You probably even poisoned Pastor John's dog, you hateful witch." Henry stated concisely as his eyes stared darkly and squarely into hers.

His hand moved the firearm until his eye was dead level on his intended target with the sight at the end of the barrel, and before his finger began the muscular action that would begin the sequence to unleash his fury, he said these last words, "Father forgive me for the sin I'm about to commit, but I find this defendant guilty of actions evil beyond the value of her life . . ."

John quickly sidestepped down the aisle toward Beverly as he pleaded a last time, "No, Henry! God doesn't want this!"

The first loud pop caused Henry's hand to flinch, and the barrel recoiled upward as his finger reflexed again, pulling the trigger with no control of where it was aimed. It continued firing as Henry's lack of control and the ease of the trigger continued to cause pop after pop, over and over, as people hugged the ground closer with several falling from being hit.

Henry's eyes were glazed over as he seemed to be in a trance, while he continued waving the gun with no apparent rhyme or reason over where the barrel was pointed or the ability to pull his finger out of the trigger ring.

\*\*\*

Somehow, Julie was able to continue the FB Live video feed that was streaming to her husband Bob as he drove with the speedometer pegged up and down the possibly slick hills toward Ash Grove, with one eye on the cellphone screen and one eye on the road while radioing an all-points bulletin to anyone listening, "Shots fired at Deliver Methodist Church, Ash Grove—multiple victims, gunshot wounds—requesting immediate medical transports. Victims with possible life-threatening injuries! Shooter is still inside and active—repeat—shooter is still inside and active. Single shooter, older, tall male. Approach with caution, no law enforcement present at this time, in route in five— multiple injuries, multiple hostages."

***

John had stepped in front of Beverly just before the first two projectiles left the barrel of Henry's semi- automatic and pierced through him, one into his abdomen and the other immediately followed, entering his chest. His eyes seemed to read confusion as they struggled to focus on Henry and then scanning downward at the pain that must have instantly erupted in his chest and torso. He had managed to shield Beverly, but the first bullet passed through him and entered the side of Beverly's neck as she had begun attempting to duck down below the pew, she continued downward as she fell into the lap of her husband Billy before rolling over and onto the floor in shock clutching her throat.

John had begun his fall backward as the first round entered his stomach area. Henry's hand had risen from the recoil, and as John began his descent, the second round entered his chest, and he fell backward over the pew behind him, rolling onto the people hiding on the ground.

Mary had sensed that Henry was losing control quickly and turned toward Shelly to protect her and her baby. She caught the fourth and fifth rounds that had left the barrel unintentionally as Henry's locked grip and lack of control of the firearm enabled it to continue firing. She was hit in the stomach and head just above her ear. She quickly collapsed onto Shelly, shielding her from any remaining rounds as they traveled wildly throughout the room, until it became suddenly silent. Henry stood there completely disoriented and unsure of what he had just done; as his right hand lowered his weapon to his side, he silently surveyed the chaos surrounding him. The chaos caused by the rage and fury of bullets that he had unleashed upon them. In a moment of silence, the sound of something rolling down the wooden floor could be heard. The small, silver, metal tube of lipstick had fallen out of Henry's hand, and the cylinder rolled down the slight decline of the wooden aisle until it stopped to a dead-rest against the sole of Pastor John's foot as he lay motionless on the floor.

Gunpowder stench filled the room as he struggled to realize what had just transpired. His ears were echoing and pounding loudly in his drums, and he had trouble regaining focus as he looked around and heard muffled moans and children crying. People were

peeking up at him, heads just above the pews, still
trying to maintain cover.

He suddenly felt sick

He suddenly felt sick to his stomach as words
stumbled slowly and loudly out of his mouth, "Oh
God! I'm sorry Pastor John—what have I done, I'm
sorry, Molly. I—I just wanted to make it, make it right
what she did to you, to me. Oh God . . ." The tears
filled his eyes as the realization of his actions began to
take hold of his cognizance. In a panic, he turned and
walked quickly toward the front door, looking back
once more in disbelief before exiting. The last sound
was the door slamming closed. *BANG.*

\*\*\*

Chief Pierce slammed his brakes on and slid to the
side, his door opening before his squad car had even
stopped. As he jumped out, he simultaneously tossed
his cellphone on the seat and drew his sidearm as he
exited his car and headed toward the front door, all
while surveying the exterior area and entrance. He was
the first on scene.

As he got close to the door, on the other side of a
large bush, he saw Henry with a weapon pointed to the
side of his head.

"Henry! Drop the weapon! Don't do it!" But
before he could utter another word, Henry looked over
at him and pulled the trigger.

A loud pop sounded, as he instantly toppled
forward to the ground with nothing stopping his face
falling into the sidewalk. He released the gun, and it slid
a few inches from the grip of his hand. His head was

turned toward Bob, and his eyes remained fixed on him as Bob walked up to him and kicked the weapon farther away from his possible reach.

It was the weapon his wife had waved wildly as she drove her motorized scooter down the street during Boone Days. The one Bob had questioned why he thought he needed it. All this passed through Bob's mind as he checked Henry's pulse and yelled to the oncoming deputies, who had just arrived, to search Henry's pockets and secure the weapon while he got up to quickly enter the church's interior. Henry had a faint pulse.

\*\*\*

Shelly was screaming for her husband frantically as Bob entered the sanctuary. Carissa had turned to Mary and rolled her over, checking her injuries and yelling for strips of cloth to stuff inside her wounds.

There were nurses that attended the church and even a doctor. As they had begun to come to their senses, they were shouting needs back and forth, while some of the women ran to the cleaning closet to fetch washcloths and whatever first-aid items they could find.

It was chaos, but people were coming to their senses and working together as they realized that the threat had been removed and were now free to move around and check for wounded. Trying their best to start triage on the most seriously injured, several had gathered around John and were trying to stop his bleeding. He was quickly losing blood as was Mary.

Bob ran up to them and quickly surmised that they needed to be taken to the hospital immediately, not having time to wait on the buses. He yelled over to Julie to pull their van around by the door and get help removing the quick release seats. She took off like lightning.

*** 

Wayne was pulling into the parking lot and couldn't imagine why all the police were there with lights flashing and people running in and out of the front door. Julie came flying past him through the grass to the front door in the van as Bob and several others carried John and Mary out in makeshift stretchers from people's coats. The sky was still spilling rain heavily.

Wayne quickly ran up and saw that they were pulling the seats out of the van and began taking them and tossing them into the yard. Carissa came out through the doorway helping Shelly, and after John and Mary were loaded, she and Shelly climbed into the back, holding handfuls of torn rags and shirts. Bob hopped in after closing the doors and took off, leaving tire trenches in the rain-soaked grass as he sped out of the yard and back onto the road toward Springfield.

Julie yelled at Wayne to help with Beverly as she had a neck wound and needed attention also. They loaded her into Wayne's backseat of his truck, along with Billy, and took off trying to catch up with Bob. He couldn't fathom what possibly could have happened, and he wondered how many others were in bad shape.

***

Jim exited the church after determining that there was no more seriously injured in the building that couldn't wait for the incoming ambulances. There were a couple of officers next to Henry, and one was administering CPR to him as the other stuffed pieces of cloth into his head wound. Somehow, he had survived his self-inflicted gunshot and was breathing, but it was labored and sporadic. His eyes didn't move much, other than quick bursts of tremors.

Several ambulances could be heard in the distance, and one by one, they sped into the lot and began treating those that were still there, including Henry.

It had been chaos, but somehow, it was being handled now. If only Bob and Wayne could get their wounded to the hospital ER in time.

***

The scene played out over and over in Beverly's mind as she lay across the back seat of Wayne's truck. Her husband Billy sat quietly holding a towel against her neck as blood steadily leaked from the tattered wound. Wayne sped down the highway, seeing Bob's van several hundred feet ahead of him with his emergency flashers blinking on and off as the darkened sky began spitting rain harder still. All he could do was try to imagine the hell that his church with its people had just gone through. How could this new plague of evil have now made its way to the small town of Ash Grove? He glanced down at his speedometer as they raced down I-44, it read ninety-four miles per hour. It felt more like forty knowing two of his best friends were possibly dying up ahead in Bob's van, racing to the same place, praying for miracles.

Beverly was thinking somewhat the same thing but realizing she had a major role in why this had happened. She kept replaying the sequence of events of how John, the man she had so much hate for, was the same man that had done everything he could do to prevent her from being hurt by Henry. Right down to maneuvering in front of her to shield her from the gunfire. Why would he do that after hearing what Henry had said she'd done?

She began to feel sick to her stomach and said, "Billy, I think I'm going to be sick . . ." And before she could say anything else, she turned and vomited onto the floor of the truck and Billy's shoes. She continued to dry heave and yelled out in pain from the throbbing in her neck.

"Hang in there; we're almost to the ER!" Wayne hollered back to her as he scanned his rearview mirror quickly. A police escort picked them up and led the rest of the way to the hospital with lights flashing and sirens blasting in front and behind them.

*** 

The scene at the ER entrance happened quickly. Julie had called ahead of time informing them of what to expect shortly when her van and Wayne's truck arrived. The nurses with gurneys were there waiting and loaded them both quickly, wheeling them inside.

Carissa was helping Shelly out of the van as Wayne's truck pulled in and slid to a stop. More attendants rushed and retrieved Beverly. As Carissa and Shelly came through the doors, nurses were trying to help them also as they looked like they were both wounded from all the blood on their clothes.

"My husband, my friend—please, you have to save my husband, please take care of them," Shelly cried out.

Shelly was hysterical now that everything had sunk in and the realization that John hadn't said a word since he had been shot. He had laid motionless for the entire trip. With the shock, the blood, the frantic hundred-mile-an-hour drive, and the chaos—Shelly finally broke down. She fell to her knees and then forward, planting her hands on the floor and dry heaving between trying to catch her crying breath. One nurse noticed she was pregnant and quickly came over with a wheelchair and told Carissa she needed to get her checked out also. Carissa helped get her loaded and said she would be right beside her if they would allow her to come. The nurse nodded and said unless the doctor says no.

***

Ten minutes later, the ambulances containing Henry and a few others began arriving.

# Chapter 33

*Later Sunday after the Chaos*
## Dealing with the Damage Left Behind

P astor Jim continued with the police at the church, filling them in with all the answers to the multitude of questions. The state police had taken control of the scene and investigation. The area was cordoned off in yellow crime tape and evidence retrieved, as well as pictures taken and witness accounts put on record. Jim was anxious to get to the hospital and check on the injured; John's condition had not looked favorable as they had carried him out to be delivered to the ER. He knew Shelly had to be inconsolable by this point. Julie had made a statement and then let him know she was going to collect clothes from John's for Shelly and Carissa and take them to Springfield. She knew they were both covered in blood. Jim asked her to keep him informed, and he would be there as soon as he could get away from the church, but so far, he had heard nothing. He also called the Methodist's district superintendent and briefly filled her in. He didn't want her to hear it on the news before he could give her some details if they tried to interview her.

The rain continued to come and go throughout the day as one by one the Deliver's attendees were able to leave and go home.

Jim briefly thought to himself, what will become of the old Deliver UMC sanctuary, would they reopen it? Would it be torn down? It had such a history, and now that history had a horrible blemish to add. He had no idea what they would do as nothing like this had ever happened in the Missouri Methodist conference before. Who would have guessed the first kind of this tragedy would be in a small community nestled quietly in the friendly Ozarks? He hated that it had, and he hated that it would be replayed over and over on the news—and surely make national coverage.

CNN, FOX, and the others would have their bright, flashy caption banners and talk every angle from every direction, bringing faith and the Methodist church into the endless headlines. He felt sick to his stomach now as he climbed into his car to check on the welfare of his good friends. He bowed his head after starting his car and prayed for God to grant good results for John and the others before he backed out and looked over one last time at the yellow tape surrounding the small, quaint house of God known as Deliver United Methodist Church.

\*\*\*

They say time heals most everything. Bob believed it was going to take a long time to heal this day. He had experienced evil in his years of police service and seen chaotic and horrific scenes but when it happened the way it did this day, among his hometown friends and family, it made it the kind of memory that you couldn't just bury and forget.

His kids and wife had been in peril in a place that was supposed to be the safest haven of comfort and love that there is. The perpetrator this time had not been a random stranger on drugs caught in a robbery; this had been a fellow church member and a normal, loving human being and long-time standing pillar of the community. There had always been stories about Beverly and Henry verbally sparring over rumors she had been accused of spreading. She, for some reason, held contempt for John and his family from the day he started leading the church, although he had never understood why.

She was just the town's wealthy, mean- natured public enemy of Ash Grove, but surely not someone capable of physically attacking an old woman in wheelchair, was she? How could he have missed that? The coroner had ruled her death an accident. They had found a brain tumor that could have been responsible for a seizure leading to her accident. Now, after today's outcome, he began to question.

He met Julie at the door of the waiting room, and she quickly ran over to him and practically fell into his arms. He leaned in close to her ear and whispered, "I'm so proud of you, Julie; you did great. You took control and acted; you saved lives today by your actions. I'm proud to call you the love of my life."

Julie leaned back to look into his eyes with tears rolling down her cheeks. "This isn't fair Bob. Just when life changes for the good and it starts becoming normal for Shelly and John. *My God, she's going to have his baby*— and Mary, the most loving and innocent woman ever— She looked so good sitting in church for the first time."

Julie's eyes were blurred with tears as she melted down from the fear and tension. She started to collapse, and Bob quickly pulled her to his chest, keeping her from sliding to the floor. She barely let a second go by as she continued, "She was proud she was able to hear John preach. It's just not fair. It—it almost makes me start to question, could there be truth to what John's mom had told him, about the devil?"

"Julie, give God a chance to heal this horrible tragedy . . . I don't think he's done with John or Mary just yet." Bob squeezed her hands with love and then said, "Let's go see if we can find anything out about their conditions."

***

John had been in surgery for over seven-and-a-half hours as Jim, Bob, Julie, Wayne, and Carissa sat surrounding Shelly trying to console and comfort her. Jim had them hold hands together several times throughout the day, once he had arrived, and led prayers of guidance for the surgeons and comfort and strength for both John, Mary, and the others.

Every time the waiting room door would open, Shelly would tense and start to jump up to find out John's outcome. Several people from the church and Ash Grove had come and gone checking on what they could do to help and give prayers and love to them. Family members' telephone numbers had been given to the church secretary so she could call them and let them know where their loved ones were being cared for. John's mom and dad were coming from Oklahoma and would be there as quickly as they could. His mom was told how serious the circumstances were, and she spent most of her time in prayer for him as his dad drove.

\*\*\*

In the operating room, the surgeons and assistants worked tirelessly repairing the damage that had occurred to the various areas surrounding John's heart, his lung, and pancreas. At one point early during the surgery, there was a moment that John had flatlined for about a minute and a half as doctors raced to restart his heart.

Later, after being moved out of recovery and into a critical care room, John would recall his memory of what was transpiring to him as he lay on the operating table. He believed it coincided with what he was told happened during his time in the OR. It was a story that brought tears to Shelly every time she heard him tell it, realizing that, if not but for the grace of God, she would have lost him that day.

In John's mind, the experience he remembered is what many who have had similar traumas in their lives have claimed to see. He was certain he had left his body for a length of time that day in the operating room.

This is John's story of what happened to him that rainy, cold, and storm-filled Sunday afternoon while doctor's struggled to restart his heart in OR 8, Cox South Hospital:

"There was darkness all around me, but a twinkling bright light lay ahead and was growing larger and more infinite as I moved toward it. It drew me in, and I felt no fear or regret as I hurriedly made my way closer. I felt called to move toward the light as if it were expected of me. My entire body began tingling as if fingers were lightly running over my skin. The closer I came to the iridescent light, the warmer my heart and soul became. The feeling was almost overwhelming, but it was still pleasant.

"I strongly desired to walk into the light. I thirsted for it as a person trapped in the desert without water would crave entering a cool body of water and swallowing it in. Once I was able to step into the light, the blurry illumination became brilliantly in focus, and I could begin to make faces out in the distant and endless hills that were covered in bright, crystal-crisp blades of green, soft grass. It felt as if I had passed through some sort of portal into an alternate world or dimension as I stepped past the light into the clarity and brilliant colors that opened before me.

"I saw friends that had left me in the past, and I seemed to recognize everyone there even if I couldn't place why I would know them. They all were so happy and content as they looked over and welcomed me with open arms. Each motioning me to join them. Intentional in their wishes to be accommodating with warmth and love. Beautiful music like I had never heard before or could describe filled the entire area above me, under me, and around me in every direction. It was like being surrounded by wind chimes of every imaginable note, lightly blowing from a sweet, aromatic breeze.

"There was a beautiful enormous tree on a hill in the distance reaching infinitely toward the sky above, and it seemed strangely alive as the leaves moved and reached out, almost beckoning me to walk toward it. It almost breathed with a heartbeat of its own.

"Near the tree was what looked like the Father sitting on a throne of shininess that had no defining boundary of a shape. It couldn't be described, yet I understood it, and it felt inviting and it was filled with a wonderful, powerful love that spilled over from its base in waves that softly rolled outward toward the people listening to him.

"The shininess from where the Father was sitting spread outward toward the people watching him, and as it touched them, everything seemed to become one. Connected in unison. It was indescribable, and I craved to move closer, becoming a part of it. I could make out a face that drew me in closer. I couldn't entirely recognize them from my memory, but I felt so drawn I moved closer in.

"The Father looked at me and smiled. I was almost unable to look away from Him; I knew it surely must be Jesus the son of God. I was so drawn to the smaller face sitting below him that I continued to walk in closer toward them both.

"All at once, like a cool breeze blowing on one's face on a warm summer's day, the wind became stronger, and the small face began to lose its blur and start to come into sharper focus. I then instantly recognized who he was. His smile was so genuine and familiar. It was my son Jason that was conversing with the Father, and as they talked, I could feel the overwhelming happiness my son felt. It was the most beautiful image I've ever seen in my entire life. I didn't want to leave. I could be happy to exist just outside of his reach without being able to touch him if that is what I had to do to stay. I had never experienced the power of desire like the one I was feeling as I watched my son's face light up with joy as he conversed with the seated Father.

"My eyes pooled in tears of love and joy like never before. It's indescribable in any way I can try to define what I felt. In a moment of beautiful joy, my son turned from the Father and looked directly into my eyes and spoke the only words that were legible to me in my memory while I was there . . .

I heard him say, 'I love you, Daddy, but it's not your time yet; I'll see you again when it is. It's okay for you to go back now; Mommy needs you, and so does Henry.'

"The deepest sadness suddenly mixed with the most ineffable happiness I'd ever felt spun through my interior. Before I could define any of what was happening, I felt I was being pulled backward in an instant, and as much as I silently pleaded to stay, the face of the Father and my son and the crisp image of the tree towering above them quickly disappeared into a blinding brightness, and my heart felt as if it would burst as I was pulled back through the darkness and then lie silently still. I remembered only a comfort of what was to come one day, and any sadness I had felt dissipated as the silence became a thundering blast that shook my body and made me heave upward violently. The next thing I remembered was a blurry whiteness with shadowy figures standing over me as I opened my eyes."

John had been placed in an induced coma so his body could overcome the shock of the damage he had suffered and to help with the healing process. He had lain silently for three days, and the figures hovering above him came into focus, and he recognized his wife, his mother, and Carissa. All had stayed with him the entire time, only taking turns to let others into the room to pray over him for healing. John was given another chance at life. *Relived* again only by the grace of God.

The first words he spoke as he began to regain clarity were, "It's beautiful in heaven; I saw Jason, and he is happy. He's with Jesus."

***

Pastor Jim had met with the Ash Grove Presbyterian church in town, and they had offered to share their chapel with Deliver UMC for as long as they needed for services until they figured out what they would do. They would now hold services at noon on Sundays until they came up with a definite plan. Jim would stay and fill in until John would be able to come back and take over his duties again.

On that first Sunday morning after the tragedy, The Presbyterian Church allowed Pastor Jim to give the message to both the Methodist and Presbyterians together so he could share the good news of the expected recoveries of all involved. Pastor Jim listed the status to each of the people who had been injured and then spoke intently on John's miracles, and as he stood at the pulpit, he spoke of the grace that God had granted Pastor John through his act of what love can truly accomplish.

Pastor Jim described the act as, "Not heroism, but an act of the love that John had been taught by growing up with parents that knew teaching the belief in Jesus Christ was of the greatest importance above all."

John's parents sat proudly on the front row listening to their son's mentor talk of John's actions that day.

Jim continued, "Pastor John acted out of that love for his brothers and sisters because he knew that is what God expected from him. It was embroiled in his very heart and soul. Pastor John never hesitated to put himself in harm's way because of that faith, that in God we can overcome—we can overcome hate and tragedy. Pastor John feels strongly about what *God's love* should mean to each of us and that kind of *love* is what this world needs more than anything." Jim stood proudly as he spoke of his good friend and shared the good news of how God had worked through him and many others through this tragedy.

He continued to speak of the particulars of how John had miraculously missed instant death by one of the bullets being directed away by mere millimeters from piercing his heart and that the other round had narrowly missed his pancreas and devastating it. One lung had been penetrated and collapsed. Upon arrival at the hospital, John had been in stage 3 blood loss. He had lost about forty percent of his blood total, or about four pints. Minutes later and he would have entered hypovolemic shock or comatose, with major organs failing. Pastor Jim went on to say it was more than sheer luck that the bullets were not defense rounds or hollow points—that they had been instead target rounds that did not expand and flatten as they penetrated, but alternatively passed through and through, causing lesser devastating wounds. As he continued, he reached into his breast pocket, and as he explained what had deflected the bullet's travel from piercing his heart, he pulled a small, damaged Case pocket knife out. A tear rolling down his cheek he showed them as he held it up in the air for all to see. It still retained its shape but the edge was gnarled and bent, the decorative bone handle portion shattered with a chunk missing on one side.

"This small pocket knife has quite a history behind it, and it is literally a miracle that it was in Pastor John's sport-coat breast pocket last Sunday when this tragedy unfolded." He continued to tell the story of how it was a childhood friend's knife they had used to become blood brothers as youth and how when Pastor John lost his son, he had dreamed of his childhood friend and the need to find that young man so he could make amends from something that had happened between them in the past. The strange path this small knife took to this point is beyond belief. John found through research where his friends last known address was and took a trip to Wichita only to find his friend had passed—but through a *(chance)* meeting with an older couple who knew by *(chance)* his friend's mother, whom then met him a different Kansas small town and passed the small knife from thirty-some years earlier to John. Full circle so to speak. John began carrying it with him every day as a reminder of how his late childhood friend had. "Don't be fooled by letting people cloud such a story as mere (*chance*) or coincidence. Chance and coincidence are only words that non-believers use to cover up the fact they are unable to explain away the ability that God still performs miracles today through the means of others he has created. It is not *happenstance* in a Christian's belief; it's *faith*."

"'*Faith being the confidence in what we hope for and the assurance about what we do not see. Hebrews, eleven, verse one.*'"

"A God inspired verse that I know for a fact is one of John's favorites and one he believes strongly in and lives daily. Knowing him and being a good friend is one of the small miracles that God has allowed myself, and in turn, I believe it's a miracle I now share with all of you in this town of Ash Grove, MO. A place that needs miracles like these to draw this community together in healing." John handed the small pocketknife to one of the congregants in the first row to look at, hold, say a small prayer of thanks if desired, and then pass it on around the sanctuary for all to see.

"And with those words of faith, now begins the process of first realizing what happened, then trying to figure out why it happened, followed most importantly by working together to make sure that we don't allow the seeds from this hideous evil that transpired last Sunday to take root and grow again.

"Ensuring that we all teach our children the value and necessity of accepting and loving Jesus Christ as our Savior and living the life of service in mission to those less fortunate is a great way to start." Jim stood tall as he looked around the sanctuary and thought it was fitting to end with a "God is good . . . all of the time"

The people answered back in unison, "All of the time . . . God is good."

"Can I get an Amen?" Jim then held his hands cupped towards the heavens much like the Keeper of the Plains, before moments later lowering them back down and holding his hands together in a thankful prayer stance. He then walked down the three steps from the alter with a loving smile as he made his way down the aisle and out the open double doors of the First Presbyterian Church of Ash Grove, Missouri. A church he was to come familiar with after this day.

# Epilogue

J ohn healed completely just in time for he and Shelly to welcome their son into the world as 'Henry Jason Austin' on March 3, 2019. He came into this world kicking and screaming on a cold and blizzard-covered Sunday afternoon. He was named after a man that John had felt close to and who had been instrumental in helping him overcome the darkness that the death of his first son had allowed him to be drawn into.

He realized Henry Tanner had been given circumstances that were beyond his control and a contributing factor to his loss of normal reasoning. He had never intended to hurt anyone. John wanted his friend's memory and legacy to be remembered as one of a man with strong Christian beliefs whom cared about his fellow brothers and sisters with the same kind of love John continues to teach about. Not to be remembered for the pain and devastation that happened in Deliver United Methodist Church on that cold and rainy Sunday morning.

He and his wife, Shelly, chose to lead the way of forgiveness and reconciliation by naming their newest precious miracle and gift given to them after the man they had known and loved and grown to know as the 'Walking Reverend.' Their good friend, Henry Lyle Tanner, loving husband to the love of his life, Molly Leona Tanner. John believed in his heart that Jason was talking about his brother when he told him his Mommy and Henry needed him back on earth. The words he had spoken to John on his heavenly visit as he sat next to Jesus.

Henry is still alive and in an adult mental facility for the imprisoned elderly. After recovering, he was found to be suffering from dementia, along with early-onset Alzheimer's disease. After the death of Molly, he had failed to maintain his medications that helped keep control of his depression and anxiety. John and his family continue today to make the trip monthly to visit him, where John ministers to Henry and many of the others in the facility every third Monday afternoon.

Sweet Mary James made a full recovery and only suffered some mild short-term memory loss from her head injuries. She, by virtue of yet another one of God's miracles, no longer suffers from 'fear of leaving' her home. She and Shelly remain the best of friends, along with Julie Pierce. Mary continues to attend Deliver UMC weekly as a member and teaches children's Sunday school, along with hosting a weekly bible study group for women in her home.

Beverly Snodgrass, after recovering from her wound, later confessed to adding to the cause of Molly's accident and was charged with involuntary manslaughter. She renewed her Christian faith, and after serving a partial sentence, donated most of her inheritance to Deliver UMC and the new worship center that is being erected. She too attends weekly as a member at Deliver UMC along with her husband Billy who stood by her and is now enjoying a renewed love together.

Carissa Mae Dean moved to Ash Grove almost immediately after the incident. She and Wayne Renfrow waited to tie the knot until their good friend John had recuperated enough to perform their wedding. They are currently building a home together as the 'Man Cave' hardly seemed like an appropriate place to call home together. They currently are fostering an eight-year-old boy whose parents and only family were tragically killed in the automobile accident that happened on Scott's Corner the day of the Deliver UMC tragedy. They are working on adopting him. His name is Corey and his personality and humor makes a perfect fit to the Renfrow's. He's a firecracker!

Bob and Julie Pierce along with their family continue to support their great friends and community of Ash Grove along with being very faithful members to Deliver United Methodist Church. Bob now volunteers working with surrounding churches to make their houses of worship safer and pro-active places of worship.

The decision to keep Deliver UMC's sanctuary was a tough decision. It now is used solely as a prayer chapel and on the alter sits a small gaslit candle that remains burning twenty-four seven alongside the Bible Pastor John held that Sunday during his sermon on God's love. It remains open to verse I John 4:19.

***

In a conversation between Pastor Jim and Pastor John one afternoon as they sat watching the construction of the new worship center—Pastor Jim looked up at the church sign and cocked his head in dismay. He then turned to John and stated, "I never noticed that before! I think we need to change the name of the church as soon as the new worship center is completed."

"What in the world for?" asked John.

"**DELIVER**—it's a semordnilap!" Jim answered back.

"What in the world is that? Are you making words up again? I can't even begin to pronounce that!"

"It's what a word is called when, spelled backward, right to left, is a completely different word than it is spelled from left to right! **DELIVER** spelled backward becomes **REVILED**." Jim looked at John and made a scowl with his mouth and furrowed his brow, and then continued saying, "I don't like that coincidence, especially with what has happened here."

John shook his head and remained silent for a drawn-out time, causing Jim to look at him with question. John then slowly and deliberately continued on, "I think what you see in that word '**Deliver**' depends on your perspective when you look at it! That's what I think!"

Jim questioned him, "Now, just what do you mean by that statement, John?"

John continued, "What I mean is if you look at things expecting to see the negative, you may see the word **Reviled**, but once you have lived through the negative consequences that life can leave you with, and not only survived but conquered them—then furthermore been given a second chance at life through grace, your perspective changes, and you start to look at the positive that can come from shaking up the negative." John smiled at Jim as he turned his focus directly towards the sign, nodding Jim to follow his lead.

And with that said, my friend and colleague in Christ—is when you look at a word like **Deliver** and see it backward, but with a **twist**. You see that it then spells something entirely different in a miraculous kind of way—the word you then see becomes **RELIVED**."

### Galatians 2:20

*I have been crucified with Christ and I no longer live, but Christ lives in me. The life I now live in the body, I live by faith in the Son of God, who loved me and gave himself for me.*

# ABOUT THE AUTHOR

I'm an example of someone who made poor choices and put himself at risk in many ways and yet God watched over me and kept me safe from the shadows I kept Him in. I must give God credit because I challenged Him so many times in ways, I should have ended up either dead or totally defeated. Still, He took me like a clump of clay and formed me into the image He had intended me to be. He has proven it makes no difference to Him where you have been, but where you are headed. His GRACE defeats all of our past burdens and leads us to happiness through serving him.

God gave me the words to write Christian fiction. They didn't come from me alone. In the many times I read my manuscript through the editing process, I would think I don't remember writing that. Other times I would be jammed in thought of how to make storyline work or segue into another part of a character, and like a gift, it would come neatly wrapped into my thoughts. Again, it came as a gift. Not something I conjured up on my own.

God does work in mysterious ways, every day, and once you become tuned in to Him—you start to smile and realize that happenstance or coincidence are just words used by non-believers to explain God's large and sometimes small almost insignificant miracles.

I hope in some way after reading these words given to me, that you gained not only some entertainment, but also inspiration and possibly a small change in your perspective of this world and how God can use you to change it for better.

*Be the protagonist that defeats his personal demons, defies the urge to crush his antagonist and instead empower them to change for the better through your faith and deeds.*
*Steve Bassett*

---

If you enjoyed this novel, please take time to write a review on Amazon or GoodReads. It is much appreciated by the author.

stevengbassett.com

~~~~~~~~~~~~~~~~~~~~~~~~~~

# COMING:

*NOVELS BY STEVEN G. BASSETT:*

### THE MASON JAR
*Christian Fiction*

### Fated Inception
*Christian Science Fiction*